When We're Thirty

Happy reading!
♡ *Casey Dembowski*

Casey Dembowski

Red Adept Publishing
Unlocking New Worlds

When We're Thirty
Red Adept Publishing, LLC
104 Bugenfield Court
Garner, NC 27529
https://RedAdeptPublishing.com/
Copyright © 2021 by Casey Dembowski. All rights reserved.

Cover Art by Streetlight Graphics[1]

No part of this book may be reproduced, scanned, or distributed in any printed or electronic form without permission. Please do not participate in or encourage piracy of copyrighted materials in violation of the author's rights. Thank you for respecting the hard work of this author.

This is a work of fiction. Names, characters, places, and incidents either are the product of the author's imagination or are used fictitiously, and any resemblance to locales, events, business establishments, or actual persons—living or dead—is entirely coincidental.

---

1. http://StreetlightGraphics.com

For my husband

Part 1

Chapter 1

Hannah

Sometimes being a Jersey girl in New York City had its benefits, like approval from her boss to order a six-layer vanilla rainbow cake from New Jersey's own *Cake Boss* for her office birthday celebration. She only turned thirty once.

Hannah's phone buzzed with yet another notification: *You have memories with Kate Novack, Stephanie Lansford, and 32 others...*

She'd been waiting for that to pop up between all the texts and birthday posts. After twelve years on Facebook, there was a lot to reminisce over. And today, there would be plenty embarrassing memories to scroll through.

She glanced around the small office, but the interns and staff writers were still enjoying birthday cake. Only the section editors—like Hannah—were back at their desks, scrambling to finish layouts. Hannah had finished her section the day before, affirming her New Year's resolution to have her section in before deadline every issue. She took a bite of cake. Sugar coursed through her, fortifying her for the mortification that was sure to follow as she clicked on the Memories notification.

Kate... Kate... Kate and Stephanie. She scrolled further, bypassing graduate school and going straight for the college memories. Kate... more Kate... Kate and Will. She paused on a picture from her twentieth birthday where she was smooshed between Kate and Will, each of them kissing one of her cheeks. Their eyes were glassy, their skin glossy with sweat. She remembered *that* birthday. The same couldn't be said for her twenty-first, though the pictures told quite the story. Hannah, Will, and Kate—the three musketeers. God, they were so unoriginal and *so* drunk.

She stopped on the last picture in the thread—her eighteenth birthday, two months into freshmen year of college. She and Kate, newly best friends, sat in their dorm room, a pilfered bottle of booze between them. She squinted at the photo—Jägermeister. Gross.

Saving the picture to her photos, she added it to a text to Kate. *We were so little,* she typed.

Kate's reply came quickly, a series of scream emojis followed by: *My eyebrows. Your hair. What were we thinking?*

Hannah snorted, looking around again to make sure no one was paying attention to her. Things were laid back at the *Deafening Silence New York* office, but she didn't need one of her interns seeing a photo of her when she was younger than them. In the photo, Hannah's hair had been a dark auburn, a look that didn't suit her complexion at all, and Kate hadn't yet learned to love getting her eyebrows waxed. But still, they had been so cute and little and skinny.

We were adorable, Hannah typed back. *And skinny. Omg!*

Kate sent several more distressed emojis. *I prefer being thirty, flirty, and thriving. Skinny thighs be damned.*

The ding of a new email pulled Hannah's attention back to the office. She glanced at her computer before taking another bite of cake. Skinny thighs be damned indeed.

Re: Arctic Monkeys Feature.

Great. Edits on her birthday. She would look at them later.

"Hannah?"

Hannah straightened at the sound of Riley's voice and swiveled her chair to face her boss. "Are you here to tell me how awesome my section turned out this month?"

Riley held a plate in one hand, and in her other, she gripped a bouquet of white carnations.

"No, but it was definitely awesome. These came for you," she said, holding out the flowers.

Hannah stared at them for too long. White carnations were her favorite, but her boyfriend wasn't the flower-sending type. In fact, she was pretty sure Brian wouldn't have remembered her birthday had Kate not mentioned it at least four times the last time they were out at McMahon's.

"Did it have a card?" she asked, clearing a space on her desk.

Riley put them down. "No card. I asked."

"Oh." Hannah fingered the petals and breathed in their familiar scent. They had to be from Kate. "Thanks for dropping them off."

"No problem." Riley shifted on her feet. "Listen, I have to go. CeCe's school just called, and she's running a temperature again. Can you assign the Atlas Genius concert to one of the interns?"

Hannah put a comforting hand on Riley's arm. Daycare was kicking CeCe's butt, and it wasn't even winter yet. And soon, Riley would have two babies to care for. "You mean, you're giving me the honor of informing Henry that he gets to cover the Atlas Genius show?"

The kid had lyrics from one of their songs tattooed on his arm. Hannah wasn't even that hardcore.

"Yes, please," Riley said, resting her hand on her ever-growing belly. At nine months pregnant, Riley looked ready to pop. Hannah didn't see how that baby girl was going to stay in there much longer. "Anyway, happy birthday! Hope you have something fun planned tonight."

Hannah waited until Riley padded away, the drag of her feet on the hardwood one of the most comforting sounds in Hannah's life, before snapping a picture of the bouquet and sending it to Kate. *Thanks for the flowers.*

I didn't send you flowers, weirdo, Kate wrote back.

What? Hannah typed. She'd been certain they were from Kate. No one else would send her white carnations.

Your parents?

I don't think so, Hannah replied. *They got me tickets to that off-Broadway show.*

That's right. Who brought them to you? Maybe you have a secret admirer.

Hannah laughed. *Riley.*

The typing ellipses appeared, followed by a flurry of back-to-back messages:

She would be the first one I'd suspect. ;-)

Heading to a meeting.

I'll pick up wine, you get dinner.

Meet you at your place.

Hannah put her phone down and looked back at the flowers. If Kate hadn't sent them, who had?

THE FAMILIAR CREDIT music of Kate's podcast, *Bitching about Boyfriends*, wound down. Hannah pulled out her earbuds and wrapped them around her phone. Leaning back against her living room couch, she went through the script again in her mind, processing it. Across from her, the television was paused on the end credits of the last episode of the sappy drama she was currently binging with Kate. The preview for the next episode taunted her with the promise of tears.

Kate had disappeared into the kitchen with an expensive bottle of wine a few minutes earlier. Hannah could hear her digging through drawers for a corkscrew. There would be no twist-off tops tonight. Thirtieth birthdays warranted high-class wine, a precedent Kate had set when she turned thirty at the beginning of the year.

The kitchen went quiet, and a moment later, Kate returned with two overfilled glasses of Riesling.

She handed one to Hannah. "So, these flowers..."

Hannah worried at her cuticles. She hadn't been able to stop thinking about the flowers since they'd arrived at her desk. Who'd sent them? Her parents didn't do that type of thing, and in the eighteen months—on and off—she'd been with Brian, he'd only ever gifted her roses. She didn't have the heart to tell him otherwise. And it wasn't as if she kept carnations around her apartment, from which he could have gleaned her preference. Fresh flowers weren't exactly part of her weekly budget. "Have you ever mentioned to Brian that white carnations are my favorite?"

"Brian and I don't exactly talk when you're not around," Kate said between sips of wine.

Hannah rolled her eyes. "Can you blame him? You talked about his penis size on your podcast and didn't even try to hide his identity."

"It's not like his parents listen to my podcast."

Hannah shook her head—Kate logic. "Still. Maybe they could be from him?"

"Brian doesn't have enough romantic sensibility to send you flowers at your job on your birthday."

"But—"

"And if he somehow came up with the idea to send you flowers, he would abso-fucking-lutely send a card, because he would want credit for coming up with such a fabulous idea."

"Kate—"

"Not to mention you have never told him that you love white carnations. And I certainly didn't tell him, and he in no way asked for my help on the matter. So no, I don't believe the flowers came from Brian, and you don't either."

Disappointment coursed through her. Hannah didn't know if it was because the flowers weren't from him or because she knew they would never be from him. "I know, okay?"

Of course she knew. She'd known for months. That didn't mean she didn't love him or that deciding to end her relationship was easy or simple.

"Can't I just pretend until I see him tomorrow?" she asked and took a sip of her wine.

Kate shrugged, her standard reaction to all things Brian. "What's one more night when you've been pretending for over a year?"

Hannah flinched. After a decade of friendship, she was used to Kate's bluntness, but Kate usually softened the blow. It was a trait Hannah sometimes loved and sometimes loathed about her best friend. Kate never meant to be cruel; it was just her way. She was a mirror, always reflecting the truths that Hannah wouldn't voice.

"Sorry," Kate said, putting her hand over Hannah's. "That was too much, and I didn't even mean it. God, and on your birthday. I promised myself I would lay off Brian for the day. It was part of my gift to you."

Hannah forced a smiled and squeezed Kate's hand. "Then I guess you owe me another gift."

"I guess I do." Kate sighed. "Brian's not even the reason I'm pissed... for once. Remember Teddy?"

Hannah wished she didn't. Teddy was the yoga instructor Kate had dated for three months back when Kate and Hannah lived together. It had been years, but the memory of walking in on Kate and Teddy attempting some insane, next-level Kama Sutra pose wasn't something she would soon forget. Hannah stared at her incredulously for a few seconds.

Kate, being Kate, stared right back, waiting for a response.

"Yes," Hannah said, laughing. "I remember Teddy, particularly his backside."

"At least it was a well-toned backside," Kate said with a shrug. "Not like the memories of flabby backsides you cursed me with."

"You've never walked in on me having sex."

"I just didn't squeal like a little girl and slam the door when I did. It's called tact."

Hannah bit back a loud laugh, but the tiniest of giggles still escaped. "Yes, because tact is your specialty."

"Anyway..." The ghost of a smile played across her face. "I ran into Teddy at yoga class. I avoided him for years and two weeks ago—poof—there he is, ass firmer than ever."

"Oh no." Hannah knew exactly where this was going. It was completely Kate. Teddy had smiled, flirted a little, and showed off his impressive flexibility. "You slept with him."

"He goes by Theo now, right? All I think of when I say 'Theo' is that guy from the *Divergent* movies, and he's just gorgeous. I mean, ten seconds into our escapade, and I'm all hot and bothered. He's kissing me, and I'm picturing hot *Divergent* guy whispering dirty nothings in my ear—"

"I get the picture." Hannah turned off the television. "So what's the problem?"

Kate focused on her wine. "He has a wife, Hannah."

Hannah's stomach roiled, the two slices of pizza she'd eaten sitting heavy in her gut. Kate wouldn't do that to another woman—not on purpose.

"How did you—" Hannah held up her hand. "Actually, hold on." With a last look at her friend, she went to the kitchen. Riesling wasn't going to cut it. This conversation required a strong red. After pouring two glasses of the best—and only—red she had, she returned to the living room, reclaiming her spot at Kate's side. "How did you find out?"

Kate took a giant swig. "He was only in town for a few weeks, which I knew. We were talking after his final class, and he just nonchalantly mentions that he's excited to get back home to his wife, who is due in a few weeks. Of course, I started freaking out, but he just stared back at me calmly before explaining that his wife understood he had to 'share his love.'"

"Jesus. What exactly has he been smoking lately?" Hannah asked, putting her arm around Kate.

"You're the one from backwoods Jersey, so you tell me." Kate smiled half-heartedly at her own joke.

Hannah took Kate's hand. "Well, there is a story about some teenagers and the poppy fields behind the high school."

Kate rested her head on Hannah's shoulder. "So yeah, I'm a home-wrecker."

Hannah stroked Kate's curls, pulling her fingers through the ever-tangled strands. "I don't think you can be a home-wrecker if his wife is aware of his penchant for sleeping with other women."

"*Pregnant* wife."

Hannah sighed, tightening her grip on her best friend. There was no easy answer to this situation—a man supposedly allowed to cheat on his wife. Was it even still cheating? Maybe not to Teddy. The growing wet spot on Hannah's shoulder proved it meant something to Kate.

HANNAH TURNED THE DEAD bolt. Kate only lived two blocks away, but Hannah always asked for a safe-arrival text. She glanced at her phone, though Kate was probably still in the lobby chatting up the doorman. Kate loved older gentlemen with character, and Ronny was a character. He knew all the residents and had taken a shine to Kate when she'd stayed over for a few weeks between apartments—and boyfriends. Hannah plopped down on the couch, wishing she had cable and could channel surf. But cable had been one of the first things to go when her rent went up last year.

The apartment had been her home for the last four years. With a little help from her parents, she'd been able to get a small, one-bedroom unit instead of a studio—a decision that she couldn't regret, even though it had cost her a dishwasher. She loved having a bedroom with a door instead of everything being in one open space. Not that paying the rent and keeping herself and Binx fed had always been easy. Journalists, especially ones working for small alternative music magazines, didn't exactly make enough money to support a New York City lifestyle. But Hannah had made it work, first by leaning on her parents too heavily and then by working too many hours at Starbucks. Now, she embraced the art of budgeting and forced herself to take an honest look at how she spent her money. It wasn't easy, but it was worth it.

Hannah picked up her untouched red wine. She swirled it around the glass, watching as it caught the rim and dripped down the sides. Wasn't there something about the quality of the wine and if it left marks?

"Happy birthday, Hannah," she said, toasting the air. Thirty. *Fuck.* On the outside, her life looked, if not perfect, certainly close to it—dream job, Manhattan-adjacent, long-term boyfriend, her own place. But something had felt off for a while. She could pinpoint her ennui to her sister's wedding. Stephanie and Charlotte had met in London in a whirlwind romance. They had married within a year. Stephanie, who was all of twenty-six, had a house in the suburbs, a wife, stepkids, and a chocolate lab. Hannah had six hundred fifty square feet, her cat, and Brian, who couldn't even be bothered to call on her thirtieth birthday.

She took another sip, glancing at her phone again. Two notifications. She clicked on Kate's message, which included a picture of Milo Ventimiglia's butt. *Happy birthday, chica.*

The other text was from Brian. A booty call if ever there was one. She was used to it by now—the late-night texts from her boyfriend—but they were seldom appreciated. Particularly because he always asked her to come to him.

Only if you come here, she typed before she could consider giving in again.

To her surprise, he answered right away. *Be there in 10.*

She glanced down at her penguin pajama pants. No one wanted a booty call in penguin pajamas.

Hannah's phone buzzed again, this time with a friend request. She stared at the name—William Thorne. The last time she'd seen him had to have been at Melissa and Tommy's wedding. That had been five years ago. It seemed like another lifetime. But they should've already been Facebook friends. She'd just seen a bunch of pictures of him from her twenty-first birthday in her Memories update. Had he started a new account or been hacked? Hannah clicked on his profile. They only had thirty mutual friends. Hannah opened her friends list and typed his name into the search bar. Will Thorne. Nothing. An inkling of a memory came back to her—graduation night, too many beers, and Will's lips on hers for the first and only time.

She jumped as her phone vibrated, shaking the thought of Will and that long-ago kiss from her mind. Brian was here.

Shit, shit, shit. Hannah scrambled to clear the mess, putting the wine glasses in the sink, the pizza box on top of the garbage, and the leftover crusts in the pail. She didn't need Binx presenting her with a dead mouse in the morning. Brian's keys sounded outside the door as he fumbled with the dead bolt. He never remembered which key went where. Penguins could be sexy. Not that it mattered. He was probably wearing Star Wars boxers.

"Hannah?"

She stepped into the living room, pulling her hair back in a messy bun. Brian leaned against the back of the couch. He was beautiful—tall but not lanky, athletic but not muscular. His light brown hair fell to his ears and hid the soft green of his eyes. It did her in every time she thought about ending things. She would miss those cheekbones, those bony hips, and the flutter she got every time he acted like the man she knew he could be instead of the boy he insisted on remaining. He'd even forgone the graphic tee tonight, opting for a fitted polo. Small miracles.

He turned to her with a smile, holding out a boutique of red roses clearly from the bodega down the street. "Happy birthday."

So much for pretending until morning.

Chapter 2
Hannah

Binx at her side, a steaming cup of coffee, and Brian's soft snores coupled with rain pattering against the building made for a perfect morning. Hannah had been sitting on the couch with her feet up for the last twenty minutes, bundled in her favorite hoodie that she'd stolen from Brian. The temperature had dropped overnight, but the heat hadn't kicked on yet. She breathed in the aroma of her coffee. If only it was the weekend. Hannah loved rainy days with their built-in excuse to stay inside under the covers. The dulcet sounds of a rainstorm calmed her, eliciting memories of childhood movie nights. Her knee, however, did not appreciate the change in pressure. It hurt the most when it rained. Lately, it hurt all the time.

Formative years filled with basketball and volleyball hadn't done her knees any favors, and a full-on, butt-in-the-air slip on some ice right after college had only added to her problems. All that had been manageable, but then there'd been the car accident last year. Hannah had been prescribed physical therapy, but the marketplace plan she had for catastrophes didn't cover such luxuries. At least, it didn't cover them enough to keep both her and Binx housed and fed. Her pain had ebbed and flowed over the last fifteen months.

Hannah had a sneaking suspicion she needed surgery. She stretched out her bad knee, pushing her leg as straight as it would go without pain. She noted the minor swelling with a sigh.

"You really need to do something about that knee." Brian stood in the doorway of her bedroom, wearing boxers covered in R2-D2s and C-3POs. He watched her with a concerned pout, as if that helped her any.

"It's just the rain," she said, bringing her knee back to a comfortable position. "Coffee's fresh."

"It's not just the rain. You've been favoring it for weeks."

Months, actually. It had worsened since that half-marathon she had known better than to run, but she wasn't going to agree with him.

Brian wrapped his arms around himself. "It's freezing in here."

He disappeared into the bedroom, reemerging in the sole pair of pajama pants he kept at her place and the zip-up hoodie he'd arrived in last night. It had been a battle to get him to leave any clothes there because of Binx and his alleged cat allergy. However, after a few frigid nights without heat, he'd brought over a single outfit and pajamas.

"I'm sure it will warm up eventually."

He zipped the hoodie all the way up. "You really need to talk to your landlord. No one should live like this."

This is New York City! she wanted to scream. She didn't have bedbugs. Her rent was a steal considering the fact that she had an elevator and a doorman. She could live with the inconsistent heating situation.

"Is my Claritin in the bathroom?" he asked when she didn't say anything.

The discontent that resided under Hannah's ribcage stirred. She lived with it much like she lived with her knee pain—never quite feeling comfortable. She told herself being with Brian was better than being alone, but right now, she felt that discontent spiraling into resentment.

"Babe."

Hannah glanced toward the kitchen where his voice had come from. Maybe he had decided coffee was more prudent, considering she hadn't heard him sniffle once in the hours he'd been at her place.

Her eyes passed over the roses she had arranged in a vase next to the television. Agitation swelled in her chest. She took a breath. The roses weren't the problem. She liked roses fine. But didn't her thirtieth birthday deserve more?

"Hey, babe. Come here for a second." Brian peeked out from the kitchen, a steaming cup of coffee in his hand. He wore a cheesy, excited smile that meant he was up to something—something he thought was romantic or epic, or epically romantic.

When she reached the kitchen, he was sitting at the table with his feet up, his toes hidden by her slippers, which he had apparently stolen. He didn't say anything when she entered but simply continued to stare at his phone. She'd played this game before. Whatever it was he wanted her to see, it was most likely in plain sight.

Nothing was on the counter except the same dirty dishes she had left there for the last two nights. The wine glasses were still in the sink, and the same banana peel was sticking out of the garbage pail from that morning. God, she wasn't in the mood for this, particularly not at five in the morning before she'd even finished her coffee. Holding in a sigh, Hannah faced the fridge. Her eyes wandered from her yoga schedule to the sandy beach magnet her parents had gotten her on their last weekend in Cape May to the My Plans Are Better than Yours magnetic clip she used to hold tickets and press passes for whatever show she was covering. The clip should've been empty, but it held a pair of tickets.

She grabbed the tickets, loving the feeling of them between her fingers. Her eyes widened as she took in the band name—Wilderness Weekend. "How did you get these?"

Brian's lips parted in a toothy smile. "Surprise."

Surprise, indeed. These tickets had sold out in six minutes, and Dave had won the straw poll to cover the show despite Hannah's adamant protest that she'd wanted—*needed*—to be at the Wilderness Weekend ten-year anniversary show at Irving Plaza. But Riley was keen on not playing favorites, and any double requests were settled with drawing straws or pretzel rods, whichever happened to be closer.

A cacophony of emotions hit Hannah—excitement, love, regret, and disappointment. She fought back the unexpected tears that came with them. Her heart ached at the perfect gift from her imperfect boyfriend. After all her traitorous thoughts yesterday, this. She clipped the tickets back to the fridge and planted a huge kiss on him. He responded in kind, but her heartache remained. Hope was a cruel companion. This wasn't the first time he'd gotten everything exactly right, and hope made her lose her resolve—he could change. He wouldn't, but he could.

"Thank you, Bri. These are perfect." She sat on his lap, running her fingers through his too-long hair. "Now explain how you got them!"

She felt him holding back laughter, and he kissed her cheek. "Well, I just called Leonard Nulty up—"

Hannah swatted him playfully.

"How do you think I got them? I was primed and ready at my computer for nearly a half hour before the sale opened. I preregistered so all my billing and shipping information was already in there. Right at ten o'clock, I refreshed and purchased them."

"Do you know how hard I tried to get these?" She hugged him again.

"Yes, I do." He laughed. "Happy birthday, babe."

She moved to her own chair and put her feet up on his lap. Why couldn't it always be like this? "So, are you finally going to come see Wilderness?"

"Uh, no."

And there it was—the Brian of the situation.

"You'll have much more fun with Kate or Riley."

"Riley is nine months pregnant."

He nodded, his expression neutral. "Somehow I don't think that would stop her from attending a concert, but fine, Kate or Stephanie."

He wasn't wrong. Kate and Stephanie were great concert partners. They were willing to get up close and personal, equally willing to find a good spot in the middle of the pack. But neither of them were Wilderness fans. Kate had gone to a show or two back in the day and would come if Hannah asked, but this show would be crazier, louder, and more overcrowded than ever—just the way an anniversary tour should be. Kate would hate it. Fans had been listening to them for a decade, and some of their songs had never been heard live before. It was a once-in-a-lifetime gift.

"Come on," she said, nudging him with her foot. "Me, you, and hundreds of other fans packed into Irving Plaza. It'll be sweaty and sexy, and there's a very good chance you'll get laid afterward. I'll even spring for dinner and ridiculously expensive concert cocktails."

She didn't know why she was pushing. Finding someone to go with her would be easy. She worked for a music magazine, after all, and she had her "Wilderness" friends, several of whom hadn't gotten tickets either. She knew there was no way Brian was going to go with her. He'd never attended a show with her despite all the free tickets and backstage passes she'd thrown at him. But he had *bought* these tickets—a *pair* of them. Somewhere in the fine print, it must have stated that the purchaser of two tickets could not turn down the invitation to attend, just like it was assumed that the receiver of the pair would take the gift giver.

"You know I don't mosh."

Hannah laughed, pushing herself to her feet. "I promise you, there is no moshing at Wilderness Weekend shows."

Brian didn't crack.

She took a final sip of her coffee and placed the mug near the sink with the rest of the dishes. She'd wash them before her shower. "Fine. I'll find someone. Thanks again for the tickets, babe."

WILDERNESS WEEKEND, like so many things currently in her life, had first shown up during her sophomore year at the University of Iowa. They were a no-name alternative rock band—emo, if she was being honest—out of Boston on the college circuit when they'd hit her school. Six months later, their lead single had smashed into the airwaves. They'd been mildly popular since then, sticking to the alternative charts and stations, which was exactly how Hannah liked it. Wilderness Weekend and their lead singer, Leonard Nulty, had been the soundtrack to her twenties, and she didn't see that suddenly ending as she started the next decade of her life. Every time she heard that first single, she was transported back to campus. Back to snowy days and too-drunk-to-care nights, Will and Kate by her side. She clicked on a Facebook photo album marked *Sophomore Year 2*. There were two of them because she was so old that albums had still only allowed sixty photos when they were created. She had most of these pictures printed somewhere, probably stashed in one of the boxes from her parents.

Will. It was so funny that he'd popped up the night before she'd gotten Wilderness tickets, since so many of her early Wilderness memories were wrapped up in him.

Her phone lit up, a picture of Kate silently flashing across the screen. Kate was on a date—the best way to wash away Teddy's bad mojo, according to her theories on dating. There were many theories, but the call wasn't a good sign.

She picked up the phone. "That bad?"

"I'm hiding out in the bathroom," Kate said in a muffled voice, meaning someone else was in there. "Can you call me back in like five minutes?"

"An 'Oh Timmy'?" Hannah asked, continuing to scroll through pictures on her computer.

"With a little more flair than usual."

The line went dead. It was bad enough when Kate called, but an Oh Timmy with *flair*? That was reaching stage-five-clinger level, or as Kate called them, "Herpes"—persistent and impossible to get rid of. The next episode of *Bitching about Boyfriends* was going to be a doozy. Hannah couldn't wait to hear the retold version of the story, always the most thorough and embellished when Kate was doing it for an audience. Kate would probably ask Hannah to reenact her phone call with fake distress, rapid breathing, and all.

Hannah jumped at the sound of someone knocking on her front door. No one knocked. Kate and Brian had keys, and everyone else texted their arrival. She stared at the door as if at any moment, someone was going barge in. She couldn't decide if it would be with a knife or a cake, but it was still early for the local riffraff, and she lived on the fifth floor. Though that begged the question of who was bringing her belated birthday cake. She walked to the door, staring at it for another second. Maybe it was just one of those annoying cable salespeople. Yes, she was perfectly happy with just Netflix and Hulu. No, she didn't miss flipping through five hundred channels for nothing to be on or to be sucked into yet another *Harry Potter* weekend. Fine, maybe she missed it a little, but not for the extra hundred dollars a month. The knock came again.

Hannah opened the door. Her mind registered the man kneeling on her doormat, but all she saw was the diamond ring.

Chapter 3

Hannah

Hannah's eyes widened at the boulder-sized princess cut diamond in front of her. Her heart dropped—Brian. A few hours ago, she'd been debating breaking up with him. Was he really proposing on the dirty hallway floor? Hannah blinked rapidly, trapping tears she knew were coming. She'd brought up engagement six months ago. He'd scoffed and disappeared for a week, reemerging with a tan and few apologies. But here he was on bended knee. She turned her attention from the ring to the man kneeling in front of her—the man who was *not* Brian.

She took in the older, leaner version of the boy she had once known. Memories flooded her brain—study sessions, drunken nights, Wilderness concerts, a graduation-night kiss, and finally, the image of him draped over yet another girl, this one in a bridesmaid dress.

"William Thorne," she said derisively. Her body buzzed, adrenaline coursing through her. She'd wanted it to be Brian—for him to have finally figured out that he wanted her for more than just the foreseeable future.

She turned her attention back to Will. He remained on one knee but had lowered the ring. A smile, halfway between questioning and amused, played across his face. "This is amazingly uncomfortable. Why do people propose like this?"

"Knights, courting, et cetera and so forth," Hannah said absently, waving him into her apartment. She peeked around the door, but fortunately, it was late enough that the hallway was empty.

Will stood, pocketed the ring, and came in hesitantly despite his initial grand entrance. Hannah watched his eyes travel around the room, taking in the small clues littered throughout the apartment before focusing on her laptop, which still had a picture of the two of them open. *Great first impression.*

"You seem surprised to see me," he said, turning his full attention and the power of his perfect smile on her.

She should've felt surprise at Will's sudden appearance, but she didn't. And not just because she'd just gotten a friend request from him—this was completely and utterly a Will thing to do. And really, she should've been expecting him.

"Well, you are a day late." *On top of the last half a decade.* Even as Hannah thought it, she knew she had a hand in those lost years. In the end, it wouldn't matter—not for them. They would still be Will and Hannah. She knew it, and by the contented expression on Will's face, he knew it too.

He pulled her into a hug, lifting her off her feet. "Hannah Abbott, as I live and breathe! I've missed you." She giggled as he twirled her around and set her down. He stepped back and gave her a once-over—not in the creepy way some guys did, but exaggerated and comical. "You used to be taller."

She rolled her eyes. Only Will would bring up the story she'd told him one snowy night on campus that, when she was seven, she'd spent a whole two months convinced that she'd been shrinking. The following April Fool's Day, he had moved everything in her dorm a few inches higher, making several things just out of her reach.

Hannah stepped further into the living room, keenly aware of Will's every move as he took a seat on the couch.

"Beer, wine, water?" she asked.

"Water would be good."

She nodded and pushed the lid of her laptop closed. "I'll be right back." As she headed for the fridge, her eyes never left Will's form.

He sat back on the couch, his hands clasped and his eyes fixed on his lap. A part of her—the part that knew and loved Will all those years in college—felt no qualms about his late-night visit. Will was Will. Even when they were best friends, he had flitted in and out of her life, always coming back just as she started to worry he never would. But underneath that calm was a rumble of discomfort. He'd shown up at her apartment—an apartment he'd never been to. She searched his face.

Will looked up, his eyes meeting hers. "Yes?"

"How did you know where I lived?" *So much for tact.*

"Oh, Kate told me."

Crap. She'd completely forgotten to get Kate out of that date. "Give me my phone."

He fumbled with the device sitting on the coffee table in front of him. "Look, I'm sorry if—"

"It's not that." Hannah took the phone from him, dialing Kate as fast as her fingers would allow. "I'm not angry that you have my address."

The line rang and rang. Hannah kept her eyes on Will as Kate's voicemail recording played. She was going to be so pissed. But right now, Hannah had her own situation to deal with.

She hung up and stared at Will. "You sent the carnations."

"Yes," he said in a tone that suggested she should've known this already.

"There wasn't a card."

"Well, it would've said, 'Happy 30th Birthday, Abbott. I believe we have something to discuss. Winky-smiley face.'"

"Will."

He placed the ring on the table between them. "*I'm* thirty; *you're* thirty."

She dropped into the chair next to him, staring at the giant sparkling rock he'd left sitting on her table. He couldn't be serious.

Heat rocketed up her neck and into her cheeks, but underneath, a hint of excitement brewed. Will Thorne had come to initiate the marriage pact.

Chapter 4
Hannah

It had happened on graduation night, post-ceremony and post–celebratory dinners at the best eateries Iowa City had to offer. After depositing their families back at their respective hotels, Hannah, Will, Kate, and Trevor, Kate's boyfriend, had met at the apartment the girls shared for one last night together. Kate and Trevor had disappeared after only an hour. Hannah hadn't blamed them. She and Kate would be leaving the following day for a European summer—a trip Hannah had somehow convinced her parents to fund as a graduation gift. No being a camp counselor at Ardena Heat. No airing her lack of any real plans to her former classmates, who undoubtedly had jobs lined up and more than a fleeting hope of keeping them. Unlike Hannah, who hadn't heard back from a single one of the New York City internships she applied to, including the coveted *Talented* internship. So, Europe it was—eight cities in eight weeks, giving her two months of blog posts to boost her writing portfolio.

With just the right amount of beer and taquitos in her stomach, Hannah's mood balanced somewhere between relaxed and giggly. Will had reached his introspective stage, meaning he'd had one beer too many and not enough taquitos. He'd lamented the fact that Hannah would board a plane for Europe in the morning and was already waxing nostalgic about their college lives. In typical Will fashion, she didn't have time to formulate a response before he was on to the next topic—the future. If there was anything Will didn't need to worry about, it was the future. Hannah could picture his whole life—law school, junior partner by thirty, a smart, attractive wife and two kids he doted on. He would be happy; it was that simple.

She'd tuned back in to his ramblings. "What if I never meet the right woman? Never experience true love? Never—"

"You will," she said, looking up at Will from her spot on the floor. She could hear the worries racking up and ricocheting in his head. She reached for his hand. "You will."

"What if I've already met her and let her slip away?" His eyes were bright, his voice returning to its nostalgic tone.

She laughed. "Then I suggest you go find her and tell her before she leaves Iowa City."

He sat up abruptly, and her hand slipped off of his. "See you later, then, Abbott."

Her eyes widened. She could've sworn he was being rhetorical. "Somehow I don't think this mystery girl would appreciate being told this in the wee hours of the morning."

He slid off the couch and onto the floor beside her. His hand wrapped around hers.

"I guess you're right. No one likes a drunk Will at two in the morning."

Hannah patted his arm. "I like you just fine at two in the morning, drunk or otherwise."

"Let's make a pact," he said, leaning his head on her shoulder. "If we're both still single when we're thirty, we'll get married to each other."

Hannah had learned the hard way that Will didn't make pacts lightly. She had once made a pact with him on a whim and ended up spending spring break building houses in Mississippi instead of partying in Fort Lauderdale.

"But I already have you penciled in as my man of honor," she said, nudging him with her shoulder.

He laughed. "I guarantee I will look much better in a tuxedo than a bridesmaid dress."

"I don't know." She gave him a once-over. "Plum would look good on you."

He turned to her, his expression playful. "Afraid to marry me, Abbott?"

She narrowed her eyes. He knew she liked a challenge. And there wasn't really a downside to this pact. By thirty, she'd either be married already or she'd get to marry Will. He wasn't bad to look at, and they had fun together. It could work.

"Fine. Let's make a pact," she said, holding out her pinky finger. Without a pinky promise, there was no pact. Rules were rules.

Instead of linking his pinky around hers, Will kissed her, soft and hesitant. He paused with his lips still on hers. They weren't friends who kissed. Hannah felt her heart speed up, confusion and longing and relief mixing in her veins. She leaned into the kiss, letting him deepen it just so. There had been a time when this was all that she had wanted. Could it be that way again?

Will pulled away, fixing her with a grin. "I thought we should know what we're signing up for."

She rolled her eyes, her heart rate dropping down to a normal pace. *Just Will being Will—that's all.* He pulled the sleeping bag over their legs. It was the two of them and the silence, and then she felt him link his pinky with hers—pact sealed.

"HANNAH?"

Hannah looked up from the blinking cursor she'd been staring at for far too long. Will wasn't thinking straight. How could he just show up with a diamond ring and a marriage proposal, pact or not, after not seeing her for five years?

"What's up?" Hannah asked, smiling up at Riley.

"You wanted to talk to me before I left for the day?" Riley said, bouncing between feet.

Fuck. This was not what she needed on top of everything else. "Oh, right, yes."

"Great, I just have to pee... again. So meet me in my office."

Once Riley was out of sight, Hannah made her way over to her boss's office and took a seat on the couch. She flipped through a tattered copy of an old *Spin* edition on the table—Riley's husband's first cover—but she couldn't focus. Instead, she leaned back and counted the cracks in the ceiling, trying to piece together what she had to say. Any way she phrased it, this was not going to be a fun conversation.

A few minutes and twenty-three ceiling cracks later, Riley ambled—waddled, when out of earshot—into the office. She patted her stomach, saying something quietly to the growing baby inside before easing herself into the oversized armchair she'd forced her husband to drag up four flights of stairs during her first pregnancy. Hannah had been an intern then, just out of graduate school, and one of only three staffers at the yet-to-publish-an-issue *Deafening Silence New York,* the offspring of the small but well-loved Los Angeles–based *Deafening Silence.*

That had been five years ago—five years of New York's finest indie music scene. Since then, the staff had bumped up to ten. Hannah had gone from intern to staff writer to columnist, finally settling in as the Long Island section editor last year. It wasn't the most glamorous gig, but she had gotten to interview bands like Taking Back Sunday, Brand New, and Nine Days—not that anyone remembered who they were until she sang the chorus of their single. It was a lot of growth for five years, and editor by thirty was nothing to frown at. Still, Hannah felt the itch for bigger things, better bands, and a salary that did more than keep the electricity on.

"What is it this time? Did Henry pitch the Halloween feature on the Amityville House again? Did Anita spell 'Hauppauge' wrong for the thousandth time?" Riley rolled her eyes, but her tone was endearing. "Do you need another intern?"

On any other day, these topics would've sent Hannah straight to Riley's office. "No, the team is fine. I'm actually... well, I'm checking in on what we talked about a few months ago."

She didn't have to look up to know that Riley was wringing her hands. Her boss had done it the entire conversation last time while making promises they both knew she couldn't keep, both of them agreeing to believe the lie. Until today.

"Nothing's changed. The management team in LA is focused on starting editions in other regions, but we don't have the investors. Without investors, we can't expand to Boston, Chicago, Austin. And without expansion, we have no money."

"Without money, you can't fund health insurance." Hannah sighed. They'd been talking in circles for a year. "I know all this, but it's been two years already. Do you know how much I pay for the barest of minimum plans right now? If anything happened, I would be in serious trouble."

"I know, Hannah. And I know I promised you I would do everything I could when we made you editor to get you insurance, but the higher-ups are just not... it's not in the plan for at least the next year. Boston is their priority right now."

A year. That meant another year of downing vitamin C at the first sign of sniffles, fearing that every ache would turn into something requiring medication, and forcing her knee into compliance with RICE.

When she'd quit Starbucks two years ago to take on the more demanding columnist position, she'd not only lost the extra income but the health insurance to go with it. As a staff writer, she hadn't needed to keep a second job, but Starbucks had kept her insured and supplied her with free coffee. It had also given her a built-in space to conduct interviews. But as a columnist, she couldn't manage both. She'd been on the cusp of leaving *Deafening Silence*—even going as far as to polish and preen her resume and collect writing samples—when the editor position had come along last year. The pay increase had also helped convince her to stay despite the lack of benefits. She hadn't planned for a car accident and a bum knee.

"How do they expect to hire a team in Boston without a competitive benefits package?" If things weren't so dire, Hannah would have rolled her eyes at herself. *Competitive benefits package?*

"They'll bring in people from the other editions, take on interns and freelancers," Riley said, still wringing her hands, "just like we did when we came to New York."

"You can't build a magazine on interns."

Riley smirked. "But we did, didn't we?"

The compliment warmed Hannah, even though she knew it wasn't the whole truth. Yes, she'd done way more than any normal intern would have been expected to. Riley had thrown her into the Warped Tour press tent in her first week with a simple "Have fun. Don't act starstruck." It had only gotten crazier from there.

"*Deafening Silence* wasn't built on me."

"No, not entirely. But without you, well... I probably would've left a long time ago." Riley sighed, and Hannah finally looked up. The tears she'd heard in Riley's voice were real. Riley moved her hands to the right of her belly where she could feel the baby best. "Which is why I should've said this to you two years ago—we can't give you what you need. If you have to leave, I can make some calls."

She meant it. Hannah knew Riley, and though Riley didn't want to see her leave, she would help Hannah go. *Deafening Silence New York* was Riley's baby—she'd literally moved across the country to start it five years ago when the editorial board decided they wanted an East Coast addition. And while her husband had continued to write for big-name music magazines, Riley had stayed the course. That didn't mean she expected anyone else to stay with her. But this was New York City—half the jobs were being covered by interns or freelancers, and the other half had thousands of applicants. It didn't help that Hannah was either vastly overqualified for many of the positions or lacking several years' experience despite her editor title.

Just as Riley had avoided saying that line for two years, Hannah had circumvented the reality of her situation. She *couldn't* stay. Open enrollment season was only a few months away. Thanks to her thirtieth birthday, the dirt-cheap plan she had would disappear, leaving more substantial plans with higher premiums. She could afford one if she sold her car.

"I should go check and make sure Henry didn't try and slip that feature into the layout again," Hannah said, turning on her heels. The weight of Riley's stare followed her out of the small office.

Hannah returned to her desk, flipping open her email out of habit. There were three new messages but nothing that required any mental space. *Damn.* A ridiculous intern email was exactly what she needed right now. Hell, she'd even take Dave's brutal edits on her article. Hannah swiped at her face, found it thankfully dry, and turned her gaze to the fading daylight.

HANNAH STARED DOWN at the bustling streets of Greenwich Village. She still sat at her desk, feet up and a piece of leftover cake in her hands, despite the workday closing. The streets, crowded at nearly any time of day, were filling with streams of nine-to-fivers ending their days and NYU students heading to local bars or the Public Theater. Life in New York City never stopped; it barely even paused. Days like today, she relished the chatter and the reminder that she'd chosen New York City and it had chosen her back. She blinked back a few lingering tears, watching a group of twenty-somethings clamor down the street, laughing and roughhousing. They wore no campus gear, but she saw them three times a week at this time. Sometimes she imagined they were law students fresh out of their torts class, their faith not yet marred by competition. Other times, they were writers just out of a workshop at the Lillian Vernon Writers House. She envied their made-up lives. NYU had been the dream, but a full-ride scholarship far outside New York trumped any hopes she had of her parents footing the larger bill.

Hannah stared at the white carnations from Will—Will, who wanted to marry her. Seriously, he was insane. They hadn't spoken in years. Not to mention, what did they know about getting married? Hannah hadn't been in a functional relationship since her post-grad days. She pushed herself back into a seated position, adjusting until her knee didn't feel like death. Brian was right—she needed to do something about her knee, though she didn't see how that was possible.

She picked a carnation out of the vase, running her fingers over the petals. She was certain Will had health insurance. He was a lawyer, according to his LinkedIn account—and a good one based on the size of the ring. And he would get something out of being married, too, right? Nothing about his online profiles gave her any clues. It didn't matter. They weren't actually getting married. She placed the flower back in its vase, smiling. He had remembered her favorite flower after all those years.

HANNAH ROLLED OVER for the fifth time, pulling the comforter tighter around her. She hated Brian's bed, with all its lumps and caverns and no Binx to keep her feet warm.

"Seriously, babe," Brian said, pushing himself up on his elbow, "I love you, but I'm about to kick you out of bed. What's going on?"

She squeezed her eyes shut and buried her head in her pillow. Too little sleep had Hannah on edge, her brain unable to decompress and let go of all the possibilities. It didn't help that, aside from a curt "Yes, no thanks to you" when Hannah asked if she was alive, Kate refused to answer her phone. Hannah had been desperate to tell her about the pact. She'd even shown up at Peace Love Yoga with a latte and the latest edition of *Talented* as penance, but Kate hadn't been at her normal Friday-evening class. Running to clear her head was completely out of the question. Even on her best days, it was hard. And with the never-ending rain, her knee hurt like hell. And what an idiotic idea spending the night with Brian had been, as if seeing him would have made everything make sense. Instead, she felt like she'd been lying to him all night.

"Kate is ignoring me," Hannah said. At least it was the truth—or part of the truth.

Brian made a face but didn't say anything.

"Why the face?"

"No, it's nothing. Sorry. I didn't know you and Kate fought... ever."

Why did that comment not surprise her? "Of course we fight. Have you met Kate?"

"Yeah, but enough to make you toss and turn?"

"It'll blow over," Hannah said with a shrug. "She called me to save her from a date, and I didn't come through."

"Good."

"Good?" Hannah asked, curling her knees up as much as her right one would allow.

"Yes, I hate that you and Kate do that. It's unfair to the guy. You think they don't know it's staged? How hard is it to spend a few hours with someone you don't like?" His expression lightened. "I'm doing it right now."

"Hardy har har," she said, slapping at him half-heartedly. She stretched her knee back out with a sigh. After two rainy days in a row and at least one more predicted, her knee was going be locked up for a week.

"Have you thought about more physical therapy?" Brian asked, falling back against his pillow.

"You know I can't afford—" She stopped, an idea suddenly taking shape. She didn't need to marry Will for health insurance if she could marry Brian. *How hard is it to spend a few hours with someone you don't like?* Hannah had been doing that for months. Brian had been sliding further down the boyfriend-quality chart for a while, but he had his moments. Maybe marriage was exactly what he needed to finally get his shit together.

"What if we got married?" she asked tentatively.

"Did you just propose to me?" he asked, his voice deep with what Hannah could only call fear.

She sat up, keeping the blanket wrapped around herself even though his apartment was always distastefully warm. "Hear me out, Bri." He didn't say anything, which, knowing Brian, wasn't a good thing. She plowed on. "I know we're not ready to be publicly married, but we can go down to city hall and make it official. No one has to know. Then I can go on your health insurance."

"I'm pretty sure that's illegal."

Hannah shook her head. "It would only be illegal if we pretended to be married."

"Okay."

Hannah's heart raced at the word. Had he just agreed to marry her after everything?

"What do I get out of this *arrangement?*"

Crap. She reached for his hand, but he held them both securely in his lap, out of reach. She'd miscalculated. He wasn't fearful; he was insulted. Cold settled into the inches between them, which felt like a chasm. Brian receded to his side of the bed, closing himself off. Frustration, rather than regret, fizzled in her chest.

"So, Hannah? What's in it for me?" His voice dripped with sarcasm, each word dipped in cruelty. "I mean, besides the opportunity to check the divorced box for the rest of my life."

"Wow." She refused to cry. Let him be mean and get it all out. There was no going back from her request. She hadn't thought that when she'd made it, but the answer was always going to be "yes" or "no." Either one changed everything irrevocably.

"This idea of yours is no way to start a marriage even if we were close to ready, which we're not."

"*You're* not ready," she said, finding herself exhilarated. They didn't fight like this. Brian usually disappeared or walked away. But this was real. She felt it down to her toes.

"No, I'm not. And more to the point, I don't want to marry you right now." Brian was on a roll and, it seemed, had no intention of leaving well enough alone. Hannah tuned him out until his voice reached his tirade's crescendo. "—between your job and Kate and—" Hannah knew the next word out of his mouth would be the dealbreaker. She'd known it since the first time he came to her apartment. "—Binx."

"If you didn't treat him with complete disdain, he might like you better." Hannah stood and flipped on the light. She reached for her clothes folded on the dresser, changing back into her jeans.

"Binx doesn't like anyone that's not you."

Brian stayed in bed, which only made Hannah angrier. She clasped her bra behind her back underneath her cami, knowing she had the hooks uneven but unwilling to be even partially naked in front of him. She couldn't look at his calm, complacent face anymore, but it was nearly one in the morning. It was going to be hard enough getting a taxi during peak hours, and she definitely wasn't taking the subway. She put her T-shirt on over her cami and fumbled with her phone as she slid into her sneakers. The Uber wait time was ten minutes. She didn't know what she was supposed to do until then, but anything was better than staying there.

"Hannah, it's the middle of the night. We can talk about all this in the morning."

Brian, her beautiful idiot, thought he could say awful things—insult her best friend and her job and her cat—and they'd just talk about it in the morning. "You just told me you don't want to marry me and basically hate everything that is important in my life. There is nothing left to talk about. Really, Brian, we should've had this conversation a year ago. It would've saved us so much time."

"I said I didn't want to marry you *right now*." He finally got to his feet and crossed the small space, wrapping his hand around her wrist.

"Well," she said, pulling her arm back. "There's someone who does."

Chapter 5
Will

Holy shit. She'd actually called. It would've been better had it not been almost two in the morning. Will had already been asleep for hours at that point. But Hannah *had* called, and there was no way he wasn't heading directly to her apartment. If he didn't know Hannah so well—or at least, he hoped he still knew her—he would be expecting a booty call. But Hannah Abbott was not a booty-call type of girl. Plus, he was pretty sure proposing with a huge diamond ring disqualified him from such debauchery. *Getting to Queens is a money suck, but at least there won't be traf*—he stopped his thought midsentence. He was going to jinx it. Now there would be overnight, all-lanes-closed construction on whatever bridge the cabbie took.

"Will, hold on!" Hannah's voice came through loudly over the phone.

He stopped halfway into a pair of jeans, the phone snugly fitting between his ear and shoulder. "Yes?"

"Come in the morning. Say, eight?" She sounded exhausted, and it was from more than being up at one in the morning. He wondered what had happened since he saw her last night. Had he caused the fatigue in her voice?

"I'll bring breakfast. The usual?" Will waited to see if she'd laugh or replace her standard Sunday-morning order from the three years they had shared that meal.

Her reply was light and appreciative. "The usual, but no sugar."

"Eight it is, then." He fell back onto his bed, kicking his way out of his jeans, grateful he didn't actually have to get to Queens and be a coherent, persuasive human.

"Good night, Will."

Six hours. In six hours, he could have a fiancée. Once they discussed the details, she'd said. He smiled to himself, burrowing back into bed. Hannah had always been a step ahead. She was astute enough to know that Will hadn't asked on a complete whim. He should've thought the proposal through more. But then he wouldn't have done it. He would've stayed quiet as he had for the past several years, silently watching Hannah's life flourish. It wasn't that he hadn't missed her—he had. But he couldn't be around her and *not* love her, which had become highly problematic for all his relationships. But then there'd been Madison. She'd made him see past Hannah and want to love someone else. So he had let Hannah go, fallen in love, and done everything right. He had made peace with the Hannah-shaped hole in his life. Those things happened—college friendships stayed in college, people grew up and apart, life went on. And it had. Until four months ago, when Madison had quite literally screwed everything up.

When he'd come out of his vodka-induced haze a month ago, he had found himself a thirty-year-old man whose life was on the brink of destruction—his girlfriend gone, his family ties strained, and his job dangling from a tightrope. After a full week of no booze or other vices, he'd woken from a dream of Hannah—a memory, really. In the dream, Hannah had slipped her hand into his, running her fingers through his hair. It had been sophomore year before he'd realized his feelings for her. She had leaned in ever so slightly, and he jumped down from his stool to greet one of his fraternity brothers and to flirt with some other girl. Lila? Lilly? A month later, Hannah was dating some asshat from the baseball team. If Will remembered correctly, the two had met that same night over a game of beer pong. But she had liked Will first. That was the important part of the dream. All these years, he had secretly loved her. Maybe she loved him back.

Will jumped as his phone vibrated on his bedside table. His heart quickened a bit at the second vibration. *Hannah?* No, of course not.

"Stop calling me, Madison," he said without bothering to hide his contempt.

"I will if you let me come over." Madison was whispering. Somewhere along the line, she'd gotten the idea that whispering was sexy. He'd tried explaining to her several times that it was dropping your voice, not whispering, that denoted sexiness. But still, she whispered. It also meant that her fiancé was home.

"No."

"I miss you, William."

Maybe she meant it, maybe not. Their breakup, her infidelity, and then her constant attempts at an affair had blurred the lines of the truth too much for him to know who she wanted. Either way, it didn't matter.

"You're marrying my brother."

"That didn't stop you before," she said, a hint of amusement coloring her tone.

He ran his hand over his face. It had been one moment of weakness. Everything that had happened between the three of them had been so fresh. His wounds had not yet cauterized and were constantly reopening at the seams. When she had appeared in his doorway, looking like the woman he loved, it had been as if he willed her into existence. The whole night had been a mistake, one of the worst of his life. It sent him spiraling, and he had only just figured out how to slow it all down again. But even with his resistance and the physical distance from Madison, the night they had shared after she'd chosen his brother lived with him, in the farthest corners of his mind, haunting him with its injustice.

"I can't—no, Madison," he said, the sudden wrongness of even this phone call hitting him. It wasn't that he couldn't be a part of the infidelity, but that he didn't want to be. Not anymore. "Stop calling."

He hung up then threw his phone onto his nightstand. She would call back and might even show up at his place. Madison wasn't used to being denied. But he would not be party to her antics, especially now. He conjured an image of Hannah in his mind. For the first time, she appeared as a thriving and talented grown woman. An inquisitive, worried, and yet slightly intrigued expression played across her features, each emotion battling for equal ground. He closed his eyes, willing sleep to come. Tomorrow, life might begin anew.

Chapter 6
Hannah

A leftover tidbit of half-and-half floated in Hannah's coffee mug, resisting all attempts at removal. Meeting at eight in the morning had been ambitious. For two nights, she'd barely slept, and now she was supposed to be making life-changing decisions. She rubbed her face. Calling Will had been a gut reaction. She'd been pissed at Brian and herself and filled with disappointment. Marrying Will was ludicrous, but as long as his reasons checked out, she was going to do it anyway. Hannah's stomach lurched. Why had she said eight in the morning?

At least the kitchen was cleaner than in recent weeks. Last night, before getting the brilliant idea to hide from her thoughts with Brian, she'd cleaned practically the whole apartment after work. Screw spring cleaning. Stress cleaning had a much better success rate. She eyed the refrigerator, scanning the assorted photos for any remaining of her and Brian. Instead, she found the Wilderness tickets still stuck in the clip. They had to be returned. It grated at her nerves. Brian would get no use out of them, except maybe through scalping. His delicate sensibilities probably made "scalping" a dirty word. So maybe she *was* still angry. She smiled into her coffee—better angry than bawling. Maybe she'd keep them and take Will. The concert was in a few months; it could be their honeymoon. Did a marriage of convenience get a honeymoon? Probably not, but an island vacation didn't sound so bad. No parents, no work, no responsibilities. Yeah, she could definitely use a honeymoon.

The clock on her phone flashed eight, and at the same time came that distinctive knock. She should've recognized it on Thursday. Will had come up with a coded knock for Hannah and Kate their junior year. It let the girls know they had approximately thirty seconds to get decent before he came in. Hannah and Kate had come up with funny retorts to the knock that year, but she couldn't remember any. She stopped in front of the door, gripping her coffee mug, and took a calming breath. If she opened the door, her path would divert from the expected. She could turn down the offer, nullify the pact, but underneath all the apprehension, a spark of excitement remained. Marriage was always a crapshoot. Maybe if more people thought it through practically instead of emotionally, fewer marriages would fail. Maybe she and Will were batshit crazy.

She shook her head, smiling. *Only one way to find out.*

Standing outside her door, a tray of coffees in one hand and a brown bag with what she hoped was an egg everything bagel with a veggie smear in the other, Will looked like a memory. He greeted her warmly, but the set of his shoulders, the tightness in his cheeks, and the dulling brown of his usually bright eyes showed his anxiety. Whatever Hannah felt for Will—nostalgia, love, or attraction—the rambling hello he offered as he handed her the coffee intensified those feelings. The Will she knew didn't get rattled or nervous. Even with their former closeness, Hannah had only been granted glimpses behind the veil. But proposing couldn't be easy, and most guys at least had years of a stable relationship backing them up. Will was flying by on his looks and the goodwill of old memories.

He stopped in the kitchen doorway, still clutching the paper bag. His eyes darted around the small space, stopping on Hannah every so often as she reached for plates and mugs. Every time their gazes met, she looked away, focusing on the plates, setting the table, or carefully pouring her coffee from the cheap paper cup into her mug. But she could still feel his gaze each time it passed over her. One of them had to say something. The conversation needed to be had, or it would be like this forever—awkward, confused, and energized. He had proposed. It should probably be him. But then again, she called him here. Hannah turned to him, ready to start the spiel she'd spent too much of the last hour going over, reminding herself that it was Will and a wedding, not peace talks between warring nations.

"You look like hell, Abbott," he said, his true smile finally appearing. "What's on your mind?"

She leaned across the table over the egg everything bagel with vegetable cream cheese. "Well, you see, this long-lost friend showed up at my door the other night with an engagement ring. Things got a bit murky after that."

"Long-lost? Really?" He leaned forward as well. They mirrored each other from across the table, elbows against the hard surface, hands clasped in front of them, and expressions sarcastic.

Hannah rolled her eyes. They really were idiots. "Last time I saw you, you were dancing the horah at a wedding. If I'm not mistaken, you left with one of the bridesmaids before cake and didn't even say goodbye."

For a moment, his expression turned pensive, but then he smiled. "I'll have you know I dated *Valerie* for three solid months."

Hannah held up her hands. At least he knew her name. "Fine. An old friend turned up at my doorstep the other night with an engagement ring." She toasted him with half of her bagel.

"Was it for you?"

Hannah chucked a piece of bagel at him. "Seriously, Will."

"You're really considering doing this?" His expression was amused yet surprised.

The hair on her arms stood up, and her shoulders tightened. "Should I not be?"

"Don't get me wrong. I'm stoked that you are considering marrying me, Abbott."

Of course he would still call her that, a habit he'd fallen into after a frat row party two weeks into their friendship. She supposed there were worse things he could've called her—such as "Nana," which was what Kate called her at her drunkest. It always started with "Hannah Banana," but by the end of the night, she would just be "Nana"—not even the whole fruit.

"It's just not your style," he said, sitting back in his chair. "I expected to get laughed out of your building. Spontaneity was never your strong suit."

Will's definition of spontaneity fell more along the lines of spur-of-the-moment tattoos than random trips to Wawa. The muscles in her back unclenched a bit.

"You're not a drug addict, a recovering alcoholic, or dying or anything, right?"

"We're all dying, Abbott," he said, his tone somber for a change. "But no, I am not actively dying. Nor am I addicted to anything harder than caffeine."

She nodded. "Okay."

He stood and took a lap around her small kitchen. "Now that that's out of the way, do you have any other questions?"

The detailed mental questionnaire she had meticulously crafted disintegrated, each question dropping from her mind as she tried to recall it. Everything she wanted to know about his life in the last five years was replaced by one blinding need. "Why?"

Hannah watched Will pick at his fingernails, his eyes trained on what must have been the most interesting hangnail ever. It was becoming increasingly apparent that Hannah didn't know this Will. He had changed since graduation, and it wasn't simply growing up. Whatever the change was, it was rooted deep in him. There were still hints of the boy she had loved all those years ago, but there was a weariness to him too. It was as if all the fears he had and all the expectations he had to meet were crushing him.

"Why what?" he asked, leaning against the doorjamb.

There were so many whys, but she would settle on one for now. "Why do you need to get married?"

"Always so on point," he said, tapping his nose twice. He sat down again and took a sip of his coffee.

"I mean, that's why you want to initiate the pact, right? There's a reason you need to be married," Hannah said lightly. She knew she was being pointed, but he was wasting time if his reasons were less than noble.

"It's not anything..." His eyes scanned the kitchen before landing on her. "Can we do this anywhere but here?"

It was an odd request, but then again, sitting at a table figuring out the details of a sudden marriage was an odd thing to do on a Sunday morning. They had always done their best talking while walking. "Where do you want to go?"

***

THIRTY MINUTES AND a subway ride later, they were almost to the High Line. When Hannah needed quiet on loud days in the office—and there were many loud days—she sometimes came here or to Madison Square Park. She'd sit and people watch, imagining the lives of whoever caught her eye, practicing her profiling skills as if she were writing a feature story that started with that very meeting. *Sitting on a New York City park bench, the man illegally feeds a pigeon...* It was weird being here with Will—or with anyone. The only person she'd ever walked the High Line with was Stephanie, on the morning before her wedding as her sister had a panic attack about becoming a wife and stepmother at twenty-four. In a city where it was impossible to ever be alone, it was important to find havens.

"Four, almost five months ago now, I found out my girlfriend was cheating on me," Will said between beats and without inflection.

Hannah paused where she stood, expecting him to say more, but he kept walking, his stride never breaking. "My dad, he likes to throw this big kickoff-to-summer party at our place in the Hamptons. It happened there in a very public manner. Life got messy after that."

Empathetic phrases bounced around Hannah's head, but none seemed quite right, and she knew from experience that those well-meaning words did little. They usually made it worse. Hearing that his emotional anguish was commonplace wouldn't help alleviate Will's pain. "What happened?"

"I tried to go back to work to keep up appearances, but after something like that, I just wasn't *there*, you know?" he said as they sidestepped a couple and their two dogs. "I work as in-house counsel for my family's real estate development company. There's a lot of red tape at the start of a project. We hire consultants to do impact and site assessments and basically to tell us if the land is going to be a pain in the ass. During due diligence, I missed something. I *missed* it."

Hannah could tell that the mistake still haunted him and maybe always would, but it would also make him better at his job. Will didn't make the same mistake twice. She remembered the night during junior year he told her that straight off a broken heart.

"We lost in court," he continued. "We didn't get the permits. It cost the company a lot of money and delayed the project indefinitely."

They walked in silence for a few minutes, stopping to take in the latest art and enjoy the view of the city whenever they caught a break in the crowd. It was nice walking the High Line with Will; he understood its pull. There was no chatter like there would have been with anyone else. Comfortable silence had always been one of the great things about their friendship. They could sprawl out on the floor of her dorm, heads touching, sharing a pair of earbuds. Hannah would be studying, with Will reading when he should've been studying. All of it, nearly every moment, had been set to Wilderness Weekend. They took a seat on a nearby bench with a view of the river.

"Things have been really bad at work since then, obviously. My dad wanted me fired," he said, worrying at that thumbnail again.

Hannah couldn't imagine ever working for either of her parents but tried to picture an instance where they pressed to have her fired. It sounded like Will had failed epically at his job, though given the circumstances and that he worked for his own family, maybe that was exactly why his dad wanted him fired. He still had to be accountable. Nepotism only went so far. Hannah didn't know enough of Will's family to say.

"My uncle—he's the CEO—convinced my dad and the board to give me another chance. But I need to prove to them that I have my act together, that I'm serious about my job. The thing is, I've been showing up in a full suit and working twelve-hour days. Nothing is working. I have practically memorized the last three reports that came in—I'm like Mike friggin' Ross right now, minus the whole fraud thing."

While Hannah was always one for a good pop culture reference, Will had done a very good job of circumventing the point. A relationship gone wrong leading to a giant mistake at work didn't add up to marriage. If anything, Hannah thought, that would make him seem impetuous, which wasn't a word usually associated with lawyer.

"I need them to take me seriously," he continued.

"But I don't see how—"

He held up a hand to stop her train of thought. "I know doing something crazy to make them see me as serious seems counterproductive, but at this company, only age or marriage gets you a seat at the table. At thirty, I was supposed to get a spot on the board. My dad did, my uncle did, and so did my older brother. They haven't invited me to a meeting yet."

Will turned had thirty in April, apparently just before everything in his life had broken down. Hannah's mind churned, going over his words again and again. For the first time since Will had shown up at her doorstep, Hannah could see how this might work. Will didn't need a pretend wife or a fiancée. He needed it to be real and binding and searchable in the public domain. She'd spent much of last night worried that Will would have the same reaction as Brian to her insurance request. But since he was the one who had sought her out, Will needed her possibly more than she needed him. "So, it has to be legal?"

"Yes, it has to be legal."

She laced her fingers with his, seeing how each finger fit into her own. She'd held hands with Will before; they'd had that type of friendship. There had also been that weekend he'd pretended to be her boyfriend when a particularly persistent law student wouldn't leave her alone. Will's hands were dry, and she felt a callus on his pinky. She wondered if he dragged his hand when he wrote. If he even wrote longhand enough for that to be possible. The texture of his hands held a story, and the longer their fingers stayed intertwined, the more she wanted to know it.

A shiver ran through her as she brought her gaze up. His eyes studied her face, not their hands as she had expected. Unbridled longing and desire and hope stared back at her. Then with a blink, each of the emotions dimmed, settling into curiosity. Before she could overthink it, she kissed him. Their lips moved against each other, clumsy and uncertain, but she couldn't deny the spark. It had been there eight years ago, and it was still there now. She didn't know what that meant for them, except that kissing Will unsettled her in ways both good and bad.

It's not going to be forever, she reminded herself. One career saved and one knee surgery later, they'd move on with their lives, both better off.

"What was that?" he asked after they pulled away.

She ignored the breathiness of his voice and shrugged. "I wanted to know what I was signing up for."

Chapter 7
Will

Leave it to Hannah to make their second first kiss sloppy and confused and flavored of everything bagel. The kiss hadn't been unpleasant—he didn't think there was any way that kissing Hannah could be unpleasant—but it hadn't been earth-shattering. It didn't live up to the memory of that graduation-night kiss; it was not a kiss you told your children about. He shook his head, chiding himself for the thought. This wasn't about that. And it might never grow into that. No matter what he had once felt for Hannah, he needed to keep his head on straight. But the little details of Hannah burned in his memory—her inquisitive golden-brown eyes when she caught him watching her, the freckle on the crest of her right cheekbone, and even the pen marks littering her right hand.

Hannah stood and held her hand out as if the kiss hadn't happened. "Come on, I want to show you something."

She chattered incessantly from the moment they got on the downtown subway until they skirted Washington Square Park. Even with the students and the tourists, the park smelled of freedom and creativity. Or maybe that was just the scent of weed wafting off half the hipsters they passed. He didn't miss the hipsters. As Hannah led them down a side street, he could already imagine her office building—quaint, classic, full of stories waiting to be uncovered. Why Hannah wanted to show him where she worked, he wasn't exactly sure. The magazine she worked for was small—he was ashamed to say he'd never picked it up, though he'd seen it a few times. It was unlikely they were the Google of magazine offices, but she'd insisted, and he was kind of excited to see how she lived.

She unlocked the office doors with a key—not a swipe or fob, but a physical key. Musty, stale air, heavy with the scent of hardwood and old city brownstone, greeted them. The scent took him back to long ago production nights in the Brown House with Hannah and a mismatched group of wannabe journalists. He wondered if Hannah had felt the same way when she first walked in, if she felt it still, and if it somehow grounded her to this publication.

She sat down at one of the smaller desks with a picture of a coworker and her girlfriend in one corner. "When I started, this was my desk." She rubbed her thumb over a worn spot that on closer inspection showed her initials carved into the wood. "I'd finished my masters, and *Deafening Silence* was just opening in New York. It looked so much like the Brown House here, and Riley was young and broken and determined. It became like home. Five years later, I feel more like myself between these walls than I do in my apartment."

He waited for her to continue, to add to the end of the statement, to give it meaning. Loving your job was a privilege not afforded to many, but to love it more than your home life felt an uncomfortable balance. Even with everything that had happened these last few months and the even more tenuous ties to his family, home was still better than work.

"There's... I-I need health insurance," she said after a few false starts. "My job doesn't have benefits. I can't afford the marketplace plans, and I have a chronic knee injury." She grimaced at his expression. "I was in a car accident and injured my knee over a year ago, but without insurance... it's been too long of me trying to fix the problem myself. Honestly, at this point, I probably need surgery."

"So, it has to be legal," he said, parroting her words back to her.

She nodded. "It has to be legal and include access to your health insurance, which I'm assuming you have."

"Yes, I have health insurance," he said slowly. Health insurance had been on his list of reasons Hannah might agree to get married, right under his good looks, pity, and financial and criminal trouble. "My brother Daniel is also a doctor, so we can get you in fast and with some of the best if you don't already have a preferred ortho."

She smiled, tentative and shy, but Will could sense the tension around her fading, an almost nervous energy radiating from her in its place. "Should we have some ground rules?"

Will's heart pounded in his chest, in his ears, and at the base of his wrist. Hannah had agreed to marry him in not so many words. He hoped she couldn't see the sweat beading at his temples or the excitement oozing out of every pore. He never dreamed she would agree. Well, maybe dreamed. He pulled his thoughts back to Hannah's actual question. *Ground rules for marriage—how romantic.* "Whatever you want, Abbott."

Chapter 8
Hannah

Ground Rules for Our Marriage:
1. *We will remain married for one year.*
2. *We won't be assholes about money should we get divorced.*
3. *We may not date other people.*
4. *Binx is allowed to sleep in the bedroom.*
5. *Our friendship is the most important thing.*

Sometimes college seemed like ages ago, another life, or a different track that couldn't possibly have ended up here. But then Hannah would make some joke that only Kate would get because it had to do with that one night at that one party with that one guy, and it felt present again. They'd aged out, not grown up. Sitting back in her apartment with Will, debating ground rules for their made-up marriage, she felt on the cusp of going both backward and forward. He sat contentedly on her couch, alternating between petting Binx and flipping through pages of Netflix suggestions. Simple actions, really, but Brian could never—would never—sit with Binx or scratch his ears. Binx didn't purr often when other people were around, but he purred now, loud and deep.

She tapped her pen against the list. Five things. That couldn't be all there was to a marriage.

"The list is fine," he said. Hannah heard the opening chords of Netflix's creepy new show. "It's not like we're signing anything into law. We can always amend it."

"Yeah, but I have a more rigorous list of requirements for the pet sitter." She put the pen down and noticed little blue spots dotting her palm.

"Well, Binx is a hard-ass." Will ran his hand down Binx's spine, causing the cat to arch his back.

Hannah rolled her eyes. "Clearly."

"I'm sure we could come up with a whole page of things to add to that if we really tried. But I do think it's this simple. We'll be married for at least a year—enough time to get me my board seat and secure it with a whole slate of meetings, long enough that we can handle anything that comes up regarding your knee, and long enough that no one will question the validity of the marriage. Neither of us will be a jerk, and we'll just find our own way. I'm pretty sure most people who get married don't have a list of rules."

"Yes, but they've usually been in a relationship for a while."

"We were best friends for three years. We basically lived together for a semester senior year."

"Will."

"Fine." He picked up the pen and pulled the paper toward him.

Hannah watched him scribble a few things, growing more incredulous by the letter. He couldn't be serious. But he was, because he was Will.

Ground Rules for Our Marriage:
Number 1: We will remain married for one year.
1a. We can choose to stay married for an as yet undecided period at that time.
Number 2: We won't be assholes about money should we get divorced.
2a. What's yours is yours and what's mine is mine.
Number 3: We may not date other people.
3a. We can choose to date each other.
Number 4: Binx is allowed to sleep in the bedroom.

4a. In a cat bed.
Number 5: Our friendship is the most important thing.
5a. No matter what, we stay friends.

Hannah looked up from the list. "How does that make it any better?"

"It gives us options. And an out—'no matter what, we stay friends.'" He gently turned her palm into his. "You might love being married to me, Abbott."

"Doubtful," she said. "I remember what it was like to live with you—boxers mixed in with my clothes and your socks hanging off the television and the Christmas tree!"

"I promise I put my socks in the hamper now," he said with a grin.

She met his gaze, allowing herself to get lost in it for a moment, recalling all those long-ago feelings to the surface. He was still the boy she'd loved—older and a bit more broken, but so was she. "Let's get married."

His expression softened, though he clearly had questions. Hannah wondered if he was afraid to break the silence until his hand cupped hers. "Why?"

"Because you're sweet and I want to help you."

Pink spots formed on Will's cheeks, and she knew she'd convinced him.

"I've missed you, Will Thorne."

He smiled his real smile—the one she'd been waiting to see since he'd shown up at her door. He closed his fingers around hers and pulled them both to their feet.

"What are you doing?" she asked as he led her behind the couch.

He didn't respond except to grin wider. Then after a quick search around the space, he found what he was looking for—the dimmer switch. The room fell into a golden hue of sunset lighting. He returned to her, dropping down to one knee.

"What are you doing?" she whispered again.

"Giving you a proper proposal." He took the ring out of his pocket and held it out to her. "Hannah..."

Hannah held her breath, waiting for the words every girl dreamed of hearing one day, but Will seemed frozen.

"I don't know your middle name," he said with a small, uncomfortable laugh.

"Guess we should've made profiles instead of rules." She waited a few extra beats before revealing the answer. "It's Grace."

"Hannah *Grace* Abbott." He put extra emphasis on her middle name, and for once, she liked it. Her parents had cursed her with a monogram that read "HAG" for the first thirty years of her life—yet another marriage benefit. She should really be writing these down. Will tugged gently on her hand, and she focused back on him and the ring and the moment. "Would you do me the extraordinary honor of marrying me?"

Her heart sped up, and despite the inauthentic circumstances of the proposal, the weight of the ring on her finger made it all the more real. Thirty years and she'd never worn a ring on that finger, and yet, as she looked down at the princess cut, the ring—which she knew must have been intended for someone else—looked like it had always belonged there.

"Yes, I'll marry you, William *Anderson* Thorne."

He groaned. "Only you would show me up at my own marriage proposal."

"I suggest you get used to it," she said with a grin.

Chapter 9

Hannah

Hannah stared at the mash of letters in her word-scramble game, swiping a random combination. The game shook, signaling an error. Frustrated, she dropped the phone onto the bed next to her. Sleep wouldn't come, no matter how many sheep she counted or how long she played that incessant white noise app. She'd read through the latest issue of *Talented*—the one meant for Kate—twice already. She knew everything there was to know about Matt Czurchy's newest role and the inspiration behind Maroon 5's latest album. She didn't even like Maroon 5, but it wasn't like *Talented* was going to have anyone remotely indie in its pages. Turning on her side, she picked up her engagement ring. It was ostentatious and everything she thought she'd never like. But she *did* like it. Maybe everyone liked their engagement ring because of what it symbolized, or because of that forever memory. Or maybe she was more materialistic than she wanted to be. A ring like that said something about who she was and the company she kept.

Will had already planned to spend the day on the golf course with one of their mutual college friends, Eddie. He had invited her along and even offered to cancel, but Hannah had wanted the day to decompress. And if Will saw how awful she was at golf, he might rescind his proposal.

Sitting alone in her apartment, she wondered if it would've been better to stay in the moment. And if she should've asked him to stay the night, considering they couldn't date other people. Will had been pretty clear that the marriage had to appear as real as possible in public, but she'd been the one to push for exclusivity. Hannah didn't want anyone to see her husband out with another woman. Marriage of convenience or not, there needed to be *some* sanctity—particularly if they evoked the clause about dating each other. Will had written it down in his clunky handwriting without hesitation. Because sex. Who wanted to not have sex for a year when they were sharing a bed? At least, she assumed they were sharing a bed. It would be too obvious otherwise, and in the city's closet-sized spaces, having a second bedroom was unlikely. Though Will clearly had money.

She opened the memo app on her phone and added a note: *Where do I sleep?* Under it, she wrote a second question: *Do I want to sleep* with *Will?*

It was a valid question. The glimpses of him she'd gotten at the various toga parties over the years had been pleasing, and there'd been that one time she'd seen his butt. And it was a nice butt—it could be his main selling point when it came to appearance, especially with the jeans from yesterday. Thank God for slim-fit, straight-leg jeans. Brian always wore relaxed fit. *Brian.* Her heart rejected the casual reference. Had it only been two days? It wasn't that she hadn't thought about him—she had. But whenever the thought popped into her mind, she banished it or let it bounce away. She needed to figure things out with Will first. That was all her brain could handle at the moment. Mission accomplished. Checklist checked. But now, she couldn't ignore the Brian in the room, even as much as she wanted to.

She wasn't callous enough to feel nothing. Things hadn't been great for a while, but she did love Brian. A fight, a night, and an engagement weren't going to suddenly change her feelings. That didn't mean she wanted to get back together, but she couldn't help checking her phone for an apology or, at the very least, an *I'm coming to get my stuff* text. Emotions whirled around inside her, and she let them grow. They extended to the tips of her fingers and burrowed deep in her gut. Each emotion demanded to be felt and experienced. Sorrow, loss, relief, fear, and clarity trickled down her cheeks. It had been time to end things—she knew that, had known it for months—but Will's arrival had pushed the issue. Anger flashed in her chest, and for a moment, she hated Will and his stupid smile and his beautiful engagement ring and his perfectly shaped ass.

But this wasn't Will's fault—yes, it definitely was. Though she had let things with Brian settle into comfortable dissatisfaction. Long-term, their life together would have been an unhappy one, filled with the differences they refused to either acknowledge or reconcile. She didn't know why she was wasting time on these thoughts. A real future with Brian had always been a moot point. Binx was only three, and she wasn't getting rid of him, and Brian would never have moved in with them. That didn't make it hurt less.

Her hand trembled as she wiped away stray tears. Her heart was bruised, but she could already feel it rebounding. The decision to marry Will—though crazy—was a good one. She believed that. She longed to talk with Kate, her fingers hovering over her phone, but Kate hadn't answered a single one of Hannah's calls in the last three days. Kate *had* posted the latest podcast episode, so Hannah knew she was alive and well. And tonight, Hannah wanted to share her news with someone, not explain it. She swiped around until she found her text conversation with her sister. She glanced up at the time in the corner of her phone—nine forty-five. Not too late, but Stephanie was an old twenty-six.

I'm getting married in two days, she typed, the words unbelievable even to herself.

Stephanie's response was fast, which usually meant she'd caught her scrolling in bed. *Ruh-roh—preggo?*

She'd have to get used to that reaction. It would be the norm, and no one was going to believe she wasn't pregnant until her belly remained flat—well, flattish. But knowing didn't help the flip-flop in her stomach as she reread Stephanie's words.

Another text came in before she could come up with a proper response. *Charli says she didn't think Brian had it in him.*

Well, if there was ever an opening, that was it. *Not pregnant, and not to Brian.*

Hannah didn't have to wait long. She'd only counted to twenty before her sister's picture popped up on the screen. She wondered if it would be Stephanie or the hybrid, "Charlanie"—Charlotte and Stephanie. The static of speakerphone came through on the other line. Charlanie it was. Hannah pushed the thought away. She liked Charlotte. But Charlotte and Stephanie had been hard to handle from the beginning, always attached at the hip, talking in that royal relationship "we." Time and marriage hadn't made it any better.

"Explain," Stephanie said in response to Hannah's greeting.

Hannah chewed on her thumbnail, regret settling deep inside of her. There was no way she could tell her the truth. Lying wasn't Stephanie's specialty, and one wrong look from their mother and Stephanie would spill every one of Hannah's secrets—she had in the past. But Hannah had to say something. "Do you remember Will Thorne?"

"Your friend from college? Yes."

Last night, she and Will had briefly discussed the need for a backstory, something along the lines of having reconnected a few months prior. But having to formulate it on the spot and have it be less than scandalous—Brian had been present at a family event on Labor Day—left Hannah at a loss.

"What's going on?" Stephanie asked.

It took Hannah a moment to realize she'd been taken off speakerphone, which meant for once, she just had her sister. She wished that changed anything.

"Will and I reconnected a few months ago. It was totally platonic, but then things with Brian took a wrong turn... and I'm getting married in two days," she said, the weight of the lie lessening with each word.

"How are you getting married in *two days*? Does Mom know?" Stephanie was getting worked up now. Hannah heard it building with each syllable.

"No, and you can't tell her, Stephanie. It's just going to be a really small thing. I thought maybe it would be better to let Mom think we were just engaged for a while. Ease her into it." Calling Stephanie had been a mistake. She should've just manned up and apologized to Kate. This news was never going to stay quiet.

"She's going to kill you."

"I know. I'm sorry. I shouldn't have involved you." Hannah hoped she sounded remorseful and not regretful, but at this point, she couldn't tell the difference. The lies and the truth were too meshed together.

"Of course you should involve me. I'm your sister." Hannah could feel the depth of Stephanie's eye roll through the airwaves. "That's like the whole point of my existence."

There had been a time when that was the unequivocal truth. A time before houses in the suburbs and model domesticity. Before midweek concerts, two a.m. deadlines, and a city had stolen Hannah's heart. Back then, it had been cute that Stephanie couldn't keep a secret instead of being a fatal flaw. Not that they weren't close, because they were, but slowly, their disparate styles had caused their lives to diverge.

"You know Mom will be mad at you simply for knowing the truth," Hannah said, shifting her phone to her other ear.

"So I won't tell her." For the first time, Hannah sensed a hint of frustration in her sister. Stephanie had definitely picked up on Hannah's subtle attempts at backpedaling. "When you show up with

Will and a wedding band, I'll act appropriately shocked. And I'll barely have to fake it."

"*You* are going to lie? To Mom?"

"Trust me, Mom's not going to be mad at me for, like, the next nine months and probably for the next few years after that."

"Wh—" *No way.* "You're pregnant?"

"Surprise, Auntie Hannah!"

"Way to bury the lede!"

"Um, where in the conversation that started with 'I'm getting married to some random guy in two days' was I supposed to slip that in?" Stephanie giggled. The lightness of her laugh carried through to Hannah, calming her head and heart. "It's still really early. I don't want to tell Mom until I'm further along. So... I'll keep your secret, and you'll keep mine. Deal?"

If they had been together, Stephanie would have had her pinky out. Without a pinky swear, everything was hearsay and words. Without a pinky swear, all bets were off.

Hannah linked her own pinkies together. "Deal."

Chapter 10

Will

Tahiti, Maui, Turks. Will scanned the Wellington Thorne database for honeymoon destinations—and there were plenty—but he couldn't decide. None of them screamed "Hannah," and all of them had been on his list of proposal vacations for Madison. Maybe Europe. Hannah had gone before. Perhaps there was somewhere she wanted to see again. There was only one way to find out. He dialed her number on his office phone.

She picked up on the fourth ring. "Hello?"

"Hello, my darling fiancée," he said, cluing her in. He hadn't considered that she wouldn't recognize his office number. "Do you have a second?"

"Not really, but what's up?" She sounded distant. Wherever she was, it was crowded and loud. He imagined her sitting in a restaurant in SoHo, waiting for some musician only heard on Alt Nation.

"Where would you like to honeymoon?"

She laughed but quieted when he didn't join in. "Oh, you're serious."

Muffled background static came across the line, followed by garbled speech, but it sounded more professional than secretive. Maybe his imagination was spot-on.

"Listen, I gotta go—impatient singer and all. But beaches are always nice," she said at lightning speed before hanging up.

A beach. Well, *that* narrowed it down and put him right back where he started. Turks, Maui, Tahiti. He pulled up the list of luxury hotels again—Hilton Head or Antigua? He opened the weather app on his phone. There didn't appear to be any hurricane warnings for the next week as of yet. Antigua. It was quiet and one of their nicest resorts. Hannah would love it. Assuming she had a passport still. He wrote himself a note to ask before he bought the tickets.

The unmistakable clearing of his older brother's throat caught Will's attention. Jon stood in the doorway in a perfectly pressed suit. It fit better than any suit he'd ever worn before. The Madison effect. It had happened to Will too.

"Everything okay?" Jon asked, stepping into the office. He stood with his hands in his pants pockets, looking heartily uncomfortable. Will almost enjoyed it, but Jon never stopped in without reason anymore.

"Yes," he said more tersely than intended.

"Well, good. Why the sudden vacation?" Jon took a seat.

Fuck. They were tracking his vacation requests. The request had been sudden, but it shouldn't have been cause for alarm. Will had more than enough time built up, and he'd been working his ass off for the last six weeks. "Dad sent you?"

"Do you think it's a good idea to be taking vacation right now? After everything?" Jon's voice was strained, but his expression remained stoic.

You mean after everything that you *caused?* He wanted to say it perhaps more than anything he'd ever wanted to say before, but that would be going backward. All the angry words had been said. There was no reason to rehash them, or so his father reminded him at every opportunity. But there was so much left to say that sometimes it made Will sick. His marriage to Hannah was a new path, one in which his father didn't see him as a proverbial screwup who couldn't even keep his girlfriend from sleeping with his brother. Yeah, that had been a Jonathan line for the books, as if his father hadn't set the bar impossibly high from birth.

"It's just a vacation. I'm not having a breakdown or doing anything that will embarrass Dad or the company." He held up two fingers. "Scout's honor."

"That would mean more if you were actually a Boy Scout." Jon laughed and unbuttoned his jacket, a sure sign that this conversation wasn't over. "Lunch then? I'd love to talk—"

"Actually," Will said, turning off his monitor and pocketing his cell phone, "I have lunch plans. Thanks for stopping in—totally saved me from being late."

"How is it that I see you eat the same salad from Susanna's every day except for the days when I ask you to have lunch?" Sarcasm clung to every word. Underneath it, Will sensed loneliness, but Jon had done this to himself.

"Just unlucky, I guess." He took his trench coat down from the rack in the corner of his office, folding it over one arm. His brother didn't move from his chair. Will wanted to leave He didn't owe Jon anything, but Jon was still his big brother, though he couldn't say what that meant anymore. "We can have lunch when I'm back. I'll see what days Daniel has off, and maybe we can make it work. We could go to that place Mom always liked."

"Valspino's. We haven't been there in ages." The tremor in Jon's voice was slight. Most people wouldn't have noticed it, but Will wasn't most people. He remembered the exact moment that tremor started—the morning she was diagnosed—and all those years later, he was still waiting for it to disappear. Of the three brothers, Jon had held on the hardest, as if retaining his grief proved he loved her the most. There was no telling Jon it wasn't a competition. Everything was a competition when you were a Thorne.

NOT TEN MINUTES LATER, Will found himself at 28th and Park, a handful of blocks from his younger brother's hospital. It had become such a routine in the last few months that he didn't even realize that's where he was headed until he arrived aboveground. As a second-year resident, Daniel kept a busy schedule, but occasionally he could spare a few minutes or a quick cafeteria sandwich. Even when he wasn't free, the area had enough restaurants and parks to keep Will occupied for his lunch hour. Sometimes, if he was feeling touristy, he'd head over to the Empire State Building or the Museum of Sex. Once, when he'd needed a particularly long break from the office, he'd gone to see a movie.

Will walked the few blocks to Madison Square Park. He remembered Hannah mentioning that it was one of her city havens. How many times had they just missed each other over the years? Sat on opposite sides of the park? Or shared the same bench a handful of minutes apart? He shot Hannah a quick text about her passport status before sending another message to his brother. He couldn't tell Daniel. He wanted to, but the less people who knew the truth about Hannah, the more likely his plan would succeed. If he could keep Hannah away from his family for the whole year, he absolutely would. But that wasn't an option—not with Jon and Madison's endless wedding events and the family weekends their father insisted on since he stepped down as CEO.

As a family business, Wellington Thorne had been passed down to his father, Jonathan, and uncle, Grayson, when Will's grandfather had passed. Per the will, the eldest Thorne—Jonathan—would act as CEO for a period of fifteen years, at which time Grayson Thorne would step into the role while Jonathan took over CFO duties. While the transition of power had been peaceful at the beginning of the year, the clout Will's father still had over the company and the board was undeniable. It was his own father who had tried to have Will fired, and he'd almost succeeded. And even though his father worked remotely from the Hamptons most of the time, letting Jon handle much of the day-to-day work, Will felt his presence more now than when they'd shared an office. Some days, he swore his father was having him followed.

Will's phone vibrated, alerting him to a text from Daniel. *Perfect timing. Meet me at Goodtimes.*

Goodtimes was the diner near the hospital. It reminded Will of Doc Magoo's with its constant flow of doctors and nurses. Daniel hadn't appreciated the comparison, but that didn't deter Will from making it every time he stepped into the place. He cut down Twenty-Sixth Street to avoid the madness of Madison and Park and jogged the few blocks up Third to the diner. Daniel stood outside chatting with a man Will recognized as one of his brother's attendings. He waited for their conversation to end before crossing the street.

"Excuse me, Dr. Carter, is it?" he said, pulling his brother into a hug.

"Dick," Daniel said with a grin. "What drove you out of the office this time?" he asked as they sat down at a back booth. Daniel reclined as much as he could in the confined space.

"It's not a *what*."

Daniel laughed, but he didn't open his eyes. Exhaustion etched the lines of his face, heavy bags under his eyes. His scrubs were wrinkled but thankfully clean of any questionable stains. Will wondered how long his shift had been—his brother usually put on a better showing than this.

"You have to give him points for tenacity." Daniel straightened up at the sound of the waitress's sneakers against the linoleum. How often did he eat here to recognize the cadence of her steps? "Adele, my love, I need so much coffee."

Adele appeared to be in her late fifties. She wore the chunky plastic frames of a hipster and a bowling shirt.

"Can't run only on coffee, doc," she said amiably.

The smile Daniel gave her was affectionate—he definitely spent too much time at this diner. "I can try, Adele. I can try."

"All right, dearie—coffee and the usual?"

Daniel nodded.

Will skimmed the menu, already missing his salad from Susanna's. Maybe he'd stop in on his way back to the office. "Just a coffee for me."

"Long day?" Will asked after Adele turned to the next table.

"I've been on for, like, eighteen hours or something. They asked me to pick up a half shift as I was walking out the door." He smiled. "It was worth it, though. I got to assist on this really cool surgery."

As he went into the literally gory details, a storm of affection and envy wrecked Will's mood. Daniel was exhausted but exhilarated as he went on about human anatomy. That excitement was something Will hadn't felt in all his time at Wellington Thorne. Will didn't see that changing anytime soon. Every day under the ever-present gaze of his father's spies, the proverbial noose tightened. Fresh air became harder to come by. But Daniel had gotten out of the family business and of being a perpetual letdown. Will and Jon had each taken the deal—MBA, JD, or MD in exchange for time in the family business. Daniel had refused and had funded his own way through medical school. Even though he was on the path to becoming a great doctor, Daniel was the black sheep when he should've been the golden child. But that was Jonathan Thorne for you, in love first and foremost with his company. Anyone who turned their back on the company turned their back on him.

During his four years of medical school, Daniel hadn't come home once—he'd wanted to, but he hadn't been welcome. It was only upon his return to New York, with Jon and Will threatening to walk away from the company, that their father had granted him reprieve. The price for their betrayal had been the mandatory family weekends. If they so wanted to be a family, then *dammit*, they would act like one.

In the almost eleven years since his mother's passing, his father hadn't softened. There'd been that first month, where they'd traveled to several hotel openings as a family, but if anything, without their mother to temper him, Jonathan had become colder and less forgiving. Will had been nineteen when his mother died, in the middle of his freshman year of college at Columbia. Her death had sent him spiraling out of New York. His father had at least given Will his pick of far-off schools where he could find his head and not make too much of a spectacle of himself—or at least far enough away that no one would notice or care. U of I had been perfect for that. And his father had been right—outside of New York, no one cared.

He didn't remember ever talking about his father with Hannah, at least not in a specific way. He had whined about the weight of expectation. She had countered with stories of suburbia and parents who were involved but not orchestrating. But he couldn't tell her what her parents did for a living or even their first names. He should probably find that out if they were going to be his in-laws, though he suspected Hannah's parents weren't quite as googleable as Jonathan Thorne.

"Uh-oh."

Daniel's voice pulled Will's focus back to the conversation. He only hoped the goriest of details had passed. But Daniel's story was long over, and his gaze was fixed on Will.

"What?" Will asked, grabbing a fry out of the to-go container Daniel had his food delivered in. It was easier for a quick exit, he'd said.

"You have that 'I'm going to do something incredibly stupid, and yes, it definitely involves a woman' look."

Will trained his expression back to neutral. "Whether it is incredibly stupid is yet to be seen, but there *is* a woman."

"Do I even want to know?" His voice was grim, but one corner of his mouth kept quirking up as he fought back a grin. Daniel was always one for the underdog.

"Probably not, though all will be revealed at our next family weekend." The weight of that sentence hit Will as he said it. The next family weekend was in two weeks—barely enough time to be settled into a routine, nonetheless proficient in love. Not that pretending to be in love with Hannah would be hard, but his family would know all the right questions to pick apart the situation.

Daniel stared at his phone as a series of large bells sounded. It was obnoxious, which was probably why Daniel had picked it. There was no way to miss those bells.

"Well, great. Something to look forward to then," Daniel said, pocketing his phone. The determined look in his eyes made it clear his mind was already back in the hospital. He stood, the to-go container in hand and not even a bite out of his sandwich. "That was the ICU. See you soon, big brother... and don't do anything too stupid."

Will grinned up at him. "Never *too* stupid."

Chapter 11
Hannah

She scrolled through Will's profile again, double-checking their mutual friends—thirty out of fifty-two. His page was active, with most of those thirty mutual friends being fraternity brothers and other college acquaintances, and the timeline for the new account worked out based on the demise of Will's last relationship. They'd broken up, and it had been awful. He'd regrouped. Somehow Hannah had made the cut, and she was going to be his wife. She rummaged around her desk for the last Hershey's Kiss. She'd brought in five from the kitchen, but she couldn't find the last one, hidden in the mess of papers. Her hand alighted instead on their freshly signed marriage license. It had been processed at 4:37 p.m.—meaning by five o'clock tomorrow evening, she could be married. She probably should've vetted him before signing the marriage license. Too late now.

Hannah picked up the license again. *William Anderson Thorne and Hannah Grace Abbott, Expected Wedding Date: October 16.*

Married. They'd have to send something to the alumni magazine.

Social media made getting a marriage license seem more romantic. Signing the license and making sure it was at the ceremony was the final step in the long process of wedding planning. No license, no wedding—no exceptions. How many times had Stephanie's officiant said that? Couples posted the obligatory town-hall picture hashtagged with their unique wedding name, a countdown to the event, and big dopey smiles on their faces. It was actually one of the parts Hannah always thought she'd look forward to—the moment when it was all officially happening, state sanctioned and everything.

Will had made them take the cheesy picture, but they couldn't exactly post it anywhere. And the process hadn't been romantic at all. A bored older woman had asked them a series of monotone questions, never once bothering to inquire about their story or why they'd waited so long to get the license if the big day was tomorrow. If Hannah spent most of her days with giddy soon-to-be-married couples, she supposed the excitement would wear off too. It was probably the forced or shotgun weddings that caught that lady's interest, where she could concoct stories about the fighting couple or the pregnant woman and her scared-shitless guy—Hannah couldn't be the only one who did that.

Hannah's fingers finally unearthed the last Hershey's Kiss. She savored the slow melt of the chocolate, the sugar providing the necessary boost of energy to bolster her confidence for the final task. It was time to go see Kate.

LESS THAN TEN MINUTES later, Hannah stood outside Kate's door. Kate hadn't answered her call on the way over, but she'd given Kate more than enough space. She knocked, shifting her ring so it was centered on her finger. Will had gotten surprisingly close to her ring size, but it wasn't exact.

Kate opened the door, her cell phone tucked between her ear and her shoulder. She rolled her eyes at Hannah's presence but stood back enough to let her in.

Hannah held out her hand, engagement ring flashing. "I'm marrying Will tomorrow."

"Patrick, I'm going to have to call you back." Kate ended her call and took Hannah's hand in her own. "Explain now."

"Patrick?" Hannah said instead. "Isn't he the Herpes?"

Kate shook her head. "Him being a Herpes wasn't the problem. I repeat, explain now."

Hannah ran through the last few days at lightning speed— the pact, Will's sudden appearance with a ring, breaking up with Brian, and her decision to marry Will benefitting both of them. Three days ago, Kate would've tried to talk her out of it. But when Hannah held up the signed marriage license, Kate only sighed, shook her head, and declared they needed wine.

"You think I'm making a mistake," Hannah said when Kate returned with two glasses of Malbec.

"Yes, I do," Kate said, her eyes going from Hannah's face to the ring on Hannah's finger. "I also think it's a mistake both you and Will need to make."

Hannah took a sip of her wine. "Meaning?"

"You and Will spent so much time talking—I mean, you two talked about everything and absolutely nothing. You never told him sophomore year when you liked him. And it was hard for you. I know it was because I was there all the nights you cried."

Hannah couldn't argue that point. She had fallen hard for Will when he'd transferred to U of I. She'd spent months forcing herself to bury those feelings as he went on to date Ana and Eva and Lilly and so on. So she'd dated, too, until eventually, the universe had given her her own love story.

"Will was so clueless about the whole thing. When he finally saw you—"

"When he what?"

"Twenty-two-year-old boys don't just make marriage pacts."

Hannah disagreed—marriage pacts were basically created by scared twenty-somethings.

"I think that maybe this marriage isn't just about convenience for him." Kate paused and put a hand on Hannah's arm. "Just something to consider."

Was she suggesting that Will was in love with her? Hannah tried to pick a memory and reframe it with that information, but it didn't compute. Will had never looked at her as more than a friend. She would've noticed.

"Did he ever tell you anything about his life in New York?" Kate asked. "About his family?"

"Just that his mom died, and it really messed him up. And that his dad was kind of overbearing." She thought of everything she knew about Will. He had two brothers and a difficult relationship with his dad, both then and now. "Nothing out of the ordinary. Is that not the truth?"

"But you know about Wellington Thorne, right? He told you?" Kate asked.

Hannah only nodded, unsure where the conversation was going. "Yes. I saw it on his social media, and he mentioned that he works for his family, and obviously, Wellington Thorne is a huge luxury-hotel developer. But I don't see why it matters."

"Wealth changes people. I just... I know you didn't know about it back in college. He never spoke about his family like that, but he's a socialite, and there are expectations—"

"He's still Will. He had money in college. He has money now. It doesn't change anything." Hannah took another small sip of wine. She meant what she said. The social media roundup had been more for her curiosity than to check him out. She didn't require the specifics beyond what she had asked and what he had willingly provided, because he was Will Thorne, the last boy she'd truly trusted.

"I know that. It's part of why I love you." Kate motioned for Hannah to follow her to the bedroom. Once there, Kate started pulling dresses out of her closet. "I'm not going to lie to you and say I'm completely on board, but I know when you've made up your mind. If you'd wanted to be talked out of this, you would've forced your way into my apartment sooner instead of letting me be a bitch about the Oh Timmy."

"I *am* sorry," Hannah said, sitting down on the bed.

"As you should be," Kate said, but a smile played across her lips. "I'll give you the details another time. All I'm going to say about this marriage of yours is that it's going to make an amazing episode of *Bitching about Boyfriends*. It might even get its own arc."

"You *can't*, Kate," Hannah said slowly. Her explanation had made it clear that the pact could not be mentioned again. "It's a secret. In no way, shape, or form can you put me and Will in your podcast."

Kate held up the cornflower-blue A-line dress she'd worn to Stephanie's wedding against herself and frowned at Hannah through the mirror. "Fine, but you owe me. I have one more question."

"Go on," Hannah said, preparing herself for the worst.

Kate put down the A-line and picked up an eggplant high-low gown. "Have you even thought about what you are wearing?"

"Probably just one of my sundresses. Something with a hint of white?" She knew there were at least two options in her closet that should fit, though neither was appropriate bridal attire.

"That's what I thought." Kate pulled an off-white fit-and-flare from her closet. It was not a wedding dress but the kind of dress every bride-to-be donned at smaller events. It had lived in Kate's closet for years—for her own eventual engagement.

Hannah shook her head. She couldn't. But Kate only smiled and pressed the soft material into her hand with a nod.

Chapter 12
Hannah

Hannah slid the folded piece of paper out of her notebook again. The letter had been harder to write than expected. Still, she felt good about the decision, Will or not. Brian hadn't texted, and enough time had passed that any texts would feel awkward and delayed. He'd said his piece and owned it. Something like pride swelled in her chest. He'd grown a lot from the young barista she'd known and fell for, but not enough—never enough. After their argument, Hannah couldn't help but acknowledge that he'd probably felt the same way about her for the same amount of time. Neither of them was quite good enough for the other, their edges always jabbing each other instead of smoothly sliding together. She knew what he would think when he heard she was married—what she would assume in the reverse situation. No one deserved to think they'd been cheated on.

She raised her hand to knock but dropped it to her side for the second time, acutely aware that she was making herself late for her own wedding. She still needed to get uptown in heels and a dress. Brian wasn't home—at least, there was no reason he would be home. On Tuesdays, he went to the gym after work and then spent an inordinate number of hours playing *Call of Duty* or one of those other inane shooter games with his buddies. As ridiculous as she found it, Hannah had enjoyed the predictability. Finally, she knocked. She'd wait ten seconds, tape up the note, and be done with it. *Eight... nine...*

A stirring behind the door, a rattle of a doorknob, and then Brian stood in front of her in his standard uniform of jeans and a graphic T-shirt, this one reading The cake is a lie. His eyes narrowed at the sight of her, but he didn't close the door in her face.

"You weren't kidding," he said, his voice unusually gruff and his eyes taking in the white dress. "I always imagined you with a subtler engagement ring."

She tucked her hand against her side. Words escaped her. No version of this scenario had involved Brian being home. Had she even considered it, she wouldn't have worn the ring and might have tried to cover the dress. "I wasn't expecting you to be home."

Could she have said something more banal? What was wrong with her? At least her voice had been steady, and she was pleased to note her heart still thrummed at its regular beat.

"I took a few days off." Brian shifted his weight between legs but didn't move from his blockade of the doorway.

She paused. Brian usually saved all his PTO for actual vacations, particularly his annual trip to San Diego for Comic-Con, where he fanboyed for three days. Hannah chanced a real look at him—heavy five-o'clock shadow, unkempt hair, wrinkled clothes. It was nothing she hadn't seen from him before, especially the opening weekend of a new game, but she always had advance notice about releases, and he hadn't mentioned one. A high-pitched, badly accented "yippee" came from inside the apartment. He was playing *Mario Kart*. He only played *Mario Kart* on his darkest days.

She stuffed the letter into his hand, ignoring the flutter in her stomach. "This will... well, I hope you'll read it."

He opened the folded sheet, his fingers brushing against the Wilderness Weekend tickets she had taped to the lower half. "These were a gift."

"I know, but after everything… You can resell them, probably for a lot of money," she said, trying to calculate how late she would be. Kate knew she was coming and wouldn't let Will think otherwise.

He skimmed the page in front of him, his countenance giving nothing away. He looked up, refolding the paper, the Wilderness tickets in his hand. "Keep them."

"Are you—no, I can't." She pushed them back into his hand, regret already filling her as she did it. She wanted those tickets. She would have to pay triple the face value to get them after this. Her phone vibrated in her purse, not for the first time. She pulled it out, mainly as a distraction from watching Brian stare down at the tickets he had worked so hard to get. *Shit.* There were two messages from Kate already and one from Will.

She gripped her phone. "I really have to go."

Brian nodded, a funny look spreading across his face, somewhere between nostalgic and forlorn. His mouth quirked at the corners, but the smile didn't reach his eyes. "Good luck, Hannah."

She stepped back from the doorway. "Goodbye, Brian."

Chapter 13

Will

She was here. In white. For their wedding. Sweat beaded at Will's temple. Kate's reassurances that Hannah was just running a little late had done nothing to quell the terror that she'd changed her mind, that he'd lost her before he ever had her. Hannah hated to be late, often chastising him for what she called "Will-time"—plus or minus thirty minutes to any arrival time, on a good day. She appeared calm—a bit harried from rushing, but he couldn't sense any doubt in her. Her smile brightened as she listened to Eddie's story of how he came to be a registered minister during pledging freshmen year and how that had earned him "Rev" as his pledge name. Hannah slipped her hand into Will's, squeezing lightly, and Eddie straightened his shoulders. Kate graciously accepted Hannah's small bouquet of paper flowers—a surprise gift from Hannah's sister. Will looked between his friends, once the most important pieces of his life. Maybe life really was cyclical.

"Are you okay?" Hannah asked, leaning into him.

He brought their entwined hands up to his lips, kissing her left hand where shortly a wedding band would rest. Her gaze remained sharp and tinted with concern.

"Never better, Abbott."

"Hey now," Eddie said, cupping his hand over theirs. "Save that for the finale."

Will hadn't told him the whole truth or, rather, any of the truth. Eddie would've still married them out of respect for his friendship with Will. Brothers didn't deny brothers unless drugs, death, or physical harm were involved. Will had assured him that it wasn't a shotgun situation, but Eddie wasn't stupid. He'd been there the day Madison and Jon's affair rocked the Thornes. He'd been there in the months after. So even if he didn't know about Hannah and Will's arrangement, he knew enough.

"Ladies and gentle*man*," Eddie began, his eyes comically sweeping over each of them. "We are gathered here today to witness the union of Will and Hannah, two of the best people I know. To know them is to love them, and though Will and Hannah haven't been together all that long, I'm not surprised that we're standing here today. If you search your hearts, I suspect you aren't surprised either."

Will wondered if Eddie had expected more people. Eddie had personalized his opening, and though he was only talking to Kate and Stephanie, who Will hadn't even known was coming, his speech still sounded as if he spoke to a room full of people. He wasn't being glib either. Eddie, for all they'd razzed on him in college, took marrying people very seriously. Once, after too many beers, Eddie had explained that, in some way, he felt a responsibility for the couples he married, be they friends, family, or friends of family.

"Marriage is a risk, a leap of faith, perhaps more so than any other choice in your life. Because it is a choice. Will, Hannah, you two are choosing each other, choosing to embrace and strengthen and grow the love you have for each other. Now," he said, pausing to give the couple a knowing smirk, "you just have to continue to choose each other for the rest of your lives."

Will caught Hannah's eye. They were as golden as ever, hinting that her mood was at the very least still good and calm.

She broke away from him, turning the full power of her smile on Eddie. "Easy-peasy."

"Easy-peasy indeed." Eddie held up his hand, and Hannah high-fived him without hesitation.

This. This was why he loved her, had always loved her. She had high-fived the officiant—friend or not. Hannah made stories in everything she did. Their wedding story would already be unique, but now, it would be fun. It would have personality. It would perhaps stand out enough to make everyone believe in their love.

"Now, Will, if you would please repeat after me: I, William, take you, Hannah, to be my lawfully wedded wife."

The words shattered Will's resolve to appear as close to neutral about the situation as he could. His breath caught in his chest, his heart raced, and his voice trembled. Hannah was all he could see—strands of light-brown hair falling across her cheeks from the wind, the curve of her lips as she smiled at him. It had always been and would always be Hannah. How had he ever thought differently?

Chapter 14
Hannah

"To love and honor you for all the days of my life." The words reverberated through her body, sinking into her skin and bones. Most people imagined saying something akin to those words while standing in front of family and friends and professing their complete love for another person.

At the start of the ceremony, she'd felt playful. The train ride across the city and the power walk up the High Line—in heels, no less, which had done her knee no favors—had boosted her confidence. Things with Brian were settled. The ceremony represented the start of a new path, unconventional though it may be. Under that excitement, she was a pile of nerves. When Eddie had talked about choosing each other, Hannah understood, maybe for the first time, that that was exactly what love was really about. Those buried emotions had bubbled under the surface and, *god*, she had high-fived Eddie. Will had clearly thought it was cute. But it was more than that—the high-five had loosened the reins, and the levity of the moment hit her. It was her *wedding*.

For better or for worse, today would always be a part of Hannah's story. Today mattered. And it wasn't how she ever expected, but standing there, hands interlocked with Will's, Kate and Stephanie at her side, in her favorite spot in her city, it was perfect. Will's vows, whether they were ones he had found or written himself, had been flawless. Instead of talking about unconditional love, they spoke of encouragement and support and laughter—all things that couples shared but also things that Will and Hannah had once shared and would share again. As she had repeated the vows, her eyes locked on Will's, they weren't a lie. She *did* promise to encourage him, to support him, and to always be open and honest with him, because they had been best friends. And in their friendship, there was no other way to be.

Hannah shifted her weight, trying to find a comfortable position for her knee in her heels. But it had been too long since she'd worn real heels, and she'd walked much too far. She'd known better.

"Are you okay?" Will whispered, turning a concerned eye toward her.

Perfect. She'd been late, and now her stupid knee was upending the ceremony. "It's fine. It's just heels and I don't get along that well."

"Here." Kate pulled out a pair of rolled-up flats from her clutch. "I had a feeling you were going to need these."

Stephanie snickered—the same sound she'd made when Hannah had arrived in the heels. Her exact words as she pulled her into a hug had been "You finally agree to wear heels today of all days?" So maybe Hannah had put up a fight about anything higher than a kitten heel for Stephanie's wedding, but this was *hers*.

Hannah slipped the flats onto her feet, expecting them to be jokingly large—Kate wore shoes two sizes bigger than hers—but no, Kate had gotten these special. "Thank you!"

She chanced a look at Will. He had his hands in his pockets and the same amused grin she'd seen on him a million times before—his "only Hannah" grin. Except now, in light of the information she'd gleaned from Kate's cryptic warning, Hannah didn't know how to take that smile. Her whole understanding of Will was being colored by Kate's admission, up to and including the marriage pact she'd so blithely agreed to all those years ago. Most people who made marriage pacts ended up in relationships. At least, that's what the internet said. Had Will's plan been to make the pact and woo her after Europe? He couldn't have planned for Paul. Only Hannah would travel halfway around the world and come back with a boyfriend from her hometown.

Eddie cleared his throat, and Hannah straightened, relinking her hands with Will's. She mouthed "I'm sorry," but Will only shrugged before directing his gaze back to Eddie.

"The rings?"

Rings? Married people had wedding bands, but there must be some protocol for ringless weddings. Wedding tattoos were all the rage now, right? Wouldn't Will have prepped Eddie for that? But no, Eddie looked at them expectantly.

"Oh, right." Will took a tiny box out of his suit pocket. It was that particular shade of purple associated with one of the city's finest jewelers.

Eddie took the box without a word, handing a ring to Hannah. It was thin and flat—not curved—and was most likely made of platinum, or maybe titanium. It would look good on Will. She attempted to peek at the ring in Will's hand, but he shielded it from her view.

"From the earliest times, the circle has been a symbol of completeness. An unbroken and never-ending circle symbolizes a commitment that is also never-ending. Will, please take Hannah's hand and repeat after me." Eddie paused while Will and Hannah reconfigured their hands.

"I give you this ring as a symbol of my commitment to love, honor, and respect you." Will's voice remained steady as he repeated after Eddie, and the ring slipped seamlessly over her knuckle.

Hannah's breath caught at its delicate beauty. With its sparkling half pavé, the slim band was the perfect complement to her left hand. It would fit comfortably under her engagement ring, but she also knew—and she bet Will did, too—that it looked even nicer on its own.

"This seemed more your style," he said, leaning close to her. "I know the engagement ring is a bit much."

Tears rushed to her eyes, forcing their way to the surface with little warning. She sucked in a breath, a few rogue tears toppling her eyelids. He'd gone out of his way to get her a ring. A perfect ring. Kate's words ran on repeat in her head—Will had loved her, possibly loved her still. All signs pointed to yes. Their wedding could've been quick and easy at city hall, but he'd made it special for her—for them. The situation was going to require careful navigation. She held Will's heart in her hands, and she refused to break it.

She exhaled, covering her nerves with a laugh, and pushed his ring onto his finger. "I give you this ring as a symbol of my commitment to love, honor, and respect you."

Eddie beamed like a proud papa. "Will and Hannah, I now pronounce you husband and wife. Will, you may finally kiss your bride."

And kiss her he did. It wasn't the uncertain kisses they had shared in the past. It was three years of friendship, five years of silence, and a weekend of mayhem rolled into a moment. She leaned into him, their lips dancing instead of clashing. He clung to her waist, his fingers warm even through the fabric of her dress. Her head was fuzzy and heavy with the weight of mixed emotions—excitement, fear, wonder, regret. The kiss had definitely lasted longer than the five Mississippis appropriate for a wedding. In the background, Hannah heard Kate laugh, Stephanie whistle, and Eddie joke about breaking it up. They broke the kiss, but Hannah remained in Will's embrace. She linked her pinky with his—pact fulfilled.

Part 2

Chapter 15

Hannah

Hannah pinned her hair back, tugging at the strands until they cooperated. After three days of Florida's most beautiful beaches, her hair was feeling the effects of the humidity. The fact that the swanky Wellington Thorne resort didn't offer flat irons almost surprised her, but the place did have an in-house salon. She sighed. At least beach waves were in style right now.

When they came in from the beach an hour ago, Will had requested she get fancied up and handed over her freshly dry-cleaned wedding dress. He'd been stingy with details before stepping into the shower, but Hannah did not doubt that it was something spectacular. For an impromptu honeymoon between platonic newlyweds, the trip was exquisitely planned. Will had pulled out all the stops—couples massages, private beaches, and chef's table dinners. And he'd been so honest these past few days. They'd always shared so much—talking about everything and nothing, as Kate had put it. But with just the two of them there, connected by their new shared secret, it was so much more.

Will told her about his family—about his father and his brothers and the Thorne legacy. He talked about his mom and how much things had changed after her death. That part she had already heard. Stories about his mom had been in Will's drunken ramblings sophomore year when her death had still been so fresh. His vulnerability had been part of what led to her crush on him—with each story he told, each moment with his brothers strained by grief, she had wanted to hold him, to shield him from the pain tearing at him. Back then, she had spent months rationalizing her feelings for Will, burying her crush so they could stay friends. And now she was his wife. Kate had hardly seemed surprised by their pact. Would that be the general consensus? Everyone would shrug and say, "Finally. We've all just been waiting on you two."

If it wasn't for the separate beds in their hotel room, it might have felt like a real honeymoon. Hannah might even have considered making it a real honeymoon, but there'd been no talk of invoking Rule 3a, and Will had been a perfect gentleman the whole time.

Will stepped into the bathroom with a short knock. He wore the same suit from the wedding, and like then, he looked stunning. She found herself wanting to touch him, to see if his cheeks felt as scratchy as they looked with his late-afternoon stubble. She clasped her hands in place, turning a smile on him instead.

"Are you coming, Mrs. Thorne?"

He'd been calling her that since the wedding, and the effect hadn't worn off. She was a Mrs. And she was married to Will Thorne, of all people. "Where are we going exactly?"

"You'll see."

Will led her through the hotel and down to the lobby. His hand clasped hers, loose but secure, always keeping her close. As they made their way down a winding hallway, music started to filter in, muffled only by distance. There were occasional loud bursts every time someone opened the door to the ballroom. They reached a vestibule where discarded table numbers sat forgotten. Will glanced through them and picked up a pair from Table 17—one she knew would definitely be in the back and on the bride's side.

"What's going on, Will?"

He opened the door to the ballroom. A familiar ballad was just finishing up, the bride on the dance floor with her father. Will grinned. "If anyone asks, I'm the bride's cousin twice removed on her mother's side."

She'd married a wedding crasher. "Will."

"We deserve a reception and a first dance, albeit a little delayed."

"We do?"

"Come on, honey." Hannah felt her cheeks heat again. *Honey*. It hadn't been patronizing or playful. It had come off his lips with some endearment behind it. "Don't you want a story to tell the kids one day?"

"Kids?" The word cut the breath from her chest. Kids were not part of their equation. Before she could wipe the shock off her face or formulate a reply, he was grinning at her again.

"Okay, fine. Don't you at least want a story to tell our friends and family over Thanksgiving?"

Good God, Thanksgiving. She knew she would have to tell her family eventually, just not in a few weeks. But, yes, she *did* want a story to tell. She wanted real memories with Will, not just ones from almost a decade ago. Tightening her grip on his hand, she let him guide her into the ballroom. Guests were crowding the bar and making their way back to their seats for the salad course. Will led her to their table and pulled out her chair before introducing himself to the only other guest at the table.

Hannah took the moment to catch her breath. The past six days had been a whirlwind. But at the same time, she felt as comfortable with him as if they never fell out of contact. That's how it was between them. That's what had made her love him all those years ago. Once, this night would've been her dream. For a small part of her, maybe it still was. She recalled the memory of the pact—the one that had been playing on repeat for so many days now—to the kiss and his drunken request that she cancel her trip to Europe with Kate and instead spend the summer with him in New York. She hadn't thought that he'd meant it. At least, not in a real way.

Will's hand squeezed her shoulder, and Hannah turned a smile on the middle-aged gentlemen sitting next to him.

"This is my wife, Hannah," Will said as if it was the most natural thing in the world.

The man nodded at her, his hands occupied with buttering a dinner roll. "Ronald Wayland. Will tells me you two are newlyweds yourself."

The lighting in the room changed from blue to red, and the music faded into a quiet ballad as guests returned to their seats for dinner. The song was one she'd heard far too often on her coffee runs. She clasped Will's hand, pulling him away from whatever conversation he'd been having. "Dance with me?"

"I thought you'd never ask," he said, his smile growing.

They fell into the sway of the ballad. Hannah felt everywhere their bodies touched—his hands on the small of her back, her fingers at the base of his neck, the length of their torsos aligning. Goosebumps rose on her skin as one of his hands came up and caressed her arm. Her whole body shuddered at the intensity of that single touch. But this was Will. Will, whom she had married for health insurance. Will, who'd had her alone in a hotel room for three days and hadn't tried a thing. There was his ex-girlfriend and her ex-boyfriend to consider. Two rebounds, a legally binding marriage, and sex did not make for the best combination. A year was a long time to be together if whatever she was feeling was a symptom of the lights and the music and the ring on her left hand.

Hannah inched closer to him. Will's hands bunched in her dress as he looked down at her, his eyes forming a question. Then the lights came up, and the song faded out. Couples deserted the dance floor as the DJ announced the main course.

Will smiled and placed the softest of kisses on her cheek. "Thank you for the dance, Mrs. Thorne."

Chapter 16
Hannah

HANNAH STARED UP AT her new apartment building. She still couldn't quite believe that she lived on the Upper East Side or that their apartment had a park view and was within falling distance of Museum Mile. The apartment wasn't actually Will's but one of the family's apartments. Will had moved in after splitting with his ex. He'd been unable to bear the constant reminders in his old apartment, so it remained vacant, as he was unwilling to give up his prime location in Tribeca.

Since Hannah didn't have a built-in nest egg, she took Will and Kate's suggestion to sublet her apartment, something she knew very little about but which both said was the norm. All she knew was that she still paid the rent, and the money would magically reappear in her checking account. Kate's query about the differences in Will and Hannah's lifestyles made more sense now. Will would never have to live somewhere with spotty heat or wonder how he was going to make rent or if that late payment was going to ruin any future renting opportunities. True, his father could ask them to move out at any point in the next year—and very well might when he found out they were married—but even a few months rent-free would give her savings account some nice padding.

Will walked out of the high-rise, his suit jacket swapped for one that looked the same as the one he claimed didn't match. But what did she know about expensive suits?

"Sorry about that, Abbott," he said, sliding his hand into hers.

She perked up at the nickname. In the five days they'd been married, he'd almost exclusively called her Mrs. Thorne, even though she wasn't changing her name. It was cute, but she'd always been Abbott to him.

"So why are you all stressed out about your clothing if you are not seeing your dad today or telling anyone that you got married?" she asked, nudging him with her hip.

He'd explained it—that he wanted to tell everyone at once at the upcoming family weekend. Otherwise, the rumor mill would turn the story before it got to his father. She understood his trepidation, as she intended to tell her family *never*, but that didn't explain his tension now.

"Welcome to my life at Wellington Thorne."

"I'm sorry."

He shrugged. "You being here is already making it better. Trust me."

A town car idled at the curb, and the driver stepped out, waiting by the back door for Will. Because Will took a town car to work.

"Are you sure you don't want a ride downtown?" he asked, his eyes imploring her to just get in the car already.

She didn't have the heart to tell him that she was already going to be early. Most of the *Deafening Silence* staff didn't roll in until ten—except for Riley, who seemed to be there no matter what time of day it was. "The subway is more than fine."

"All right." He kissed her on the cheek. Always her cheek. She worried how they were going to make people believe they were in love if their lips never touched and they didn't even share a bed. Then again, apparently everyone had known they were in love in college even when they hadn't.

"See you after your show tonight," he said with a tip of his imaginary hat.

"You don't have to wait up." She thought about how late she usually got home and how much she smelled like stale beer and weed and sweat. And how they would go to separate rooms to sleep.

"But I do." He grinned and dropped his briefcase in the trunk. "It's my husbandly duty, Mrs. Thorne."

"HANNAH?" RILEY'S VOICE rang through the small office, louder than usual considering no one else was in yet. She would suspect Riley slept at the office if Hannah didn't know she had a husband and a toddler and couldn't possibly fit on her office couch at nine months pregnant. But even Riley had her limits, and missing Cecilia's bedtime was one of them.

"Be right there!" Hannah dropped her bag onto her chair and poked at the wilting carnations. She'd left two at her desk in her *Write Like a Motherfucker* mug. Whenever her mother saw the mug—mainly in pictures whenever Hannah moved desks—she scoffed at its utter lack of professionalism. That it had come from Riley via an online journal they both loved or that it was one of Hannah's most prized possessions was irrelevant. The carnations hadn't fared well in the week she'd been away. Dumping them seemed callous—they were her first flowers from her now-husband—and the full bouquet hadn't survived Binx and then the move.

The sound of the overpriced, overcomplicated espresso machine pulled Hannah from the flowers. Riley leaned against the counter, a pen dangling from her lips as she read from a proof of the next edition. Hannah could see the red marks from across the room.

"That'd better not be my section," she said, walking over and reaching for the regular coffee grounds and percolator. Hannah liked lattes as much as the next person, but the machine they had made mud. That was coming from someone who had tasted all the roasts Starbucks had to offer via French press. And for the last eight months, it had been decaffeinated mud. *Gross.*

"No, I finished your section last night. Henry's story turned out better than expected." She wrote something then, with a shake of her head, scribbled it out and wrote a hasty *stet* at the end of the line.

"I know." Hannah wondered when Riley would look up and notice the diamonds encircling her ring finger or even ask how her vacation had gone. She knew from experience it could be several more minutes. When Riley was editing pre-coffee, there was little else she noticed.

"Do you think we should hire him after graduation?" She looked up finally, her eyelids heavy with lack of sleep. Hannah remembered Riley's ninth month the first time around. There had been days when she hadn't slept, kept up by back pain and heartburn. And Baby Sutton the Second didn't like to cooperate, just like her big sister.

"How long have you been here?" Hannah aerated Riley's milk to tournament-quality foam.

She shrugged. "I couldn't sleep, and CeCe was having a sleepover at my mom's, so I just came in… maybe around seven?" Riley accepted the coffee mug from Hannah with a contented sigh. "You always make the best lattes."

"Job security," Hannah joked, angling her hand so her wedding band was out in the open. She should've worn the engagement ring too. No one could miss that thing.

"How was your trip?" Riley asked, taking a seat on the battered couch they used as a coffee lounge. She put the proof down, but Hannah knew her mind was still going over whatever edit she'd left dangling. Stets didn't last long in Riley's world.

Hannah sat down across from her, leaning her elbows on her knees. It was no use—not when Riley was in one of her moods. Nothing would draw her attention—not a sparkling diamond band, not any subtle hints.

"Well, I actually—" Hannah took a calming breath. Despite Kate and Stephanie knowing, the official marriage license, and the honeymoon, saying it out loud at work made everything real. She plastered a giant grin on her face and held up her left hand. "I got married."

Riley blinked at Hannah's outstretched hand a few times before meeting her gaze uncertainly. "You and Brian got married?"

She'd walked into that one. The trial run with Stephanie clearly hadn't taught her anything about prepping the announcement. At least Riley hadn't assumed she was pregnant—out loud anyway.

"No, Brian and I broke up." Hannah ran through the story she and Will had crafted to perfection before letting it spill out. "His name is Will Thorne. We went to college together and reconnected a few months ago. It was totally platonic until it wasn't."

"Sounds like the tagline to the next big rom-com." Riley gave an exaggerated sigh, holding up her hands as if setting the scene. "Hannah and Will's friendship was completely platonic... until it wasn't. Flash to big heated first kiss followed by sad girl sitting in the window, sad boy out with his friends. Will things between them ever be the same again?"

"Maybe I should write the screenplay." Hannah sat back and took a sip of coffee, her heart rate finally coming down a few measures. Thank God for people like Riley—people who loved love and loved their friends, and just went with it. No matter what Riley might really be thinking, she wasn't going to share it without a direct request. Sometimes you needed a Kate, and sometimes you needed a Riley—having both was a blessing.

"A *Deafening Silence* production. Written by Hannah Abbott... Thorne?"

"Abbott. At least for now." Hannah didn't have strong feelings either way about changing her name. She had always assumed she would change it—that was what people did when they got married and started a family unit.

"Oh, you millennials and your contemporary notions. Next you're going tell me that you and this Will character are creating a new last name. Thabbott or Abborne."

"Not exactly." Hannah scrunched her nose at the names—they were awful. She'd have to present them to Will later. "But if *I'm* a millennial, *you're* a millennial."

Riley stood up as quickly as someone with another person living inside them could, her hands on her hips. "You take that back, Thabbott. Take that back right now."

"Or what?" Hannah smirked as Riley's countenance cracked. This was her favorite Riley. The Riley when the rest of the office wasn't around, when she wasn't worried about budgets and press checks and keeping solid writers without a benefits package.

Riley looked her dead in the eye. Whatever she was about to say was a trump card. "Or I'll let Henry run his Amityville story as the lead in your section."

Touché.

Chapter 17
Will

Ten days. They'd been married for ten days. And even the last four back in society were excellent. Work pulled them in too many directions, but there'd been breakfast every day. And no matter what time Hannah rolled in, no matter what she smelled like, Will was awake and waiting. Those small moments made his days bearable. Even sans wedding ring, he felt it in his breast pocket, and it was enough. Work had been enjoyable, and Jon less grating—they'd even shared a lunch with Grayson where Jon had spent thirty minutes trying to find out why Will was in such a good mood. Well, in one more day, he would know.

Getting out to the Hamptons on a Friday night was a bitch any time of year, but that didn't stop their father from requesting an early arrival to maximize Saturday mornings. These were Will's last hours as a secretly married man. Putting that ring on and never taking it off was going to feel amazing. How did other men feel trapped by their rings?

Will watched the numbers rise as the elevator lurched to the top floor. It had been a trying day, spent buried in contracts and reports. All he wanted to do was fall onto the couch and watch bad TV, not get in the car and drive three hours. At least Hannah would be with him. His wife was his key to keeping his footing at Wellington Thorne and to proving he wasn't the proverbial screwup his father had cast him as so many years ago.

Will stepped out of the elevator, and voices floated down the hallway from the direction of their apartment. Maybe Mrs. Schumacher had finally come to meet Hannah. She'd mentioned it that morning when they'd passed in the lobby.

But as he got closer, he could see the door to their apartment open and a few boxes of stacked outside. Most likely books or clothes since Hannah hadn't wanted the movers packing either. That meant their visitor must be Kate.

"You are *so* Tally Atwater," Kate said.

Will stepped closer as Hannah made some snarky reply. They stood in the doorway, Kate leaning against the jamb, Hannah standing just inside. They would've noticed him if they were paying attention. Kate and Hannah, in their element—it had been too long.

"What?" Kate said, rubbing her arm. "It's a compliment. You made it. You dreamed the impossible dream."

Kate and Hannah had to be the only thirty-year-olds to casually reference *Up Close and Personal* without being prompted. He hadn't escaped their repeated viewings of it either. He'd immediately caught the reference.

Hannah giggled, her gaze sliding past Kate to Will standing outside the doorway. She straightened, but her expression stayed light and playful. "Hey."

Kate turned around. "Hubs!"

Will laughed. Only Kate. At least she was on board with it. They were going to need allies, and Kate had always been a good one.

"We were wondering when you were getting home," Kate said. The statement was so simple, and yet, nostalgia washed over Will. How often they'd said that to him in college, as if him sleeping on their apartment floor for a semester was completely normal.

"Well, here I am," he said, hugging Kate. He hadn't seen her since the wedding and was surprised to find that he missed her. He turned his attention to Hannah just in time to see a blush fading from her cheeks. Was it from the "hubs" remark? Or had it been something else entirely? Sometimes he could read the world on Hannah's face.

Other times, those missing five years had created a chasm that he couldn't cross. He kissed her lightly on the cheek. "We should get those boxes inside before we go."

"I will. Kate brought them since there's this dress I thought would be perfect for tomorrow. A good first-impression dress."

"Definitely a parent pleaser," Kate added with a nod.

"Plus, she needed to see Binx's new setup." Hannah gestured toward the kitchen, where they'd added Binx's food station.

"Are you sure you want to come all the way up here?" Will asked, calculating the cost and time for Kate to come uptown twice a day to feed the cat. "I'm sure Mrs. Schumacher would feed him."

"He's still not used to the apartment," Hannah said, picking Binx up as he rubbed against her legs. "I don't want to add another stranger to the mix." She paused on the word "stranger," perhaps realizing she'd implied that *Will* was included on that list. Though in truth, he was. Binx might be far friendlier with him than others, according to what he'd heard, but their relationship still involved hissing. Will was nursing a nasty scratch from when he had tried to relocate Binx from the foot of his bed one evening.

"It's fine. Really," Kate said with a shrug. "As long as you don't mind me borrowing your flat-screen for a few hours?"

"Kate doesn't have cable," Hannah added. "And the Jets are playing against Tom Brady on Sunday."

"Watching Brady get sacked in high-definition would be the highlight of my week."

"Then consider it yours," Will said, finally slipping his bag off his shoulder. "Just no parties. As I'm sure Hannah told you, the place isn't actually ours."

"She did, and noted." Kate crossed her heart. "I promise to not throw a rager in your squatter's haven."

Before he could even formulate a response to that comment, Hannah laughed. "Your idea of a rager is two bottles of wine and binging *Dawson's Creek* on Netflix."

"A promise is a promise. I will not destroy your Netflix recommendations with my nostalgia." She hugged Hannah and patted Will on the shoulder. "Goodbye and good luck, lovebirds."

The front door had barely closed behind Kate before Hannah fell back onto the couch, limbs akimbo. "Do we have to go? I never—and I mean *never*—have two weekends off in a row. Let's go back to Florida, or just stay here. You, me, some beer, and bad TV. I'll even let you pick the first binge session as long as it has nothing to do with a Kardashian."

"That's not bad TV, that's god-awful." He slid in next to her, letting her legs drape across his lap. "Long day?"

She ran a hand over her face. "We had to fire one of the interns. She was using our name to procure concert tickets for her friends. She didn't take it well."

He squeezed her foot. "That sucks.

"Yeah." Hannah sat up, tucking her feet under his legs. She glanced back toward the guest room—her room. "Do I have time to throw in a load of clothes before we go? I'm seriously low on everything."

"I guess you could bring some with us. Clara's not back until Monday otherwise, and she usually handles my laundry on Wednesdays." He stumbled through the end of the sentence as he looked up from his traffic app. Having a cleaning lady was another thing he'd taken for granted and not told Hannah about. By her expression, she was not too happy about it.

"I'm perfectly capable of walking my clothes down to the laundry room," Hannah said, crossing her arms.

He considered his response for a moment, but there was no way around explaining their lack of options. "No laundry room. Each apartment has a dedicated laundry area, but Dad took it out years ago to expand the kitchen."

"The wine fridge?"

"Yes, partly." Heat rushed through his cheeks. The luxuries of his life had become too commonplace and the company he kept too equally wealthy to even bat an eye at a maid. "If you bring some for the weekend, Dad's housekeeper will take care of it for you."

"I am not bringing laundry when I meet your family for the first time ever." She rolled her eyes. "But when we get home, we are finding the nearest laundromat and reintroducing you to a washing machine."

He laughed at her mock outrage, glad that her derision seemed only half-hearted. "As you wish, Mrs. Thorne."

Chapter 18
Hannah

The Hamptons were a hike. Even with all her years as a New Yorker and her current role as the Long Island section editor, she rarely had a reason to travel out here. Jersey had better beaches and also her family. Jersey Shore traffic was a bitch. But this ride? *Damn.* They might as well have gone to Boston or Binghamton for the amount of time they'd been in the car. And the Thornes didn't even live that far out according to Will—or William, as he'd told her his family called him. That was going to be an adjustment Hannah wasn't entirely sure she'd be able to make.

The song on the radio changed, the opening chords causing a twitch in Hannah's fingers. It wasn't her favorite, and they had to have heard it four times already.

"It's all right," Will said, not taking his eyes from the road. "You can change it."

"Thank God," she said, hitting a few of the presets but finding nothing worth stopping on. She hit another button, the station name piquing her interest. "You have Z100 as a preset?"

He laughed as the annoying night DJ chatted away. Commercial-free did not mean chatter-free. "I like the morning show."

"Your driver listens to NPR. I know because it almost put me to sleep when he picked me up the other day."

Will smiled in the darkness. "Is this how it's always going to be?"

"Absolutely."

"Good. Someone to call me out on my bullshit is actually what I need."

The DJ finally stopped talking, and the opening lyrics of the latest Ed Sheeran ballad filled the car. Will's hand covered hers, his fingers sliding between Hannah's. Goosebumps raced up her arms. "It's our song, Abbott."

Too many perfect retorts sprung to her mind, but she found she didn't want to make them. Having the top wedding song of the year as their song was as cliché as it came, but it was one of the few things that was truly and honestly theirs. She leaned back against the headrest, letting the song wash over her. A smile spread across her face as the chorus peaked—the memory of their "wedding reception" filling her with uncensored joy.

They drove in comfortable silence for several miles. It was enough to be in this moment. It always was with him. So much had changed yet remained exactly the same. But then, that had always been the nature of their friendship.

"WE'RE HERE," WILL SAID as they turned onto a circle drive.

Hannah's breath caught as she took in the mansion. She'd heard about the wealth of the Hamptons, had seen it on television shows, but it was all Hollywood magic and hearsay until now. "Holy shit."

"My dad bought it for my mom for their twentieth wedding anniversary," he said as they pulled in next to a Mercedes. And she thought his rarely used Lexus was a luxury. "It was her favorite place in the whole world."

"How old were you then?" She wondered if he noticed how his voice changed whenever he spoke about his mother. It took on a soft and faraway tone, his memories showing through.

"Thirteen or so? We'd always vacationed out here, but this place was obviously something completely special."

His mother had only had her haven for five years. Not nearly long enough. Or perhaps perfectly long enough because she'd shared it with all her boys. Hannah wished she knew. For all the drama with his father, the original Mrs. Thorne seemed the picture of an affectionate and caring mother, the best you could hope for in this world.

She placed her hand over his again. "Is it hard coming here?"

He laughed lightly, turning his hand over and intertwining their fingers. "It was at first. But now, it's where I feel closest to her. This was her house. She had a hand in every aspect of its design and decoration. I think—I *know* that's why my dad can't sell it."

They stepped out of the car.

"I wish I could've met her."

Will rested his elbow on the roof of his Lexus. In the driveway lights, she could just make out the wistful expression playing across his face. "Well, I like to think that in some mystical way, she brought us together. Nothing else could've driven me out of New York—especially not to the cornfields of Iowa."

She rolled her eyes. "We were hardly in the cornfields."

He walked around the car and took her hand in his. "Are you ready to face the firing squad?"

She glanced up at the mostly dark house. "Is anyone even awake?"

"Oh, I'm sure *someone's* awake." He led them toward the front door. "Daniel isn't even here yet."

Daniel, the doctor. Hannah had a running list of Thorne family members in her head as well as the creative and not-so-nice descriptors Will had given each of them, Daniel being the exception.

He squeezed her hand, and she was surprised to note that she didn't feel the weight of his hand in hers anymore. She'd already gotten used to it. It was the same with his sweet pecks on her cheeks. But as much as their natural flow and banter filled in enough blanks to make people think they were in love, she knew they were going to need more than that to get through an entire weekend with his overly observant family.

She stopped him at the base of the stairs leading to the house. "Will, wait."

"Everything okay?"

Hannah took in the sight of him—the rigid set of his shoulders, the stress lines near his eyes. He was putting on a good show for her, but Will was nervous. She stepped closer and, without overthinking it, pressed her lips against his. His lips parted slightly, letting her in, but she felt him holding back, even as a spark shot through her.

She stepped away. Will stared down at her, awestruck. He hadn't been expecting that. And why would he? Hannah hadn't dropped hints that she wanted more than Will was giving. She wasn't sure if that's what she did want. There was so much at stake—most importantly, their friendship. She didn't want to lose it again and not over kissing. "I just thought... I imagine we're going to have to lay it on pretty heavy this weekend, and we haven't—"

"You're right." He leaned down and kissed her again. It started light, but Hannah leaned into him, letting her arms come up around his neck. He smiled against her before breaking the kiss and running a cold finger across her flushed cheeks. "Good thinking, Abbott."

"You probably shouldn't call me that in front of your family," she said with a smile.

"Right again." He started up the steps, reclaiming her hand as he did. "Have you been in a fake marriage before?"

She laughed, though her nerves were getting the best of her. She took a breath, trying to calm her quickening pulse and the clamminess coming over her the closer they got to the door. It was silly to be this nervous. Even if Will's family didn't believe they were in love, there was nothing anyone could do. Their marriage was legal and binding. Will would secure his place at Wellington Thorne. But she wanted them to like her. Disapproving in-laws would only make everything harder, particularly with eleven more mandatory family weekends ahead of them, not to mention his brother's wedding. If the mansion proved anything, that event was going to be like nothing Hannah had ever seen.

"Should I call you William?"

"Please don't," Will said, leading her into the house. Her eyes scanned the space, taking in the picturesque staircase and the giant chandelier. Seriously, they could host weddings in this place. "I prefer Will. It reminds me of better times." He squeezed her hand. "My mom always called me Will."

She flushed at the comment, her racing thoughts silencing and her heart calming. Romantic or not, she held a special place in Will's heart. The urge to protect him swelled in her again.

She kissed him on the cheek. "Okay. Will, it is, then."

With a final deep breath, Will led her through the labyrinth of the mansion. Every so often, he would point something out or tell her a story. She wondered if there was a map to the estate. What if she had to pee in the middle of the night? Who was she kidding? In this house, every bedroom probably had a bathroom.

They finally stopped at the entrance to what could only be called a den. A large wood fireplace burned low in the hearth. A couple that had to be Jon and Madison sat on one of the three couches, their backs to the door. They leaned into each other, heads almost touching as they talked. The Thorne patriarch was nowhere in sight.

Will cleared his throat. "Jon. Madison."

They pulled apart enough to turn and look at Will. Hannah envied that level of comfort—to not be ashamed of your affection but to bask in it.

"Good evening, William." Jon's eyes lingered on Hannah for a beat too long. "And...?"

"This is Hannah... my *wife*." Will's smile reeked of something akin to smugness. She had expected that with his father, but not

Jon—she didn't know the whole story, but whatever was between them, it was big.

Silence ricocheted around the room, bouncing from Jon to Madison and back to Will and Hannah. She hadn't thought Will would be so direct, though there wasn't really a subtle way to introduce your new wife to your family. Maybe it was better to just tear the Band-Aid off.

After another excruciatingly long exchange of confused looks, Jon cleared his throat and lifted himself from the sofa. He offered Madison a hand, and Hannah saw the silent conversation between them. With a *what the hell* shrug, Madison accepted his hand and allowed herself to be drawn to her feet.

And Madison was gorgeous—all dark waves and deep brown eyes and curves.

They came around the sofa and stopped in front of Will and Hannah. Will's hand slid down Hannah's back, and she had never been more grateful for his touch.

"Congratulations, little brother. Hannah, it's a pleasure to meet you. William hasn't told us a thing." He grinned. "I suppose we'll get the whole story in the morning? It must be intriguing."

Hannah took Jon's outstretched hand, glad he hadn't gone in for a hug. She didn't think she could bear it.

"This is my fiancée, Madison," Jon said in his booming voice.

Madison dragged her eyes away from Will and met Hannah's gaze. She took Hannah's measure, though Hannah had no idea why. "What a surprise," Madison finally said. "William never mentioned he was seeing someone."

Hannah plastered on a smile to cover her nerves. "It was all kind of fast."

The corners of Jon's mouth quirked up, but he swallowed whatever he was going to say. Instead, he clasped Will on the back. "Congratulations, William. Really."

Despite all the pleasantries, Hannah felt an undeniable awkwardness fill the room, both in the overly polite nature of Jon's words and in the way Madison stared at her and Will's intertwined hands. And then there was Will's haughty smile.

Hannah yawned exaggeratedly. "Will, honey, can we head to bed? I'm wiped."

Will tore his gaze away from Jon and Madison and kissed Hannah lightly on the temple. "Of course, Mrs. Thorne. Let me show you to our room."

Chapter 19

Hannah

Hannah rolled over, her arm sinking into the still-warm pillow on the other side of the bed. In the split second before her brain caught on, she wondered if Brian had already started the coffee. Then she opened her eyes to the opulence of the room. Will, the Hamptons, long-standing family feuds. *Right.*

"Good morning, Mrs. Thorne."

Hannah glanced around the room. Barely any light was peeking through the slats of the blinds. "Is it even morning?"

"For those of us not accustomed to working until two in the morning, yes, it is." He sat at the edge of the bed, his foot resting on the bedframe while he tied his sneakers. She scooted over toward him. All the hairs on her arm stood up as she brushed his. He hadn't had this effect on her in a decade—*why now?* It was more important than ever that she keep it all in check. A year didn't seem that long until she was stuck in an unhappy situation because she couldn't keep her pants on.

Hannah peeked at his shoes, ignoring the thrum running through her veins. They were running sneakers—nice ones too. Brooks were not a casual runner's shoe.

"You run?" she asked, jealous she hadn't brought her own pair but at the same time knowing there was no way she could go very far.

His face brightened. "Yeah. Daniel got me into it. We get up before the 'state of the union' brunch and do ten miles. It's a family weekend tradition."

"Ten miles." He definitely was not a casual or occasional runner to pull that off on a Saturday morning.

He touched her arm lightly, and Hannah felt it again—that spark between them. Did he feel it too? She wondered again if what she was feeling was real or simply a side effect of their forced proximity.

"I'm sorry I didn't tell you. It seemed insensitive since you clearly miss it. But if you think you're up for it?" he asked, wrapping his headphones around his neck.

She shook her head. This weekend was no time to push her knee past its limits.

"Okay, well, brunch starts at nine. There's always coffee in the kitchen."

"Is there a map?" She laughed, but truthfully, the last thing she needed was to run into Jonathan on her own. Because *that* wouldn't be awkward or confusing.

Will stopped playing with his Forerunner watch and glanced over at her, his cheeks still pink but paired with an expression somewhere between bashful and sympathetic. "I can take you down there or bring you up a cup."

She sat up, attempting to comb through her bedhead with her fingers. "What are the odds that I would run into, say, your father who has no idea I exist?"

"I wouldn't put it past him to already know." He strapped the watch to his wrist. "Though Jonathan sightings are rare before brunch."

HANNAH FOUND HERSELF surrounded by stainless steel in a kitchen larger than her old apartment. On a large piece of butcher block acting as a table was a coffee setup and an oversized bowl of fruit salad. Off to the side covered in plastic wrap was a plate of English muffins and what looked to be orange marmalade.

Will picked the plate up. "Renata is too good to me."

Renata, Hannah had learned, was the housekeeper, cook, and general head of the staff— a staff that had dwindled to just Renata and Jonathan's assistant, Arthur, in recent years.

Hannah sat down on one of the stools surrounding the table. She popped a grape into her mouth as the scent of the coffee made its way through her system, awakening her mind. The smell brought back memories of stumbling into Starbucks half-asleep, waiting for that first batch to brew, the sun not yet up but the city still awake. This was no Starbucks coffee. The steam coming off her cup smelled bold and bitter, and she detected a hint of other flavors—vanilla, cinnamon, and possibly lemon. But she'd never been one for strong roasts. She'd trudged through the mildest of roasts those early mornings at Starbucks because she had no other choice.

"All right," Will said, wiping crumbs from his shirt. "You're good? Can you find your way back?"

She nodded as she poured half-and-half into her coffee, watching it go from black to muddy to the edge of drinkable. "Have fun."

The second the door swung shut, she dropped the smile and let her shoulders slump. Will was a runner. Hannah had never even seen him in workout clothes. Any other morning, she would've been happy for him, glad that he'd finally told her and wasn't depriving himself of something he loved. But why this weekend? She was already the odd one out, and their best chance of being believable was to tell their story together. And yet, she wasn't surprised. This was the Will she had always known, somehow always adrift and yet a constant in her life.

She stared down at her coffee, the color still one shade away from drinkable. If she put any more milk in this cup, she was going to have a very weird latte on her hands. She speared a piece of mango with her fork, wishing for plain old cantaloupe, then judged her coffee again. Any coffee had to be better than no coffee. *Right?*

Two knocks sounded from the entryway, pulling Hannah's attention from her coffee disaster. Madison stood in the doorway. Her leggings and cowl-neck sweater looked much too warm for the weather, even with the ocean breeze. "Hannah, right?"

"Uh, yes. Good morning, Madison." Hannah ran her fingers through her hair. She'd noted last night that Madison was gorgeous, but in the daylight, she was even more striking. Her chestnut hair, which had fallen in thick waves last night, was pulled back into a messy bun. Her eyes were bright, her face already made-up. Hannah had barely had time brush her teeth and wash her face before Will had escorted her downstairs.

Madison plucked a strawberry out of the bowl. "Please tell me you aren't actually drinking that stuff."

"I wasn't aware I had a choice." Hannah gave the kitchen another look but didn't see any other means of procuring coffee.

"Well, I have ten bucks and the keys to the Mercedes. What do you say?"

"Oh, thank God." Hannah hadn't really gotten a read on Madison from Will—he'd mainly stuck to his blood relatives—but she seemed nice enough, and it would be helpful to have a female friend among the brood.

"Good," Madison said, closing her hand around the keys. "You are going to need to be well-caffeinated to handle brunch with the boys."

CARS HAD NEVER BEEN Hannah's thing, but she couldn't deny the appeal of the Mercedes. Everything was sleek lines and leather.

But Madison was awful at driving it. It was no wonder she'd had to steal the keys.

"Your New Yorker is showing," Hannah joked as Madison reattempted her parallel parking job.

"Hey, you've lived in the city your entire adult life. That makes you a New Yorker too."

At least someone had accepted her into their ranks. Hannah was starting to wonder if it would ever happen. "Queens, Madison. We use cars in Queens."

Madison rolled her eyes but didn't say anything as she attempted to straighten the car out in a spot that could more than accommodate the coupe. After a few more maneuvers, Madison slammed the car into park. "Whatever. We're going, like, twenty feet, and we're in a town full of rich people. No one is going to hit the car."

That was probably true, but Hannah couldn't help but laugh when she stepped out of the car and onto pavement rather than the sidewalk. She'd seen some bad parking jobs in her day, but wow—at least the car was straight.

Hannah followed Madison down the street to a small café called the Peach Pit. The resemblance didn't go much past the moniker—leave it to the Hamptons to outclass even fake Beverly Hills. The café was quiet, with an older couple and a few teenagers sitting at tables on opposite sides of the room. It was nothing like the Saturdays she had experienced at Starbucks, but this wasn't the city, and it wasn't in season. Hannah didn't know how much of the town's population was permanent. Maybe it was like Jersey Shore, where the BENNYs— tourists from the north that the locals only liked for their patronage—descended each summer, making the months between October and May the only bearable times to visit. Hannah stopped midscan of the menu. If she was officially a New Yorker, did that make *her* a BENNY?

"Are you okay?"

Hannah blinked a few times, Madison's small frame coming back into focus with a coffee cup held out her to her. "Yes, sorry. I was just contemplating something horrid." Hannah took the too-large cup, breathing in the wondrous smell of drinkable coffee.

"Well—" Madison eyed her up and down. "Please refrain from thinking such things. It is far too early, and we're decaffeinated."

They sat at a table near the older couple, as far from the teenage girls as they could get—not that that helped keep their squeals out of earsplitting decibels. Oh, to be sixteen. Beyond the clamor, the chorus of one of Hannah's favorite songs was fading out.

Music found her everywhere. She might not be able to hear someone across a table from her in a crowded restaurant, but she'd be able to pick out the song, know the lyrics, and find it again throughout the course of a conversation. Wilderness Weekend's latest track started up. A calmness came over her, as it did whenever one of their songs came on. It had been that way since she'd found them. It would be that way always.

"Oh god," Madison said, breaking off a piece of her scone, apparently unable to wait for breakfast. "William found himself another Wilderness fan. Okay, okay, let me guess." She paused dramatically. "You and William met at a Wilderness Weekend concert. You both went to sound check and then to the bar next door, where Leonard Nulty was having an early dinner. Your eyes met, and the rest, as they say, is love."

That would've been a fabulous story. Hannah almost wished she'd thought of it. Of course they would've reconnected over Leonard Nulty's soul-crushingly beautiful words.

"Not quite." She sipped her coffee, caffeine and relief filling her veins. She liked Madison. She was fun and quirky and owned it. The last time Hannah had felt this comfortable with a stranger had been with Riley, and the time before that, Kate and Will. "Are you a Wilderness fan?"

"God, no. No offense. They just aren't my thing." Hannah could only imagine the music Madison listened to. The car radio had been set to something innocuous, but that didn't mean anything. "But it's impossible to know William without knowing Wilderness."

Hannah laughed. "That is true. Will introduced me to them back in college."

"Ah, so you two have a history." She winked as if Hannah had slipped up and spilled a secret.

"Yeah. We were best friends in college, lost touch for a while, then a few months ago we ran into each other... and the rest, as they say, is love."

"Shame you two didn't run into each other sooner. Manhattan's not that big, after all." There was a hint of contempt in Madison's tone, but Hannah couldn't place it. Yes, she'd given her a detail-free version of the story, but she'd tied in Madison's own phrasing, made sure her "ran into each other" sounded wistful.

"I know, but there are a million people on that island—my best friend and I live a few blocks apart, and I swear, if we didn't seek each other out, we'd never accidentally run into each other. Will and I actually crossed paths down the Shore." That was the part of the story they had crafted generically enough so it couldn't be questioned or verified, unlike a concert or a fundraiser or even something as simple as being in the same bar to watch the same game. "My parents live ten minutes or so from the beach, and I was down for a weekend. Our shared loved of funnel cake brought us together, really."

"Kismet," Madison said, her eyes glued to her phone. She still seemed off, but all Hannah had to judge by was the bubbly woman she'd been with for the past thirty minutes, and no one could stay that way indefinitely.

"Everything okay?" Hannah asked finally, unwilling to let the weird vibes she felt go unnoticed.

Madison pocketed her phone with a grimace. "Yeah. Just work and wedding stuff. Jon and I are meeting with the florist tomorrow before we head back to the city. She agreed to a Sunday-night meeting, and now she's being all bitchy about the timing. But there are ten other equally qualified florists in the area, so whatever."

"Wedding planning sounds fun."

"It's god-awful. I swear, if you can get through planning the wedding, marriage should be a breeze. You seriously dodged a bullet."

Hannah laughed, knowing that what Madison said was one hundred percent true after her sister's wedding. "And work?"

"Oh." She rolled her eyes. "I'm a physical therapist, and apparently there's some insurance issue and they need paperwork, and *ugh*. Can I just fix people, please?"

"Whereabouts?" Hannah asked, her pulse quickening. Could she have found a physical therapist after all this time? Madison was someone Will knew and who she would want on her side.

"Union and Nineteenth."

She could walk there from her office if she wanted. "I've actually been looking for a PT for a while. Do you take new clients?"

"I do." Madison looked her over. "What's wrong with you?"

"Bum knee."

"Let me check my schedule, but I'm sure I can fit you in. We're practically family." Madison swigged her coffee. "Speaking of, we should get back. You don't want to make a bad first impression by being late to brunch."

"Then I guess that means we can't try and sneak in a coffee refill?" Hannah asked, swirling the last of the coffee around in her cup. It had gone cold, but the tiniest part of her wanted to drink it if her only other option was that sludge back at the house.

Madison shook her head. "Bringing in outside coffee is basically treason."

Chapter 20

Hannah

"Where were you?" Will's tone was near panic as Hannah stepped into their bedroom.

She eyed him, sitting at the foot of the bed in slacks—not jeans—and a long-sleeved polo. It was far from the usual Sunday brunch attire. She guessed today would be the day to wear the dress she'd brought.

"Madison took me to get coffee since the pot in the kitchen practically melted from whatever your dad likes."

"Madison?"

Hannah pulled the dress out of the closet and glanced at her watch. Blowing out her hair wouldn't be an option, but she still had enough time to get presentable. "She's cool. It's nice having another woman here."

"Right." He pulled his phone out of his pocket and started scrolling.

"Hey." Hannah sat down next to him despite the ticking clock and pulled his hand into hers. "It's going to be fine."

He smiled, but it didn't quite feel real. "I know, Abbott. How could it not be with you by my side?"

Normally, she would've rolled her eyes at such a comment—Will made them often enough—but this one rang true in a way the others hadn't. She kissed his cheek as he had hers so many times that week. The surprising intimacy of that small gesture sent a shiver down her spine.

"I'll be right out," she said, giving his hand one last squeeze.

Less than twenty minutes later, Hannah sat beside Will at the dining room table across from Madison, Jon, and Daniel. It felt intentional, and she wished someone would move to their side. The head of the table was open, awaiting Jonathan's arrival—apparently getting there before the patriarch was not just a ploy on Will's part. Will hadn't introduced her to Daniel, which made sense, but the youngest Thorne kept looking over and grinning into his coffee. Either he knew that shit was about to hit the fan gloriously, or more likely, Will had told him the news on their ten-mile run.

Hannah and Will kept their hands hidden under the table. There would be no deflecting the gleam of their wedding rings or hiding the rock on her finger. She was just about to force down another sip of the household coffee—Madison making faces at her across the table—when the door swung open and Jonathan himself entered. It was such a formal entrance, she had to stop herself from standing as if he was a judge entering his courtroom.

It took about two seconds before Will's father's eyes landed on her. He took her measure in those seconds. She knew by the dismissive way he averted his eyes that she had been found lacking.

"Good morning," he said, sitting down and pouring himself a cup of coffee. His eyes raked over each member of the Thorne family before landing squarely on her and Will. "And who is your lady companion, William?"

Will, to his credit, didn't even hesitate. "Dad," he said, thrusting their entwined hands toward the head of the table, a huge and convincing grin brightening his face, "this is my wife, Hannah."

Despite working for a magazine called *Deafening Silence* for years, Hannah herself had rarely experienced the phenomenon. But there it was—the silence was screaming at the Thorne breakfast table. Jon, Madison, and Daniel collectively held their breaths, waiting to see Jonathan's reaction to the marriage. The silence unnerved Hannah. In her house, there would be laughter or tears or yelling, or something. When Stephanie had arrived home engaged, their mother had laughed and then cried at her baby growing up. Their father had outright cried, shameless. But all Jonathan did was place his coffee cup back on its saucer.

He considered the two of them, then the rings, and then Hannah herself before his gaze finally settled back on his son. "Ah. Well, I see you did more on that little impromptu vacation than drink by the pool."

Hannah laughed. It nearly echoed in the large space where no one else had said a word or even made a sound to Jonathan's retort. She cut her laughter off, clearing her throat. Next to her, Will took a sip of water.

"I suppose congratulations are in order then," Jonathan said. "Renata?" She was at Jonathan's side in an instant. Hannah hadn't even noticed her in the room. "Champagne. Unless... Hannah can't partake?"

She felt Will stiffen beside her. Hannah turned a smile toward her father-in-law. "Champagne would be great."

A nod from Jonathan sent Renata to the kitchen. Hannah hoped she was keeping notes—this family needed an unauthorized biography. But then the staff probably had confidentiality agreements.

"So, if I may," Jonathan said, returning to his coffee, "why the rush?"

"It didn't really feel like a rush to us, Dad," Will said, reigning in their hands but keeping them front and center on the table. "Hannah and I were best friends in college. I'm sure you remember me talking about her."

Jonathan nodded.

She cut a look at her new husband, disbelieving. Sure, her family knew who Will was in a cursory way—that "friend from college"—but this seemed more than that. Much more.

Keeping his eyes on his father, Will continued, "When we met again this summer, everything just fell into place. It was like, why had we wasted all these years fighting it? A perfect fit, like Mom used to say." That was a new addition to the tale. "We didn't want to steal the limelight from Jon and Madison's wedding, and we didn't want to wait when we knew we wanted to be together."

The first somewhat real smile appeared on Jonathan's stiff face. "You've always had your mother's whimsy." He turned his attention back to Hannah, the spark of curiosity clear on his face. "And what is it you do, Hannah?"

Telling people she was a journalist either elicited "wows"—the job had a built-in coolness factor, especially when her beat was alternative rock music—or came with an implied sympathetic shoulder squeeze for the trampling the industry had taken in the last decade. Sometimes both. But Jonathan did neither when she said she was an editor for a music magazine.

"Really?" he said, clasping his hands together. "William always did have a soft spot for the creatives. There was that writer in high school, the artist when you were at Columbia, and Melody—sweet girl—wasn't she an aspiring singer?"

"Which magazine?" Daniel asked from across the table. No one but Jonathan had spoken for so long that Hannah had nearly forgotten they had an audience. Will was still tense beside her. She rested a hand on his shoulder, squeezing softly. It was going to take more than innuendos and old girlfriends to ruffle her feathers.

"*Deafening Silence New York*," she said. "I'm the Long Island section editor. There's a pretty big alt rock scene out here, believe it or not. Plus, everyone still loves Taking Back Sunday."

Will laughed and turned his attention to Jon, who was nodding enthusiastically. "Uh-oh, you just said the magic words."

"Jon's a huge fan," Madison said, rolling her eyes. "It's not quite at the level of William's obsession with Wilderness, but seriously, I'm starting to think it's hereditary."

"Hey now," Daniel said, pointing his finger accusingly at Madison.

They bickered some more, taking jabs at each other and laughing. Based on Will's grim description of these weekends, she'd expected a family that hated each other's company. But the brothers seemed at ease with each other. Even Will, whose shoulders had been near his ears since they arrived, had relaxed back in his chair. She studied their alliances, which were constantly shifting. Will and Daniel always seemed to come back to each other against Jon. But then that made sense. Jon was four years older than Will, making him six years older than Daniel. There was a point when he'd probably wanted little to do with his younger brothers. It had happened with Stephanie once Hannah had moved up to middle school in fifth grade.

Intentional or not, Daniel had shifted the attention away from the two of them without even trying. He regaled the table with a blow-by-blow account of one of his recent trauma cases. Hannah wanted to hug him for knowing Will needed an out, even as Will cringed every time his brother used medical jargon. He started biting his hand when Daniel described inserting a chest tube. Binging *ER* was not in their future.

Renata arrived with the champagne after a too-short reprieve. The joking ceased. Will clutched her hand like his sanity depended on it. Jon sat back and slung an arm around Madison, who leaned into him easily. Daniel eyed his father warily.

Jonathan clinked his fork against his glass. "To Will and Hannah. May your marriage be much longer than your courtship and a shining example of what can happen when you follow your heart."

From anyone else, that line might have been humorous and cutesy, but from Jonathan, it was throwing the gauntlet. He didn't believe for one second that they were in love. Determination spread through her, taking root in the pit of her stomach, and from the shadowed look on Will's face, he felt the same way—challenge accepted.

Chapter 21
Will

Try as they might, no one in the Thorne family was a night owl. Not even Daniel, despite a lifetime of overnight shifts ahead of him. Will wasn't either, but this house never let him sleep. He liked to think that it was his mom's way of letting him know she was there, choosing him to keep her company like he had as a surly kid and then a teenager terrified of losing his mother. He'd always stayed awake for her, listening to her stories and telling his own. She knew his greatest secrets, which as a fairly normal teenager hadn't been that big. He knew her fears, regrets, and hopes for each of them.

Even lying in bed next to the girl he'd dreamed about for the last eight years, he felt the pull of the house. Hannah, though she must have been accustomed to sharing a bed at least some of the time, was a bed hog. It was adorable. Last night, she had tossed and turned, almost taking out his knee cap. Tonight, she was sprawled across the bed, her arm slung over Will's torso, her head resting next to his shoulder. At any other house, on any other night, this would be heaven. But Hannah had done her telltale giggle by the time they returned to their room after accepting Jon's offer for a nightcap, and this house and all its memories haunted him. At least he didn't have to worry about anyone spilling the Madison beans—if there was anything his family understood, it was secrets and decorum. Not to mention he'd spent the entire day threatening Jon and Madison within an inch of their lives. And while his father hadn't sought him out yet, Will knew Jonathan would keep the truth in his back pocket, a grenade waiting to be detonated.

Will sidled his way out of bed, pulling the comforter up over Hannah's shoulders. She immediately flopped over, pulling it even tighter around herself. It would be nice to stay there and pretend that her cuddles were more than tipsy sleep habits, but he wouldn't sleep for many hours. Maybe he wouldn't sleep at all if he stayed here. He leaned down and pressed a kiss to Hannah's cheek, whispering a good night. She turned back over, her arm stretching to where he would've been if his restless mind had let him stay.

Will didn't bother wandering the halls anymore. He knew where he had to go to settle his mind. He walked directly to the back of the house, down a long hall to an old sunroom that had been closed off and redesigned by his mother. All these years later, he couldn't think of it as anything other than "Mom's Room." In the past few months—since Madison and Jon—he had finally come to understand why she loved it so.

The room had picture windows perfect for viewing the expanse of the yard and the woods beyond it but also a fireplace for the chilly nights. His mother designed it so she could go from reading in the natural sunlight to reading by the firelight. There was no television or phone, only a desk nestled into a nook opposite the picture windows and a small stereo she'd never let Jonathan upgrade. He turned the system on now, hearing the whir of the CD in its cradle. It was weird to think there were people who'd never known that sound. Wilderness Weekend filled the space, loud enough for him to relax into the melodies he'd long ago memorized but quiet enough that he wouldn't bother anyone and no one would bother him.

He ran his finger across the desk—not a speck of dust. His mother had always kept her laptop and stack upon stack of papers there. She kept information about the various charities she and Jonathan contributed to and lists of key members and prominent clients—everything she needed as a wife of the wealthy. It sat empty now, all of her responsibilities long ago assigned to an assistant.

Though the room was cleaned weekly, it was otherwise left untouched, a relic of another life.

"I thought I'd find you here."

Perfect. Madison.

"You don't look happy to see me," she said, shutting the door behind her.

Will touched his wedding band, kneading the metal as if willing Madison to turn around and forget they'd ever been a thing. Harsh had been his perpetual tone with Madison for months, but when he committed to Hannah, he made a promise to himself that he would go for simply standoffish, if not cold. He didn't have to like Madison, but he was moving forward with his life, and he couldn't properly do that if he was stuck in the past. That was why the next words out of his mouth weren't "leave me alone."

"Thank you for not saying anything to Hannah about us." His voice stuck on every part of that sentence. He hadn't thanked Madison for anything—not even passing the creamer at brunch—since everything happened. It had been a small act of defiance that made him feel the teensiest bit better, petty as it might have been.

"Of course. Though I don't know how long you can get away with keeping that secret." She paused, studying him. "You are planning on telling her, right?"

He had planned on telling her on the drive up, once they'd arrived, or any time in the last two weeks. But when was the appropriate time to tell his wife her sister-in-law was also her bajingo sister, a homewrecker, and the person who had utterly destroyed his life? He couldn't bear the look that would cross her face the moment the truth came out—not from Hannah. She was the only important person in his life who didn't pity him like that, who still believed only great things for him.

"Hannah likes you," he said. "She's excited to have another woman to help her, and I quote, 'navigate the intricacies of the Thorne boys.'"

"That's not—"

"Come on, Madison. What if the situation was reversed?" He met her eyes, which were locked on him. It had been so long since he'd really looked at her, but they were the same eyes— still adorably wide and mesmerizing green.

"Yeah, yeah, I'd hate me."

He looked away, his stomach roiling. This wasn't him. This couldn't be him—agreeing with Madison, keeping secrets. All that lying was what had gotten him here. Hannah deserved the truth. "I'm going to tell her."

Without him realizing it, Madison had crossed the room. She stood inches from him. "I won't say anything, William. Not unless she says something first."

"Why?" He wouldn't have questioned anyone else, but meddling was one of Madison's specialties, and the sanctity of commitments was not high on her priority list. She had barely shown any remorse for her actions both to and with Will. Her hand had slipped from one Thorne to the next, and that was that. Except in the middle of the night when she had clearly missed the younger model.

"Whatever you may think, I do care about you." Will braced for Madison's touch, but her hand didn't move from the arm of the chair. "And if Hannah makes you happy, then I'm happy for you."

He almost believed her. But Madison was ever the actress. The glint in her eye hinted at ulterior motives. He could guess at them, but he couldn't go down that road anymore. It only led to more despair and lies and messiness. He would warn Hannah about Madison. It had only been a day. It wasn't like the two women were exchanging friendship bracelets.

"Do you think..." she said, hedging. Madison never hedged. "Do you think your mother would've hated me?"

Had they been in any other room, it would've been as far out in left field as you could get. But she knew why his wanderings always brought him there. Madison knew everything.

"I don't know," he said after several seconds of silence. The question had crossed his mind, but he'd never come up with a sound answer. Hating Madison betrayed Jon—loving her hurt Will. It was a lose-lose situation. He was glad Mom wasn't here to decide between her sons.

"Do you hate me?"

Will crossed the room to the picture window and stared into the darkness. "Let's not do this, Madison."

"So, you *do* hate me," she said, and he swore there was melancholy in her voice, a quiver to the statement that didn't fit.

"No good would come from my answering that question," he said, trying to be diplomatic. What answer could she have possibly expected? Of course he hated her. He hated her in the way he could only despise someone he had loved—deeply, completely, and sometimes not at all. "You're about to be my sister-in-law, so whether I hate you or not is irrelevant."

"It's not irrelevant to me."

He turned to face her, relieved to find her standing by the doorway. Madison might be a meddler, but she also knew when to fold. "I hated you a little less today."

WILL DIDN'T KNOW HE could have an emotional hangover, but after only a day and a half in the Hamptons, his head felt like it was in a vise grip, and he was literally itchy. He'd woken up to an empty bed and a note that Hannah had gone to find sustenance. She wasn't in the kitchen, though according to Renata, she'd been there earlier. Will sat down by himself in the dining room with a heaping plate of eggs, bacon, and two full English muffins slathered with orange marmalade. He shot Hannah a quick text before diving in. He didn't often get to claim this table as his own. It was rejuvenating. Bit by bit, he was taking back what Jon and Madison had stolen.

As the first sips of coffee hit his system, his head started to clear. He tried to cast off the memory that had been haunting him since his late-night conversation with Madison. Memorial Day Weekend, during the first big party of the summer, he'd found Madison and Jon locked in an embrace deep within Renata's kitchen, the sounds of the party muffled by all the stainless steel. Jon's pants hung low on him, and Madison's dress was scrunched up over her hips. Will had dropped the bottle of wine he'd retrieved, shattering—

"Morning, little brother," Jon said, sitting down across from Will.

Will blinked twice, snapping out of it. He should've known better. There was no being alone at the Thorne mansion, and even when he was alone, the weight of expectation was a constant companion. And Jon had built-in Will radar. If Will wasn't hiding out in his room—as far away from his family as he could get—Jon found him. Will knew what his brother was trying to do. He also knew it would never work. There was no going back if he married her—*when* he married her. Jon thought that the fact that his love for Madison was the real thing would make everything better. Maybe it would to the outside world, but to Will, that only made it more unforgiveable.

"And now my appetite is gone," Will said, piling his silverware on his plate.

"Can I have your muffin, then?" Jon reached across the table, but Will pulled the plate back toward himself. "Come on. Don't act like a child. You sat in a public space."

Will wanted to argue more—his brother could've kept walking, found literally any other place to sit—but he also wanted to finish his breakfast. He glanced at his phone, still no word from Hannah. Maybe she'd made a run for it. It wouldn't be the first time his family had scared a woman off in a day. He picked his silverware back up and scanned the latest headlines in hopes of deterring his brother from further conversation.

Three bites into his eggs, Jon cleared his throat.

That couldn't be good. Will looked up expectantly.

Jon stared at him, his expression hesitant and curious. "Hannah seems cool," he said after a beat. "You two are a good fit."

"We think so," Will said, returning to his breakfast. He couldn't be nice to Jon. Once he opened that door, Jon would lodge himself inside and wouldn't give an inch. Well enough wasn't in Jon's repertoire, and the longer Will shared a room with Jon—literally and metaphorically—the more likely he was to punch him in the face.

"I was thinking, you know, now that you're married—" Jon paused, uncertainty flashing across his face before he plowed on. "Maybe you would consider giving a speech at the wedding or the rehearsal dinner?"

What. The. Fuck?

Will took a breath then another. He counted to ten, twenty, and thirty, giving his brother a chance to take it back, giving himself the self-control to not leap across the table. Jon couldn't be serious. And yet, it was clear from the open expression on his face that he thought it was a reasonable request.

Will ran a hand along his forehead, stopping to massage his temple. He tried to keep his tone as neutral as possible and devoid of the well of sarcasm brewing under his chest. "No, I will not give a speech at your wedding."

Jon had the audacity to look surprised. "But you're married now. You're happy."

"Yes. I'm happily married to the woman of my dreams. But I'm still not giving a speech at your wedding to my ex-girlfriend," Will said through his teeth. *Fucking Jon.* "You are lucky I even agreed to be in the bridal party. I tolerate you at work and these godforsaken weekends because I have to. But if I never had to see you again, I would be fine with that."

"You don't mean that, William. No matter what happened, I'm your brother." Jon took an infuriatingly calm sip of his coffee. "I will always be your brother."

"Unfortunately."

Jon pulled a face. "I don't see why we can't be adults about this and agree to put everything that happened behind us."

"Wow," Will said. "That's a real apology right there—*I know I destroyed your life, but let's be adults about it.*"

"I've already apologized to you."

"Actually, Jon, you have *never* apologized," Will said, shaking his head. "You never even bothered to speak with me before proposing, like you marrying her made it all better. It didn't—it doesn't. You can't wish this away with a wedding and forced lunches and acting like everything is fine."

Jon put his coffee cup down and met Will's gaze. "I never wanted to hurt you."

"Still not an apology!"

"I'm not going to apologize for falling in love with Madison." Jon stared at him incredulously. "And I'm sure as hell not going to spend the rest of my life apologizing for marrying her."

Will stood up. He didn't have to sit here and have this conversation. Jon thought what he'd done was okay because it was for love, and there was no telling him otherwise. Maybe he had to see it that way. Maybe that was all that kept him from hating himself every day.

"Everything okay in here?"

Will and Jon both looked up at the sound of Madison's voice. She stood in the doorway in her tennis outfit, a small plate of fruit in her hands. Hannah would've had bacon. Madison met Will's gaze, not Jon's. It was an awful representation of the mess they found themselves in.

"Fine," Will said as a means of getting Madison to break her hold on him. "Have you seen my wife this morning?"

"She went for a walk with Daniel earlier. I believe she was heading to the Peach Pit after that."

At least Hannah was fitting in and comfortable enough to head out on her own. Not bothering to look back at Jon, Will walked past Madison and into the hallway. He sent Hannah another text, letting her know he was going out for a run. If he didn't get some miles under him, all the emotions roiling inside were going to explode to the surface. That was the last thing he needed to happen in front of Hannah before he told her the truth about Madison.

"Oh, Will." He stopped in his tracks at Madison's voice. "Can you make sure Hannah has a copy of your insurance card with her name on it for our first appointment? I can't get her in without it."

A shiver went through him. He knew Hannah had set up an appointment with Madison, but he had to find some way around it. He wondered how he could he manage that without spelling out the truth. And if Madison was in—which she so clearly was—there was no turning that train around. He took a deep breath and glanced at his phone again. There was still no response from Hannah. With a curt nod to Madison, he headed back toward his room, considering exactly how many miles he could fit in before Hannah returned.

Chapter 22
Hannah

Hannah pulled the Lexus into the circle drive, sliding in between Jon's Mercedes and Daniel's Acura. The doctor had the cheapest and least luxurious of the luxury vehicles. There was a joke there, but she didn't know what it was. All of that was completely out of her realm. Her car was six years old—paid off only last year—with nearly one hundred thousand miles on it. It wasn't flashy and still had that boxy shape that cars had back before every company remodeled for a sleeker look. But it was hers.

She wrapped her hands around the large coffee from the Peach Pit. Madison had warned her it was a bad idea to bring it back, but after that weekend, she didn't care. But how best to get it into the house unnoticed? Was there a side door? Though she had no idea where in the house her father-in-law resided. She bit her lip and examined the house again.

Oh, fuck it. She was a grown woman. If she wanted to buy coffee, Jonathan would have to deal with it like an adult. She smiled to herself, the cup warming her hands and self-righteousness warming her soul. She was going to find the largest mug possible and hide the shit out of that coffee.

Hannah peeked in the front door. No one was in the vestibule. Not that that meant anything in a mansion—someone could be in the next room, and she'd never hear them. She shouldered the front door closed and weighed heading straight to her room or detouring through the kitchen. Her stomach growled. The kitchen it was.

Maybe there would be some breakfast left out since they apparently didn't eat lunch on Sundays. *Heathens.*

"Pardon?"

Hannah slapped a hand over her mouth, swallowing a squeak at the voice. She'd apparently said that last part out loud.

"Did you need something, miss?"

"Oh, Renata," Hannah said, turning to face the older woman. "No, thank you. I'm fine."

Renata stared at her—judging or calculating, Hannah didn't know. She counted the seconds before the woman finally spoke. "You don't like Mr. Thorne's coffee?"

"Umm... it's just a bit strong." The urge to shield her offensive outsider coffee from Renata overwhelmed her, and she wrapped both hands around the paper cup.

Renata's eyes narrowed, but then the smallest of laughs escaped her lips. "Can't say I don't agree. Come with me."

Hannah thought her wanderings from that morning had given her a solid understanding of the house layout, but she had no idea where Renata was taking her. They might as well have been crawling through a secret passage behind the walls.

They went through a part of the house with its own vibes. Nothing was dusty, but everything seemed older, from the style to the personal pictures of the boys as kids—something the rest of the house lacked. She stopped to pick up a picture of a young Will curled against the hip of his mother. Will resembled Jonathan, but *wow*, he was his mother's son.

"Miss?"

Hannah took a few quick steps and found herself at the back of the kitchen. She followed Renata through the pantry, past the appliances, and to the front where breakfast had been set up that morning. She grabbed a plate and a cranberry muffin, taking a seat on one of the stools. Renata placed an oversized mug in front of her. It wasn't anything she would have expected to find in this house with its fine china for a continental breakfast. Hannah spun it around. University of Iowa was on the other side. It was Will's mug. It had to be. She distinctly remembered the morning he chipped the handle and his resolve to use the mug through graduation anyway. That had been October of junior year.

"Has Will been down yet?" Hannah asked, sipping her still-warm coffee.

Renata nodded, her attention focused on the vegetables she was chopping. "I saw him heading out in his trainers right before you came in."

Right. Of course he'd be out for another run. Hannah pulled out her phone and found a text message confirming this information—a series of messages, upon further review. She typed out a quick text with one hand, picking up Will's mug with the other. She stood up, raising the cup to Renata in farewell. She smiled back, laughter playing across her face. Was Renata like this with all the women the boys brought home? Probably not—Madison had barely registered Renata's existence. Hannah held her coffee close to her chest. She had found another ally.

She meandered through the halls, certain if she kept going straight, she would find a room with a fireplace. It would be nice to sit in the glow of a fire, relax, contemplate life—or at least text Kate the latest details. She'd promised a live-texting event but had sent only two texts since Friday night. Fate had other plans. The door next to her opened, revealing none other than Jonathan himself. *Crap.*

She smiled wanly and waved with the hand that didn't hold her contraband coffee. Jonathan did not wave back or smile but rather nodded. "Ah, Miss Abbott," he said, his tone placid. "Or I suppose Mrs. Thorne?"

"Hannah is fine," she said, trying to keep her tone neutral. Jonathan was prickly and could insult a person without ever saying anything negative and keeping a completely sanguine smile on his face. Will had warned her. She was prepared not to react, but seeing it in action and having it directed at her created quite an exercise in self-control.

"As you wish. I was hoping to chat with you without my son, if that's amenable?"

She nodded her approval and then followed him into what appeared to be an office. In the middle of the room sat a giant mahogany desk whittled to spectacular detail. It was every writer's dream desk and something a writer's salary could never afford—at least, not her salary. Jonathan took a seat behind the desk in an oversized leather chair. He motioned for Hannah to sit across from him. Even the chairs were designed to intimidate. They were low to the ground with equal heights in the arms and the back. They created a George Bailey-versus-Mr. Potter dynamic. Well, the joke was on Jonathan—the Mr. Potters of the world never won.

"I have something for you," Jonathan said once they were both seated. He held out a large manila envelope.

Hannah glanced at it warily before accepting it. "What's this?"

He motioned for her to open it, but she left it in her lap. Whatever was in this envelope, Hannah knew instinctively she wanted no part of it.

"Please," he added when she didn't move.

She pulled out the document, taking in the top line: Petition for Marriage Annulment.

Hannah's eyes flicked up to his, anger and shock warring inside her—anger because how dare he make assumptions, and shock because it was Sunday morning, and he'd only found out yesterday afternoon.

"My son can be quite impetuous," Jonathan said to her silent accusation, "especially after a broken heart. And I must say, his last broken heart was quite thorough."

"I am aware," Hannah said curtly.

"Are you? Well, then you can see why I might find it suspect that my son was in his right mind when he married you. And if I'm not mistaken, you yourself only just got out of a relationship."

He'd had her looked into? Who did this man think he was? Hannah waited a moment before answering him. Her response needed to be perfect and not the string of profanities she wanted to hurl at him.

"There's no harm in taking a step back if, perhaps, you feel you two rushed things," Jonathan continued before she could respond.

"Will and I are happy, *sir*." She added the salutation after a beat, hoping it sounded as petulant as it felt. "There was no mistake in our decision."

"Be that as it may, I can't have my son risking half his fortune because the girl he once fancied himself in love with decided to glance his way."

She trained her expression to neutral, though her heart pounded—both because of the delicate situation and the implication that Will was indeed in love with her. Jonathan would not rattle her. She would not give him the satisfaction.

"And if you actually love each other, why not annul the marriage now and give it a go the old-fashioned way? Then get married again with a prenuptial agreement in place. No harm done."

Hannah swallowed the rage boiling inside her. "I do love your son."

"And the fact that you could gain a significant manner of wealth if this marriage should go south in a year, a few years, or if an heir were to come of it, had nothing to do with the brash decision to marry him?"

"I didn't marry Will for his money." Hannah's pulse pounded in her head. She'd expected plenty of things from that weekend, but

Jonathan's attempt to overturn the marriage wasn't one of them. "I was doing just fine on my own."

"Ah, so 'just fine' is now underpaid editor for a no-name magazine that doesn't even offer health insurance? Interesting."

Hannah didn't know if she was more insulted at the dig at her integrity and her livelihood or at the fact that he had figured her out in less than twenty-four hours. "I have loved your son for close to a decade. Three months ago, that love turned romantic. He asked me to marry him. I said yes, but I didn't want to spend two years of our lives planning a wedding. He agreed. End of story."

"I'm sure that's not the end of the story." His tone was icy and contemptuous. He wasn't playing polite now. He wanted those papers signed.

"And if I sign the papers?"

"You can *date* William, if you like." Jonathan Thorne wasn't a frivolous man, but his comment held all the attributes of a good shrug.

Hannah realized then that he didn't care about the aftermath. He wanted his son's money—*his* money—handed down and protected, and he wanted to discredit Will. Could this still be about the board position?

"Or go out and find your true love and forget any of this happened," Jonathan said. "You'll both be better for it. If anything, I'm sure of that. William is too much heart. He always has been. You and I both know this—that is how he ended up in Iowa, after all."

She *did* know that, and it was precisely why she loved him. The world needed more men to lead with their hearts. Hannah stood up, finished with Jonathan and his insinuations and presumptions, and dropped the annulment papers back on his desk. "I know who Will is. Nothing you do is going to make me change my mind about him."

THE DOOR CREAKED OPEN, and with it came a rush of warmer air from the hallway and Will. Hannah finished her Chaturanga, transitioning into an imperfect Upward-Facing Dog. She smiled at her absentee partner in crime. His eyes were alert with post-run high, but there were bags where there hadn't been before. A snarky remark about how he'd left her to the wolves died on her lips.

"How was your run?" she asked instead, pushing back into Downward-Facing Dog.

"It ended up being more of an errand. As I was heading out, Dad asked me to pick up some stuff at the farmers market. It's only about two miles away, down by the beach." He stripped off his shirt, revealing a nearly flat stomach and speckles of chest hair. Hannah's insides stirred. Will shirtless wasn't a new sight, but this was a new Will—a manlier Will, with those defined hip bones sticking out of his too-short running shorts. Her husband was *hot*.

She stood up from her pose and adjusted her cami, wrapping her arms around her waist to stop from running her hand down Will's chest. The yoga had cleared her head, but it had also brought on a fabulous or terrible idea. She hadn't decided until he entered. Jonathan was going to do anything he could to pick apart their relationship. Will had told her as much, but she hadn't understood before. They needed to be better. They needed to be believable. They needed to be in love.

"Well, are we at least having something yummy for whatever this midafternoon meal is?" she asked, sitting down on the edge of the bed.

"Everything Renata makes is yummy," he said, looking up from the pile of clothes he was digging through.

She gave him a dubious look.

"Everything besides the coffee." He sat down next to her, the brush of his bare arm once again causing the hair on hers to stand up.

"Are you okay? You seem a little weird," he said, balling a clean shirt in his hands.

There was her opening, but Hannah still didn't have the words. She wasn't even sure what she was asking. She straightened her shoulders and rested her hand on Will's chest.

He went rigid at her touch.

After another moment, she ran her hand up over his shoulder and down his arm, finally linking their fingers. "We need to do a better job of convincing everyone we're in love."

"We have the papers." His voice was breathy but steady. He didn't look directly at her. "No one can dispute our marriage."

"Oh, I'm sure there's no doubt that we're legally married. But we're supposed to be madly in love, so much so that we got married in less than three months." She scooted closer to him. Their knees touched. Everything touched. "Kiss me."

Will leaned forward and pressed his lips to hers for a brief moment. It was nice enough, like the kisses they had shared lately, but that kiss wasn't going to convince anyone. It barely convinced Hannah.

"Kiss me like I'm someone you actually want to have sex with."

"That might be difficult." An amused and yet wary expression played across his features.

"Just do it." Hannah put both her hands against his chest. His heart beat a steady course under her touch. She leaned in when he didn't move, parting his lips with her own. Will deepened the kiss almost immediately, his tongue greeting hers. Hannah's body lit up as his hands found the soft skin between her waistband and her cami. She pushed herself closer to him, her hands climbing up his torso, over his shoulders, and wrapping around him. His muscles tightened as her hands passed over them, Will's kiss becoming more urgent with each caress.

This was exactly how she imagined Will's kiss to be. Their chemistry was not going to be an issue. She started to retreat, her mind winning over her body. They needed to take this slow. It had only been two out of fifty-two weeks. But Will pulled her back in, his hand coming around her neck and tangling her hair. She breathed him in. Hot and a good kisser. Did she want to sleep with Will? Yes, yes she did.

Will broke away, and Hannah scooted back. Her heart pounded. Adrenaline coursed through her veins. He was too good at following directions. Will's eyes bored into her, questioning, wanting.

"Yeah, that's what we need to show people," she said, still breathless.

Will shook his head, his mouth quirking at the corners. "We can't do that in polite company."

"You know what I mean," Hannah said, shoving his shoulder playfully.

"Maybe we should start by sharing a bed when we get back to the city. You know, before we complicate things."

She narrowed her eyes at him. He was trying so hard to be a gentleman, which was adorable. "Are we going to complicate things?"

His cheeks pinkened. "Maybe... eventually."

She giggled, feeling the kiss in every part of her body. She would have dreams about that kiss—dirty, sweaty dreams. "Okay, hubs, let's share a bed."

Chapter 23

Hannah

Hannah's hand tingled as she pulled open the door of the physical therapy office. It was really happening—PT, the doctors, all of it. Daniel had booked her an appointment with a coveted orthopedic surgeon. That wasn't until January, but after waiting over a year, two months seemed like nothing. And it meant she got to give physical therapy a try with Madison. She hadn't pegged Madison as a PT, but aside from being a future Thorne, she also came highly recommended.

There was no receptionist when Hannah walked in. The sign on the door had indicated it was after-hours, but Madison had definitely said six o'clock. She pulled out her phone to check her calendar but instead found a text from Kate.

Come on, you have to let me put Father Thorne on the podcast. He handed you freakin' annulment papers. Who does that? No one, Hannah. No. One.

Kate was seriously low on material if she was asking to put Will and Hannah's Hamptons adventure on *Bitching about Boyfriends*. Hannah sent back a pair of emojis, the eye roll and the raised hand.

"There you are," Madison said, stepping into the lobby. She wrapped Hannah in a hug. "I was just getting set up."

Hannah followed Madison back into the main room. Bikes lined one wall, exam benches another. Exercise equipment was scattered throughout the space. Madison handed Hannah some paperwork before taking a seat on top of a balance ball.

Hannah sat on the mat in front of Madison and rummaged through her wallet until she found her newly printed insurance card. "Your boss doesn't mind our session being after hours?"

"Nah, I cleared it with her. She's a hard-ass, but I told her you were family." Madison grinned. "It was close enough to the truth, at least."

Hannah felt herself relax as she filled out the forms, writing in the drab details. There was no primer with Madison. She'd jumped right in, happy to accept Hannah since that first morning coffee run. A week later, Madison texted Hannah more than Kate.

"You know, I met Jon here," Madison said. She rolled almost off the ball and held a tricep dip.

"Really?" Hannah asked, transcribing her ID number.

"Yeah, he hurt his shoulder playing tennis." She glanced back at a grouping of equipment. "We fell in love over TheraBands and the rowing machine. I was sitting on that bench when he kissed me for the first time. It shook my whole world."

"That's adorable."

Madison rolled back into a seated position. "You must know what it's like. I mean, William's kiss must have really been something for you to marry him so fast."

Hannah blushed about five shades of red—of course Madison would fish for details. "Our first kiss was in college, but our second kiss..." Hannah paused. It was best to stick to the truth as much as possible. "It was actually kind of clunky and unexpected, but there was a spark."

"Ah, the spark. Can't deny it."

"No, you can't," Hannah said, handing over the completed paperwork.

Madison looked over the paperwork. "You hurt your knee in a car accident, right?" Hannah nodded, and Madison wrote a few notes in the margins. "Did you know what grade the tear was?"

"Two?"

Madison scribbled another note. "Well, I think the key here is to properly build up the muscles around your knee, giving you a good foundation for healing. Since you haven't had any official PT, we'll start slow and see where your triggers are. We'll meet once a week here, but you'll have homework to do every day, and I will know if you don't do it."

Hannah laughed. Madison's boss clearly wasn't the only hard-ass on staff. "Homework. Got it."

"All right, hop on that bike for a quick warm-up."

Madison sat on the bike next to her, alternating between a slow cycle and resting her head against the handlebars.

"Can I ask you a personal question?" Madison asked from her headrest.

"Sure."

"I know you knew William before..." She waved at the open air in front of her. "But how did you just marry him without missing a beat?"

Hannah considered her answer. The truth and the lie, in this case, were the same—because it was Will. Will was and always had been her person. It was as simple and as complex as that.

"There was definitely a beat," she said. "But Will and I, we had all these missed opportunities in college. Ones we didn't even know about. Then he was there, standing in line for funnel cake, and it was like this part of myself fell back into place. And that was before it was ever romantic."

"It couldn't have been anything else," Madison said, a wistful smile on her face.

Hannah shrugged. "Maybe, maybe not. I mean, he was fresh off heartbreak, and I was in a relationship. It could've gone a different way, I suppose."

"That didn't scare you? His broken heart?"

Hannah had learned Madison was in love with love and fate and destiny. Otherwise, she would've suspected she was trying to pick apart the story, to find the flaw that would pull it all apart.

"I guess it scared me a little," she said, glancing over at her future sister-in-law. "But we didn't go from out-of-touch friends to lovers in an instant. And as we got closer and shared a bit more about our feelings for each other—from then and now—I knew Will could never use me as a rebound. We're about more than that."

"Clearly." Madison smiled and went back to pedaling. "Pick up the pace a bit. Focus on how your knee feels."

Hannah pedaled for a minute, training her thoughts on her injury. She hoped she remembered these answers. She'd have to fill Will in and make sure Kate understood the timeline of their supposed relationship too.

"Any pain?" Madison asked.

Hannah shook her head.

"Good. So, to be clear, you broke up with your boyfriend to be with Will?"

Hannah rolled her eyes at the intensity with which Madison had asked the question. Holding it in to focus on her job must have been killer.

"Yes and no," Hannah said, aware she was treading a fine line and this story could go completely off the rails. "Brian and I had been ending almost since we started. When Will showed up, and I realized how I felt—how I never felt that way about Brian—it was an easy choice. And it's not like I woke up with one boyfriend and went to bed with a different one. Even though everything happened so fast, it was still slow."

"So, what? Like forty-eight hours before you jumped his bones?"

If only. They were closer to that in the week since they started sharing a bed. It had been agonizing. She felt every movement of his throughout the night. She woke up sweaty from vivid, mostly naked dreams to find the star of them with his arms wrapped around her, his bare chest warm against her back. The other night when he'd leaned in and kissed her goodnight, she had wanted to pull him down on top of her. He'd even lingered over the kiss, their bodies gravitating toward each other. Hannah felt her cheeks brighten at the memories. Another night, one with more drinks and less editing, and it might have gone another way. But they were carefully treading the line of uncomplicated for now.

Madison stared at her expectantly. Hannah tried to imagine their proposal in a more romantic fashion—one where it wasn't so clearly platonic, where the lines were already blurred. They wouldn't have waited very long, if at all. She met Madison's gaze head-on. "Sixty-three-and-a-half hours."

Chapter 24
Hannah

The city was already awake, though the sun was barely rising on Central Park East. Hannah had gotten used to the relative quiet of Queens. She could go out for an early-morning jog, and the neighborhood would be stirring with her—teachers bustling to get to school, corporate types walking their dogs, and millennials like herself pounding the pavement. It was rarely quiet on Central Park East, but there was something nice about the scene outside her window. It was different than the one she had in Queens and different than the one she watched each night from work, and yet they all offered her the same comfort. It was her city; they were her people.

She sipped her coffee, letting the mix of vanilla and hazelnut draw her closer to being awake and warm. She burrowed deeper into her college hoodie. *God, she wanted to be in bed.* She'd gone right from PT to a show—because that's what her knee needed—and then Riley kept her late last night to go over a too-long and too-detailed list of everything Hannah might need to know in her absence. Hannah hadn't said they'd survived her first maternity leave and they would survive this one, but the truth was that they would. They'd gone over the list twice, and after the next day, Riley would turn her attention to all things baby—supposedly. Hannah had her doubts.

Her phone vibrated, and she glanced down at the text from Madison. *Did you have any questions about the exercises I gave you?*

Of course Madison was up. She was probably doing interval workouts in her living room. *No, I got them. Still on for Tuesday night?*

You mean for date night with the brothers Thorne? Hell yes!

Hannah laughed. She didn't know what was so exciting about dinner with both Jon and Will, but Madison had been practically bouncing since Hannah suggested it at the end of their session. It would be nice to have a break. November had already kicked into high gear a week into *Deafening Silence's* annual "30 Concerts in 30 Days" event. The schedule had been set for weeks, but Hannah had no idea how she was going to manage it.

A yawn wracked Hannah's body. As much as she enjoyed her nightly dream romps with her husband, the truth was that she'd forgotten what living with Will was like. In her memory, everything about Will was rosy and happy and silly. He had promised her when they wrote their marriage rules that he now picked up his socks. And that much seemed true. His dirty socks were in the hamper every morning since she moved in. She pulled herself to her feet and came back inside. Irritation sparked as she walked through the living room. Will's suit jacket had been flung across the back of the couch, and a collection of ties covered one of the kitchen-nook chairs. Binx batted at one, his nail catching it before Hannah could shoo him away. *Great.* A thread had pulled from the silk fabric, and Hannah dreaded showing Will what Binx had done—again. But she'd told him to put them away every day since Binx had wrecked the first one, and he'd left them out anyway.

Hannah collected the ties and placed them on the counter. She took in the pizza box Will had left out the night before, the last slice still inside. She hoped this bachelor lifestyle was a consequence of living in his father's apartment with a built-in cleaning lady and not his norm. It wasn't like her apartment had been spotless, but this situation was unsustainable. Between Clara's weekly cleanings, laundry accumulated in the hamper, dishes festered in the sink, takeout filled the fridge, and empty cartons stuffed the trash bin. Was it that difficult to walk down the hall to the trash shoot?

Two stacks of reports sat on the coffee table. The dining room table was cluttered with leftover takeout plasticware, napkins, and ketchup packets. Her old bedroom still housed all her boxes, and on the kitchen nook was an inordinate amount of mail addressed to Jonathan Thorne, which Will never went through. That was why she had been sitting outside before sunrise in November. The apartment was submerged, and if Hannah spent waking hours inside it, she felt like she was drowning too.

She shook out her shoulders, trying to roll out the frustrations. She would be better about cleaning too. She'd take the pizza boxes to the recycling room on her way out and empty the dishwasher before bed no matter what time she rolled in. She'd unpack. Tidying up could become part of their Saturday-morning ritual.

Another yawn hit her, and Hannah contemplated trying to go back to bed. Riley wasn't there to see her comings and goings, and the other editors were just as ransacked by November as she was. That was another problem: Hannah wasn't used to sharing her living space. She wasn't used to someone's morning routine disrupting her sleep, and Will—despite having had a live-in girlfriend—was not used to being quiet in the morning. She hadn't slept in since the honeymoon. Will's morning routine, weekday or weekend, was far too loud for that. He hummed while he picked out his clothes, he turned on lights, and things—she couldn't even tell you what—clinked around the bathroom as he got ready. And Hannah was by no means a late sleeper. She loved waking up early, but she also needed to compensate for her late hours a few days a week.

She refilled her mug. Her fatigue was showing in her skin, in the bags under her eyes, and in her mood. Will had noticed that their easy banter was not quite so easy lately, but he hadn't said anything directly. Were they always so passive with each other? A memory of college-aged Will, backing away from her, his hands held up haltingly, came to her—she'd cleared out space in her closet for his clothes, unable to take the spray of wrinkled boy clothes across her and Kate's living room for another minute. Two weeks later, his clothes hadn't moved, and half her closet had remained empty.

"Morning, Mrs. Thorne." Will leaned against the door jamb. He wore suit pants and an unbuttoned shirt. Her stomach fluttered despite her bad mood, and she shivered as she conjured up the dream version of her husband, who pulled her into the shower and did dirty things to her. Real-life husband still hadn't brought up Rule 3a and resolutely stopped every kiss just when it was getting good. It was a special kind of torture. Because she knew he felt every kiss, but something held him back. Maybe Kate and Jonathan were wrong. Maybe Will didn't love her. Or maybe he was considering all the same things she was—mainly, what if something went wrong? How could they stay friends after sharing that intimacy?

Will held up the light-blue tie with small purple flowers that Binx had just clawed. "Another one bites the dust."

"I told you not to leave them out." She took a sip of her coffee to try and hide her frustration. Maybe she *was* immune to him a little.

Will started to button his shirt. "Eh, I never liked this tie anyway."

"That's not the point." She knew what he was going to do before he did it. College Will imposed himself over the adult Will and put his hands up.

"Don't do that," she said. "God, Will. I hated it in college, and it's even less attractive now."

Will grimaced and dropped his hands. "What is going on with you?"

"The apartment is a mess," Hannah said in a huff. "I'm not a neat freak by any means, but this isn't your all-expenses-paid bachelor pad anymore."

If her words had bothered him, Will didn't let his reaction show it. Instead, he looked back into the living room, his eyes narrowing into slits as he stared at their home. "I can see if—"

"We are not bringing Clara in for a second day," Hannah said, making sure her tone left no room for negotiation.

This time, Will did take a step back, though his hands remained at his sides. Hannah watched him consider his answer, his brow furrowing in thought. If she'd been in a better mood, she would've found it sexy.

"Is this about the mess or the money?" he asked finally.

Wow. Just wow. Hannah brushed past him without saying a word. She wound her way through the mess and into their bedroom, which was surprisingly tidy. Will had this thing about making the bed every morning, as if he started his day that way, he would do all the other things he was supposed to throughout the day. *As if* indeed. She pulled the first thing her hands touched out of the closet and then locked herself in the bathroom, which was still steamy from Will's shower. The sound of the running water blocked out any remaining noises from the apartment, including Will coming into the bedroom. She heard him knock on the bathroom door, but she couldn't talk to him now.

Was it the money or the mess? One of Will's ties cost more than most of Hannah's outfits, his bathroom was nearly as big as her bedroom in Queens, and yes, having a cleaning lady chafed at Hannah's sense of adulthood, but it wasn't the money. It was the lack of respect for the money.

Fifteen minutes later—five of which she had spent sitting on the vanity, scrolling through overpriced secondhand Wilderness tickets—Hannah emerged from the bedroom feeling steadier. Will had heard her, and maybe calmer heads could prevail. She expected him to be gone. He'd been leaving earlier and earlier for work all week. But when she stepped into the messy living room, the stacks of paper had been organized into two piles that only took up a corner of the table. The sound of water running pulled her toward the kitchen. Will stood at the sink, the sleeves of his shirt rolled up to his elbow.

"What are you still doing here?" she asked.

Will glanced over at her. "I told Jim I'd be later than usual."

"You didn't have to do that."

"I think maybe I did." His tone had an edge to it, but it wasn't exactly anger or contrition. Either way, it wasn't particularly on the nice side. She'd annoyed him.

"Can I help?" she asked instead of pressing the issue.

He held out a towel. "Dry?"

She accepted it and picked up a frying pan from the rack. They worked side by side in silence for a few minutes, Will handwashing dishes that could've gone in the dishwasher and Hannah drying them and putting them away.

He handed her the final coffee mug, her own from this morning. "I did ask Clara to stop back in today, if she could, to finish cleaning up. I figured that would give us a fresh starting point."

Hannah nodded. They were both busy. It made sense to only have to keep the apartment clean, not clean it from scratch. And they had at least tackled the dishes together. They could get into habits. They could make this apartment their own with baby steps. It had only been three weeks, and the first few days, they hadn't even been in the state.

She dropped the towel over the empty dish rack. "I'd like to unpack this weekend."

"That sounds like a great idea." Will shucked off his shirt, which was practically see-through with dishwater. She averted her gaze. "Why not start tonight?"

Before Hannah could answer that she'd have to trek out to the Stone Pony and back tonight, Will shook his head. "Right, you have to go out to Jersey tonight. Anything I can unpack for you?"

"It can wait another day."

He kissed her softly on the lips. The gesture shocked and thrilled her with its simplicity and care. "Then it's a date."

Chapter 25
Will

"No, Frank. I'm a lawyer, not an environmental specialist. Send me the report, and I'll let you know if I think there are any legal tie-ups." Will doodled a spiral in his notebook, his tenth in this dragging conversation. He listened to the man's continued request. "I'm not a project manager. I don't need to visit the site. Just send me the report."

He hung up, writing a note next to the newest spiral to follow up in two days. Frank was notorious for requesting unnecessary site visits, and when the higher-ups declined, he always tried to get Will to visit. It was a flaw that kept him from getting promoted, but no amount of encouragement from Will, who had come up through the ranks with him, increased his confidence. Will turned back to his computer, where a list of overpriced tickets to the Wilderness Weekend show waited. He would buy them for that cost just to see the look on Hannah's face when the first notes of "Away From You" filled the venue, but she'd been strict about the budget, and triple the ticket price was definitely not within her perimeters.

A knock on his door brought Will back to himself. It was nearly lunch, so it had to be Jon. He had taken that one unplanned lunch with Grayson to be a standing invitation.

"You don't look happy to see me."

Will's head shot up at the sound of Hannah's voice. "You."

"Me." She leaned against the doorjamb, looking entirely out of place at the Wellington Thorne offices in her skinny jeans, Chuck Taylors, and a vintage Dashboard Confessional tee. It was awesome.

He could already imagine the whispers. Everyone knew he'd gotten married. No one had met Hannah, but the picture on his desk was from the wedding.

Under the smile, her appearance showed the frenzy and stress of the last thirteen days. Thirty concerts in thirty days didn't seem like that much to Will when there were five editors covering shows, but between Hannah's boss going out on maternity leave and one of the other editors getting mono, the month had quickly gone from manageable to messy. Hannah practically lived at concert venues, and he was almost surprised she didn't sleep at the office. He wondered if any of it had to do with the growing pains their marriage was currently experiencing.

There'd been the argument about the apartment being a mess, where Hannah had made her feelings on Will's lifestyle abundantly clear. And then Hannah had delayed their plans on Saturday to unpack her things and canceled tonight's dinner with Madison and Jon, almost requiring him to have dinner with them on his own. Will was less than gracious at that news, and she was quick to point out that she didn't need Will's permission to adjust her schedule. Workaholic meet workaholic. Things between them were by no means bad, but they also weren't easy. It didn't help that every time she scrunched her nose at him in frustration, he wanted to pull her down onto their bed and spend the next several hours getting to know every inch of her body. Except there would be no going back for him the moment he had sex with her.

"Welcome to Wellington Thorne, Mrs. Thorne," he said, coming around his desk to greet her.

"I brought lunch," she said, holding up a paper bag.

It had no obvious markings, but the smell of grease hit the moment he got closer. "You didn't."

"I did." They sat as she started unpacking the containers, laying out the spread on the small table in the corner of his office. "Burgers and fries from your favorite Village hole-in-the-wall."

If this was a peace offering, it might be the best there had ever been. It even came with fountain drinks.

"I knew I married you for a reason."

"Yes, for my incredible taste in music, not for my ability to successfully drag five pounds of beef and fries across the city."

She scooted her chair forward until their knees touched. He had barely processed her closeness before she pulled him in by the tie. Their lips crashed together, and Will let her take the lead. She parted his lips and slid her tongue across his own. His body stirred, wanting so much more—it always did when Hannah kissed him.

"Hannah." He pulled back, the word barely a whisper. They couldn't do this here—not like this.

"Tell me you feel it too," she said in a low voice, her forehead pressed against his.

He stared at her hands, that single word—*too*—rolling around in his head. *Tell me you feel it too.* Which meant *she* felt something for him. "You know I do."

"I want to invoke Rule 3a." She'd said it plainly, but to Will, she might as well have exclaimed her love for him from the rooftops.

"What?" *Great*, now he sounded like an idiot.

"We've been sharing a bed for two weeks and practicing kissing and..." She took his hand in hers. "I want to be able to do what we just did and feel what I just felt without wondering what it means and what we're doing, and if I'm jeopardizing our friendship and the pact by thinking that I want more. Because I want more, Will."

Holy shit. He was not expecting this when she walked in the door. "I-I completely agree."

She nodded, and a shy smile lit her face. "So, husband..." She kissed him again, and he prayed that no one decided to walk into his office right now. "Will you be my boyfriend?"

His heart swelled. Those words were perfect in their ridiculousness. Nothing could be more *them*.

"Yes," he said, sitting the slightest bit back. He had to say the rest of it before there was no going back. "But I have one stipulation—consider it Rule 3b."

She scrunched her nose in confusion, and Will tightened his grip on her hands to keep from pulling her into his lap and forgetting all rational thought.

"Okay?"

"I'd like to take it slow, make sure our hearts are in it too." Or until he was sure her heart was in it—his was already there, ready to drop those three little words and mean them forever. But he'd loved Hannah for years, and she'd only had him back in her life for a month.

"But we can still do this?" She kissed his neck, the edge of his chin, and the corner of his mouth before bringing their lips together in an earth-shattering kiss.

Will's hands shook in his lap. Taking it slow was going to be *difficult*. "Yes, we can still do that."

"I'll add it to our agreement," she said, sitting back.

Will watched her, still not believing this was happening. But it was. He had married Hannah. And that was about to mean so much more. "You know, you didn't have to butter me up with burgers before asking that."

She grinned. "Those were actually for my next request."

"Uh-oh."

"What would you say to lunch with Kate and her new guy one weekend?" Hannah asked as she stole yet another fry out of Will's container.

"Oh, there's a new guy?"

"Yeah," Hannah said around her straw. "Actually, it's crazy, because he started as a Herpes."

"A *what*?" Will's voice went too high at the shock of the word.

Hannah bent over herself laughing. She held a hand up, signaling him to wait for an explanation as soon as she caught her breath—which he wasn't sure would ever happen. Her cheeks had turned bright pink with laughter, and it hadn't died down. She had to be exhausted to laugh like that.

"Sorry to interrupt."

They both froze, and Hannah's laugh cut short at the sound of Jonathan's voice. Will suppressed a shudder. Jonathan, who never came to the city, had appeared on the one day Hannah surprised him for lunch. Maybe his father *was* having him followed.

"Dad?" Will had spent years training himself to address Jonathan by his name at the office, but something told him this wasn't a professional visit. For one thing, Jonathan wasn't wearing a tie, and two, he didn't just drop in. He expected others to come to him.

"William, Hannah." He nodded at each of them respectively. "How fortuitous that you are both here. I have a few things to discuss with you."

Hannah straightened next to him, but when he looked over, her face was placid, even expectant. After a moment, she turned away from Jonathan altogether, taking care to pack up the food.

"Shall we go to my office?"

"Of course, we'll be right in," Will said.

Jonathan turned and left the room, though his presence still hung heavily. Hannah hadn't said a word, but her jaw was tight, her eyes practically slits.

"I have to tell you something," she said after a few excruciatingly long moments. She sat down, head in her hands. A jumbled mess of words came out of her, but they were muffled by her hands.

Will drew them from her face, tucking them into his own. "Tell me, Abbott."

"He gave me annulment papers when we were in the Hamptons," she said, her eyes trained on their hands. "He thinks we're going to have an heir and I'm going to take the Thorne fortune."

"Oh." A mixture of emotions went through him. It wasn't surprising. What had been surprising was that his father hadn't made a move yet. And annulment papers were far from the worst thing he'd done to a girl Will had brought home. He'd most definitely paid off two of Will's prospects in his early twenties. "So that's why you said we needed to act more like husband and wife?"

She nodded and gave him a wry smile. "That, and I really wanted to kiss you again."

"Why didn't you tell me?"

She shrugged. "It didn't matter. I gave him the papers back, told him I loved you, and said he could go screw himself. Okay, I implied that last part, but still."

He was impressed—not many people took on Jonathan Thorne. "You went toe-to-toe with my father over me?"

She flushed. "The thing is, I kind of like you."

He kissed her because he wanted to and because he could—she was his girlfriend *and* his wife. "You just like having someone to keep your feet warm at night."

There was a sheen in her eyes he'd never seen before. She shook her head, showing a bashful, adorable smile. "Let's go see what he wants."

Will had walked the halls of Wellington Thorne his entire life—running through them as an unruly kid, handing out mail as a petulant teenager, and following around the project managers as an ambitious college student. Aloof employees became invested coworkers. Their attention wandered. Will wasn't the heir—that was Jon, destined by a chance of birth order and a penchant for business and finance. The younger Thorne would be general counsel and would fix their mistakes, but he could also be one of them. Will had been one of them for years. Walking down the hall with Hannah, her hand wrapped in his and her punk-chic style clashing with everything Wellington Thorne stood for, he had their attention again. Not a single eye stayed on its screen. Phone calls and conversations paused as they passed. The prodigal son had returned with a wife.

Sarah, Jonathan's secretary for as long as Will could remember, sat at her desk outside his office. She glanced briefly between the two of them, her expression warming. Sarah had always had a sweet spot for Will. "He's ready for you."

Hannah kissed his cheek. "Here goes."

Jonathan sat at his desk, flipping through papers. "Good, you're here. I don't want to take up too much of your time, as I'm sure you both have to get back to work."

"Of course," Hannah said, sitting down in one of the chairs opposite Jonathan.

"Well then, I would like to host a small gathering honoring your nuptials." He folded his hands in front of him. "And I understand you two don't want anything big, but there are certain customs we should still try and honor. We'll need to run an announcement in the *Times*, and then a dinner at the house—I was thinking Thanksgiving weekend. A few of our closest friends."

Will knew that "closest friends" meant at least a hundred people and expected that the *Times* announcement was already in the hands of the social editor, awaiting approval. The Thorne name demanded action in those circles. The only problem with all of this was that Hannah hadn't told her parents yet. Did they read the *Times*? And if they did, would they check out the social section?

"Would that work for your parents, Hannah? I know all families have their holiday traditions, and I wouldn't want to impose."

"I think the date would be fine," she said with hesitation. "But it's probably over three hours one way."

"I see. Well, they are more than welcome to stay at the house. Your sister too. Whoever has need."

That was generous. The same offer had never been extended to Madison's family. Though perhaps Jonathan, knowing everything he did, had realized about Jon and Madison all along. Maybe he had given everyone an out by not offering to host her family that fateful weekend. Still, inviting Hannah's parents felt like a trap.

He knew Hannah felt the same way. Her affirmation that she would ask her parents about the party had held obvious wariness. She hadn't even planned on telling them until Thanksgiving. A houseful of guests would have her parents on, if not their best, at least good behavior, she'd said. Will had asked for clarification, but she'd shaken her head and moved onto the next topic. He'd thought their biggest hurdle would be Jonathan. He hadn't considered that Hannah's parents might be anything other than supportive. They seemed like sitcom parents from all the stories Hannah told him over the years—loving, open, and progressive. But Hannah's whole body shrank any time the topic came up, and each time her sister called, Will watched her visibly exhale whenever it wasn't Stephanie saying she'd spoiled their secret. Now, the fierce woman, who had moments ago stared down the man who had tried to push her out, retreated into shadow.

"This all sounds great, Dad." He took Hannah's hand securely in his own. Her palm was sweaty against his. "We were planning on visiting Hannah's parents this weekend. We haven't had a chance to share the news with them yet with Hannah's work schedule, so can you hold the announcement?"

He hadn't wanted to give his father that information, but there was no other way out of the situation. Jonathan had laid down his conditions for his acceptance—or possibly the first phase of his war plan—and they couldn't be circumvented. But Will would fight to get them on his own terms.

"Certainly. Let me know when it's taken care of." Jonathan's eyes alighted in the knowledge he'd received. Already, Will saw the wheels turning on how he could use this to his advantage.

Will hated that he knew that about his father. He despised the chess game his life had become and that he was still only average at it despite years of experience. Jonathan had checked them into a corner.

Chapter 26
Hannah

Hannah poured another round of wine—rosé, in memory of summer. Kate and Madison had come over for an evening cocktail since Will had a business dinner on her first Friday off in two weeks. They sat on the balcony, the sights and sounds of the city washing over them. Madison clinked her glass against Hannah's and Kate's.

"What are we toasting?" Kate asked, though she didn't wait to take a sip.

Madison waved her glass toward the view. "Global warming, for giving us this fabulously warm day in November?"

"But the polar bears," Hannah said with a giggle. There'd been too much wine and not enough food or sleep.

"We'll make a donation," Madison said. "In lieu of wedding favors, we'll donate to the polar bears. I'm texting Jon right now."

Hannah snatched the phone from her hand. "They are at an important dinner."

Madison rolled her eyes. "Please. This is just another way for Jonathan to force the boys to spend time with him. He calls up some golf buddy and acts like he wants to invest, blah, blah, blah. He hasn't invited Will to one in ages."

Hannah tried to keep her expression neutral, but inside, fireworks were going off. The pact was working.

"Drama, drama, drama." Kate took another sip of her wine. "I don't know how you two deal with it."

"Wine, a poker face, and *The Real Housewives*," Madison said.

"*The Real Housewives?*" Hannah and Kate asked at the same time, causing another round of giggles.

"Trust me, it will make you feel so much better about yourself and your life choices."

"Hannah prefers streaming *Jersey Shore* for that."

If she'd had something to throw at Kate, she would've. Hannah settled for giving her the finger. Kate stuck her tongue out.

"They're from New York," Hannah said. "Do you think we Jerseyans like the New Yorker descent every summer?"

"We talked about this." Madison pointed her finger precariously close to Hannah's nose. "You *are* a New Yorker—say it!"

"What?"

"Scream it from this balcony."

Hannah looked to Kate for support, but her best friend motioned toward the railing. "You heard her."

There was no way out of this. Both Madison and Kate stared at her expectantly. The longer she waited, the more likely one of them would make her yell something worse. Soon, they would be playing the Penis Game or yelling "tampon" at the top of their lungs. That wouldn't endear her to the neighbors—not in this neighborhood. She put her wine glass down and stood up, setting her shoulders.

Hannah gripped the railing and shouted, "I AM A NEW YORKER!"

Hoots and hollers sounded behind her. Triumphant, she whirled around and found herself staring into the tired and confused eyes of her husband.

"Hi," she said. God, he looked hot in that suit. A part of her wanted to skip across the small space and wrap her arms around him, pulling him down into a much-too-public display of affection. The rest of her—the part not muddled by wine and warmth—knew that tonight was not the time for that, not when he had that completely drained look in his eyes. "Everything okay?"

He scanned the small party on the deck, his eyes hovering on the empty bottles of wine, on Kate and Madison, and finally making his way back to her. The night had been planned. He knew girls' night was happening since both he and Jon would be MIA all night, and yet he still looked surprised—*concerned?*—at Madison's presence.

"What are you doing?" he asked, his tone not angry but not sounding happy either.

"I..." She blushed. "Madison—"

"She was owning her New Yorker status," Madison said. "And it's about time."

"I didn't realize shouting from the rooftops was a way to *own your New Yorker status.*" Okay, that definitely held more than a hint of anger.

Madison shrugged. "It was the best I could come up with on short notice."

After a too-long moment, Will's eyes left Madison and landed on Hannah. They softened as he took her in—messy bun, Wilderness Weekend tee, skinny jeans—and then finally, he smiled. "And *are* you a New Yorker now?"

Had she owned her status and shed her New Jersey? Could she be both? "I'm a New Yorker."

"Shall we show her the secret handshake?" Kate asked dryly.

Hannah rolled her eyes but otherwise ignored her friends. She walked the length of the balcony and pulled Will into a hug. "How was dinner?"

"Long," he said. "Madison, Jon is waiting for you downstairs."

Madison downed the rest of her wine. "Guess that's my cue. Ladies, this has been wonderful. I'll see you Tuesday, Hannah. Can't wait to hear how your parents take the news." She turned to Will. "William."

He didn't respond, not even a nod of acknowledgment. Hannah eyed him. Tensions between her and Will had eased in the last few days—near-constant making out would do that. Had something happened at dinner?

"Well, I better catch an Uber," Kate said, peeking over the rail at the traffic below. "Hannah, *William*."

"Don't call me that," Will said.

"Can't I even try it out?"

He shook his head. "Trust me, Will is a much better person than William."

Hannah shot him a look, but he wouldn't meet her gaze. What was going on with him tonight?

"Are you sure everything is okay?" she asked after Kate had secured her ride.

Will shrugged out of his coat and pulled her into a lingering kiss. There was an intimation of longing in the slow movements of his lips against hers. His hands tangled in strands of hair that had escaped her bun. She wondered if this was the moment he would slip her shirt over her head and let them move beyond kissing, but it wasn't.

He stepped back and wrapped an arm around her waist. "Just a long night, and I wasn't prepared to see you shouting into the abyss."

She blushed. "Well, wine, a challenge, and—"

"—Madison." They said it at the same time, Hannah with amusement and Will with mild weariness.

"Do you..." She paused. It was such a weird question to even have to ask. "You don't like Madison?"

There was an abnormally long pause where Will's face tensed and relaxed. Hannah thought he might not answer. "I like Madison fine. Sometimes she's just a little much. I worry that she's... bigger than Jon."

"Well, yeah. But I think that's probably their strength. Jon tempers her, and she brings him out of his comfort zone." Hannah followed him into the apartment. Something about his answer was still off, but she saw the tiredness in his eyes and the set of his shoulders and decided to tread lightly.

"You're probably right," he said through a yawn. "I'm going to take a quick shower."

"That sounds fun." She placed a hand on his chest and fiddled with the top button on his shirt, popping it open. Will sighed as her finger slid just inside his shirt. "Can I join you?"

His hand caught hers, stopping her from undoing another button. He kissed her again, pushing her back against the wall. It was hard and desperate, and she wanted so badly to touch him again, to slowly strip him of every piece of clothing he had on. But Will held her hands between them.

This time, she broke the kiss. She glanced up at him, expecting his eyes to be wild after everything she'd felt in his kiss, but he was perfectly in control.

He backed away, dropping her hand. "Ask me again when you're sober."

HANNAH ROLLED OVER, her arm slamming into something solid and warm. Will. She'd almost expected him to sleep in the other room after her tipsy attempt to seduce him. But there he was, sitting in bed, reading the morning paper.

She nudged closer to him, and he let her, even wrapping his arm around her. Maybe they didn't have to talk about it. Maybe it could just be a thing that'd happened and never got mentioned again. Though it's not like there was anything wrong with propositioning her husband, especially with Rule 3a in effect.

"About last night," he said.

Or not.

"I'm sorry." Hannah pushed up until she sat face-to-face with him. "I know we're supposed to be waiting until our hearts catch up."

He kissed her lightly. "If we're going to turn our marriage into a real relationship—and I want to, Hannah, so much—let's do it right. Our first time shouldn't be when you're tipsy and I'm frustrated."

"I agree."

"Well..." He paused and cut a glance at her. "You're sober now."

Her heart pounded in her chest, and her whole body sprang to life. She throbbed with anticipation and desire. Her voice came out in barely a whisper. "But you just said—"

"There are plenty of other things we can do."

She grinned and slipped out of bed, pulling him with her. "Will you join me in the shower, husband?"

Chapter 27
Hannah

As soon as they pulled off the highway and into the backroads of Ardena, Hannah had the sensation of being eighteen again. Eighteen because that was the first time she'd ever truly left home, and returning that first Christmas break, her car stuffed to the roof with her belongings, she'd realized she'd never really be able to come back. In twelve years, that feeling hadn't gone away.

"Kate said you were from the backwoods, but, um, where exactly do you live?"

Kate *would* say that. She spared him a look of derision, keeping her eyes locked on the road. "We prefer rural-fringe."

It was true that Ardena didn't give the best first impression from this direction, with its abandoned buildings and an old overgrown farmers' market lane. But like so many exits, this was a crossroads. Going left would wind through small towns to the beach, the right would lead to municipal buildings and the business district, and straight ahead were farms and parks and endless developments. The light changed, and they continued straight into the heart of suburbia.

"Did you just make that up? Rural-fringe?" He placed his hand over hers on the gearshift.

"What?" She glanced over at him. "No."

"Rural-fringe, who knew?"

"Anyone who lives outside New York City." Hannah laughed and turned onto a road lined with horse farms.

"Do you have horses?" he asked. "Should I have brought my chaps?"

"If I ever see you in chaps, there will be divorce papers in the morning."

"Your loss, Mrs. Thorne. I look damn sexy in chaps."

"Please never tell me how you know this."

A few minutes later, Hannah pulled into the open spot in her parents' driveway. They got out and saw Charlanie's car parked on the other side, bags of groceries piled in the open hatch. Will grabbed all the bags at once as Stephanie walked out of the house.

Stephanie wore loose clothing, but because she knew to look, Hannah could detect the tiniest of baby bumps under her sister's shirt.

"Hey, lovebirds," Stephanie whispered as she got closer to them.

Hannah enveloped Stephanie in a hug. "How's my little niece or nephew?"

"Good. Really good." Stephanie's smile spread ear to ear. Hannah was so excited for her. Stephanie would be a great mom. She was already a fabulous stepmom to Charlotte's boys. "We're finding out the sex in a few more weeks, and then if everything is still progressing well, we'll tell Mom and Dad. I mean, it's not like I can hide it much longer."

"Nonsense, sis," Will said as if he'd been calling Stephanie that all his life. "You look amazing."

"Mom and Dad are in the back room," Stephanie said, pulling some toys from the backseat. "How do you want to do this?"

That was the one part of the trip Hannah hadn't pinned down yet. Planning it had been hard enough. Neither Stephanie nor Hannah lived particularly close, and they weren't ones to randomly plan visits, especially that close to Thanksgiving. But as it turned out, Stephanie and Charlotte weren't going to be with the Abbotts for Thanksgiving, so Hannah had been able to angle a pre-holiday get-together in her favor. All that planning, but how to introduce Will? They would have only seconds. They'd be expecting Brian. Between Will's wedding band and Hannah's engagement ring and band, there were going to be a lot of questions.

"Let's just do it." She held up her hand. "They aren't going to miss this."

Stephanie pulled Hannah's hand into her own, running a finger over the diamond. "Jesus, it gets more beautiful every time I see it."

"Funny," Will replied, pulling Hannah into him. "That's what I think every time I see your sister."

Hannah kissed him, letting his warmth and confidence seep into her. They could do this. She pulled away from Will at Stephanie's overly loud throat clearing.

"Ready, husband?"

His hand found hers. "We've got this."

Hannah paused at the threshold and took a calming breath while Will followed Stephanie into the kitchen to drop off the bags. They were going to love him. She repeated it like a mantra, drowning out the sounds of the kids and her dad's deep laughter, giving herself an extra moment to collect her thoughts and rehearse. *Mom. Dad. This is Will. My husband.* Straight to the point. *Hi, everyone. Remember my friend Will from college? Well, we have some exciting news.* That option at least framed Will's connection to her life before the last month and maybe didn't make her seem completely insane.

Too soon, Stephanie and Will returned. Will reclaimed her hand and kissed her temple. "Ready, Mrs. Thorne?"

She nodded and led him through the house to the back room, where she could hear the adults talking and the boys running around.

"Hi, everyone," she said loudly enough to catch their attention. She waved with her right hand, her left still secured—effectively hiding her diamond—in Will's hand.

The adults in the room turned at the sound of her voice. Charlotte stopped midsentence. Her gaze swung between Hannah and Stephanie, back again, and landed on Hannah and Will's entwined hands. Hannah's parents seemed only to have eyes for Will. And she couldn't blame them—she'd brought Brian to the Labor Day barbecue.

"Who's *that*?" Aiden, Charlotte's youngest son, asked. He crawled onto his grandpa's lap—Hannah wasn't sure she would ever get used to her dad being a grandpa—and waved shyly at Will. Will wiggled his fingers back with a big smile.

"This is Will, you remember—" Hannah stopped short at her mother's laser gaze on Will's hand. He was holding Hannah's hand with his right, so he'd waved at Aiden with his left, wedding band gleaming. *Damn platinum.*

Hannah disentangled herself from Will. She was either a homewrecker or crazy. She preferred that her parents think her crazy. "Will and I are married."

"Are you..." Hannah's father said. "This isn't funny, if it's some sort of joke."

She held up her left hand, ring out. "It's not a joke, Dad. We got married about a month ago now. It all happened so fast, and then work exploded. I've wanted to tell you."

"You could've called." This was from her mother, who hadn't moved from her position on the couch.

Conversely, Hannah and Will stood awkwardly in the entrance of the family room, with Stephanie leaning against the doorjamb.

Hannah crossed her arms and curbed the urge to tap her foot. "We wanted to tell you in person."

"Well, task achieved," her mother said, crossing her legs. "A month and a day too late."

Ouch. They probably deserved that. This was why she'd wanted to tell them they were engaged first and work up to the marriage part. But Jonathan's upcoming party had stopped that idea in its tracks.

Will shifted next to her, and she sensed that he was about to come out with some endearing response to try and win her mother over. It wouldn't work.

She took a small step forward, but before she could say anything, Stephanie moved in, taking up a position next to Hannah. They stood shoulder to shoulder, exactly how they'd stood when Stephanie had returned home with a fiancée and stepfamily in tow.

"*Mom*," Stephanie said with enough attitude that the single word conveyed a paragraph's worth of conversation.

"Did you know about this?"

"All right, boys," Charlotte said, scoping Aiden up. "Let's go check out those new Nerf guns Grandpa got you."

A round of squeals came from the boys as they headed upstairs to Stephanie's old bedroom. Her parents had converted it into a playroom complete with a fort.

"Will, is it?"

Hannah turned at her father's voice. She hadn't noticed him approach.

His eyes were locked on Will. "Do you drink? Because I could use a drink."

Will caught Hannah's eyes. She saw the struggle—he didn't want to abandon her, but they both knew her father's request wasn't optional.

"I'll be fine."

He nodded and lightly brushed his lips against hers. She felt it down to her toes.

"A drink would be great, sir," Will said, following her father out of the room.

Hannah returned her attention to her mother, who was needling Stephanie. Clearly, her mom did not believe that the youngest Abbott had no idea about her sister's activities. Or maybe she was shocked Stephanie had kept a secret, if only her mother knew Stephanie was keeping two.

"Mom," Hannah said, drawing her mother's ire away from her sister. "Stephanie didn't know. Will and I fell for each other and decided to get married. There was very little planning involved."

"*Clearly.*" Her mother's tone was harsh and a bit sarcastic. She had yet to move from the couch.

Hannah couldn't stand being read a riot act like she was a teenager breaking curfew. She sat down on the ottoman her father had vacated. "Can we talk about this like adults, please? I didn't mean to hurt your feelings or upset you—"

"Are you in trouble? Is that what this is about?" The subtext to that statement was more than clear.

"No, Mom. There's no baby on the way. How could you even ask me that?"

"How could I *not*? You show up at our house with some strange man you married since we last saw you a few months ago? What happened to Brian? We liked Brian."

"I was never going to marry Brian," Hannah said dryly.

"Why not?"

She hadn't confided in her mother for years. Kate and Riley fulfilled that need. But still, how had they gotten so far off base that her mother couldn't tell Brian wasn't long-term? She debated what to disclose. "Because he didn't want to marry me."

Her mother crossed her arms. "So you cheated on him?

"I didn't cheat on him," Hannah said, throwing her hands up in the air. She had spent a lifetime making smart decisions and safe choices—her mother's voice lived in her head, guiding her down the expected road. Wasn't she allowed a detour? Stephanie had taken several, and their mother had never questioned her integrity.

Stephanie was all heart, but Hannah always led with her head. She still was, but her mother didn't deserve to know that now.

"When I realized I had more than platonic feelings for Will, I broke up with Brian—before anything happened," Hannah continued. "God, Mom. Who do you think I am?"

"I don't know at this point, Hannah! Why did you get married to someone you barely know? Where did you even find him?"

She hoped against all hope that Will was far enough away that he couldn't hear her mother. Maybe her father had taken him out to the garage to show off his midlife-crisis sports car. She could hope.

"*Where did I find him?* He's my friend. Will Thorne, remember, from college?"

Her eyes narrowed. "That boy who lived with you rent-free for almost a year?"

Now wasn't the time to inform her that Will had indeed paid rent. He'd paid most of it, allowing Hannah and Kate to pocket nearly all the money their parents had funneled into their rent fund.

"What does he need now?" she asked. "Or is he paying you? What have you gotten yourself into?"

"Hannah." She jumped at the sound of Will's voice and at the weight of his hand on her shoulder. She wasn't used to hearing her actual name out of his mouth. It shook her more than his somber expression. He had heard, if not everything, enough. She knew he would argue for her, use every skill in his lawyer toolbox to talk her mother down. It wouldn't work, but he would try. Which was exactly why he was worth it.

"It's okay, Will." It wasn't, but what else could she say in that moment? "Mom, *please*. I'll tell you the whole story. It's not a bad one."

She shook her head. "Honestly, I don't want to hear it. How could you do this?"

Hannah straightened. Was her marriage unexpected? Yes. Would she have gotten this reaction if she'd come home with Brian's wedding ring on her hand? Probably not. She pushed herself to her feet and took Will's hand. Her eyes shifted to her father, standing in the doorway. His expression was clouded—whatever he thought, he wasn't going to save her now.

"I thought you'd at least be a little happy for me." Tears welled in her eyes. "Because I'm happier than I've been in years."

Neither of her parents spoke. Her father stared down at his shoes, and her mother glared at the family portrait hanging over the mantel.

Only Stephanie stepped forward. "Hannah."

She shook her head and turned to Will, meeting his worried gaze. "Let's go home."

Chapter 28
Will

Will might not have been party to a full-on Hannah meltdown in several years, but he still knew how to handle them. He called in the big guns—meaning he had texted Kate an SOS before they even hit the parkway. Kate and Hannah had been locked in the guest room for over an hour. At first, there had been the occasional sob or laugh, but it had been quiet for too long. He was starting to worry. Hannah had left with him, had asked to go home, but that didn't mean she would *stay* with him. Complete parental abandonment nullified any agreements they had made. After all, Will had a heart. He'd told her as much in the car, but she only shook her head and continued clicking through his radio presets.

He wanted to knock. He'd stood in front of the door, hand at the ready, more than once. But he was probably the last thing Hannah needed right now. He sat down at the kitchen nook. Clara had left a note about the dry-cleaning delivery for Wednesday morning. She'd sent in his tuxedo for the party—his father had insisted on black tie. Hannah's dress—he had no idea how she'd found time to go to a boutique—was being hemmed as they spoke. She'd refused to show him a photo of it. Traditions, she'd explained. He wondered if he'd ever get to see it.

Will flipped through a stack of unopened mail. She'd never taken him to the laundromat. It had come up again during their conversations around keeping the apartment clean, but there hadn't been time. He wished they had that experience. He should've made the effort. But time had seemed like the one thing they didn't need to worry about.

"Will?" Hannah stood in the doorway of the guest room. Her eyes were puffy and red and her hair in a messy bun, strands sticking out everywhere. Her feet were covered with fuzzy pink cat socks, and she wore loose yoga pants and a tattered, faded University of Iowa shirt. He'd seen Hannah like this before. It was never good. He walked up to her and enveloped her in his arms. He felt her stiffen before relaxing into his embrace.

"I'm sorry I shut you out," she said against his chest.

"Don't apologize." He squeezed her tighter. "Are you okay?"

She laughed against him. "Not really, but Kate and I are going to drown my sorrows in *Twilight*, and I know watching it without you is grounds for divorce."

"That it is," he said, his lips quirking up at the sides. "Please tell me we're skipping the awful first one."

"We can't watch them fall apart before we watch them fall in love." She'd said it with a perfectly straight face and not a hint of irony. And he loved it.

"I hate when you have sound logic."

She smiled against him. "I always have sound logic."

"That is *so* far from the truth," Kate said from within the guest room. "I'm all for skipping awkward Jacob and going straight to hot Jacob."

Hannah straightened and marched back into the bedroom. "Excuse me, but we are drowning *my* sorrows, and I say we are starting with creeper Edward."

***

THEY WERE HALFWAY THROUGH *Eclipse*. Kate had passed out before they'd even gotten to the opening meadow scene, and

Hannah, despite her best efforts, kept dozing off. Will clicked off the television. They hadn't said much during the movie, but he'd gotten out of them that most of their earlier conversation had been about whether to invite her parents to the party. That meant she didn't want to end things. Or maybe she didn't think she could. He needed to be sure either way.

He nudged her awake. "We should go to bed."

Hannah, sleepy-eyed, peeked over at Kate and nodded. After carefully untangling themselves from the comforter, Will led her to their room. As soon as they got into bed, Hannah draped her arm across his chest and rested her head above his heart.

"Before you go to sleep," he began, knowing the conversation needed to be had, no matter the outcome, "you should know I meant what I said in the car. We can get the annulment."

She yawned again. "Tell me why it had to be me."

"What do you mean?"

"Why did you ask *me* to marry you? It wasn't just because of the pact."

He'd never outright told Hannah how he felt about her, but it had to be more than obvious, and Kate had known. "Kate told you."

Hannah was quiet. Had she fallen back asleep? He shifted to check and found her staring up at him.

"I want to hear it from you," she said.

There had to be a better time to tell her that he loved her. Her parents had basically accused her of being a harlot. None of that conversation had been easy for him to hear. He couldn't stomach standing by while someone hurt Hannah. It didn't help that Hannah hadn't exactly told him about the extent of her relationship with her ex-boyfriend. Will knew he existed—there were pictures in her apartment and a few on Facebook, but nothing that led Will to believe it was serious enough for her parents to think they were on the marriage track. Though clearly, they weren't if Hannah had dropped him so easily. That was a conversation for another day, or maybe it wasn't. Hannah could have her secret ex, and he could have his. *Shit.* That was an awful thought.

"Will?"

"You're right. It wasn't just because of the pact," he said, running his fingers through her hair. There was so much to say and yet so little. It was simple when he really thought about it. Hannah was his person. "The pact got me in the door, but it could only have been you. You get me in ways no one else ever has. I mean, you like me as I am. I woke up from my post-breakup haze one day to a dream about you. And I knew that I had to try. I'd wasted my opportunity senior year to tell you how I felt and distanced myself from you to make up for my own cowardice. I missed you, Abbott."

Hannah inhaled, sudden and sharp.

Perhaps he was being too earnest, but it was too late to stop now. "It had to be you. There was no other consideration. And now—"

His words were cut off by her lips meeting his. It was quick but meaningful, conveying everything he'd been about to say—that he *couldn't* go back. There was still no other consideration.

"It could only have been you too," she said so quietly he almost believed he imagined it.

She ran a hand down his arm. Every part of their bodies touched, but that simple caress sent a shudder through him, rocking his remaining equilibrium. He stayed still, fighting the urge to pull her into him—to give in and see what happened, damn the consequences. Under Hannah's unwavering gaze, her fingers running slow circles up and down his arms, his body stirred.

But they couldn't consummate their relationship after her parents' negative reaction today. Absolutely not. "Hannah?"

She looked up at him, her gaze clear and decisive. "Tell your dad to release the announcement and invite my family to the party."

He started to protest, but she held a finger to his lips. "They already know, Will. We can't change what happened today, and the thing is, I kind of like being married to you, Will Thorne."

She cupped his face and then kissed him so slowly he thought his heart might explode. When he broke the kiss, she returned her head to his chest, where his heart beat wildly under her touch. She took his hand, placing it over her chest—her heart beat at the same fast rhythm as his.

Chapter 29

Hannah

"You look amazing, Mrs. Thorne."

Hannah twirled in her wedding dress, the skirt lifting and falling around her legs. The plan had been to get a respectable whiteish dress for the party, not a gown. But the sales lady had been insistent that Hannah try on at least one gown. She'd picked a simple one without a train and with less embellishment than the usual wedding gown but with beautiful three-quarter-length lace sleeves. Hannah hadn't tried on another dress.

"And you look quite ravishing yourself, Mr. Thorne." She scrunched her nose. "Doesn't work the same way."

Will laughed. "No, not really."

He led her through the winding maze of hallways, the sounds of the party growing louder with each turn they made. Randy, the event planner, had insisted that they sit at a sweetheart table where people could come to them. The idea made Hannah itchy. She needed to walk around, to mingle, and to have Madison whisper the truth about guests in her ear while Will put on his most dazzling smile. *Hell*, she needed to show off this dress.

When they stepped into the main hallway, Hannah squeezed Will's hand and let out a low whistle. The Thorne mansion was beautiful, decked out in plum and silver with hints of festive seasonal décor. The party was split between three rooms—the dining room, the back den, and the study across the hall, which had been set up with lounge furniture. It rivaled every wedding reception she'd ever been to. Guests wandered between the rooms, chatting, drinking, and requesting more appetizers from the waiters.

"Can we do a round before we're relegated to our table?" she asked, fingering a floral bouquet of purple and white carnations. Jonathan thought carnations weren't a worthy flower, but Will had insisted on her behalf.

"If Randy sees us, we're in for a world of hurt," Will said but extended his hand.

"We'll be stealthy."

Will quirked an eyebrow at her. "In a wedding gown?"

Hannah's retort was cut short by the arrival of two guests. They looked oddly familiar, though Hannah was certain she'd never met them before.

Next to her, Will went rigid, and his voice dropped its usual flair. "Mr. and Mrs. Hart, my father didn't tell me you were coming."

Madison's parents. She could see the resemblance.

"We're not staying," Mrs. Hart said, patting Will's arm. "We're heading up to Westchester for a second Thanksgiving. We just wanted to wish you well and meet your wife."

"Right." As if remembering she was there, Will drew her close. "This is Hannah. Hannah, as you've probably already figured out, these are Madison's parents."

Madison's name seemed to catch in his throat. She shook off the weird feeling. Tonight night couldn't be easy for Will. Everything that happened with his ex had happened right there, at another party, probably with a similar guest list. People loved gossip, and William Thorne getting married suddenly was definitely a commodity in this circle.

"It's so nice to meet you!" Hannah said. "Madison has made the transition to becoming a Thorne so easy for me."

Mrs. Hart looked from Hannah to Will, confusion clouding her expression before her smile softened. "I'm glad to hear that. William"—she pulled Will into a hug—"we're so happy for you."

Will backed away from Mrs. Hart as soon as was polite. "Thank you. Have a safe trip."

With the Harts out of sight, Hannah followed Will further into the party.

Will let out a heavy breath as they broke into the main hallway. She squeezed his hand. "Madison's parents seem nice. I didn't realize you knew them."

"They're around often enough," Will said, his eyes on the guests. "I was just surprised to see them. They weren't on Jonathan's guest list."

"You saw the guest list?"

Will stopped walking and turned to her. He ran a hand through his hair, and worry lines creased his forehead. "Yeah." He glanced to his right and stealthily pointed at an older gentleman in a well-fitted suit. "I wanted to know who to warn you about. Like Mr. Johnson over there. He's touchy-feely, so stand at least an arm's length away."

Will cast another look around the room. "And this guy here"—he pointed to a well-dressed man who looked so much like Daniel he must've been a Thorne—"is bad news."

"Ah, my free-spirited nephew." The man pulled Will into a bear hug. "Didn't think I'd see you in one of these penguin suits so soon."

Will grinned. "Hannah, this is my uncle, Grayson, CEO of Wellington Thorne and perpetual thorn in my father's side. Pun fully intended."

"I bet Jon says the same about you," Grayson said, giving Will what could only be called a meaningful look.

Will returned it with a wan smile. "I'm sure he does." Hannah knew she was missing something, but there wasn't time to consider it before Will held out his hands, putting her on display. "This is Hannah."

Hannah extended her hand, but Grayson hugged her. "Welcome to the Thorne circus."

She laughed and continued to watch Grayson and Will interact. Will and Jonathan, and to some extent Jon and Daniel, were so cold with each other. But Grayson was loud and boisterous and happy. He reminded Hannah of Will when his family wasn't around. This was the man who had fought to save Will's career and who had clearly had an influence on Will over the years. The thought that someone was in Will's corner calmed a worry Hannah hadn't even consciously known she'd had. With everything going on with her parents, she'd still had Kate and Stephanie and Riley, and even Madison. But Will seemed alone so much of the time.

She scanned the room again. Their friends and family—Kate and Patrick, Eddie, Stephanie and Charlotte, Madison and Jon, and Daniel—stood in a cluster in the den. Her parents weren't there. They'd RSVP'd no—Hannah had seen the card herself—but she'd expected them to change their minds. Maybe they had. It was still early, and traffic getting into New York was probably a bitch right then. They would come. They couldn't miss the closest thing she would have to a wedding reception.

"Our guests of honor, there you are." Hannah turned at the sound of Jonathan's voice, so formal compared to Grayson's. What had caused these men to go in such different directions?

Will straightened at his father's approach and linked his hand with Hannah's. "Hi, Dad."

"Can I steal you two away? I'd like to introduce you to a few people from the board."

Will nodded like it was a death sentence. But it couldn't be that bad. She didn't believe for a second that Jonathan was sanctioning their marriage. She hadn't come close to forgiving him, but for Will's sake, and for the sake of his future at Wellington Thorne, she would spend a few minutes schmoozing with Jonathan's peers.

"COME WITH ME." WILL tugged at her hand, and after excusing herself from the most boring conversation she'd ever had with the touchy-feely Mr. Johnson, Hannah let Will lead her through the party. He took her past the den and into a hallway with a series of rooms. She knew the first one on the left was Jon and Madison's. The sounds of the party were muffled there, even so close to the den. Will pulled her into one of the rooms, flipping on the light as he did so.

"Sorry, I just needed to do this." He kissed her hard, his arms drawing her to him. They fell back against the closed door, Will's lips never breaking from hers.

She pushed his jacket off and untucked his shirt. Slipping out of her shoes, she wrapped a leg around him, feeling the intensity of this moment through her whole body.

Will trailed kisses down her neck and into her cleavage, sending waves of excitement rushing through her body. She undid his belt and then the button on his pants, weaving her hand into the waistband of his boxers. He gasped as her hand slid down his perfectly sculpted hip bones.

"Knock, knock, lovebirds. I know you're in there."

Hannah and Will broke apart at the sound of Kate's voice and the repeated knocking on the door. Kate jiggled the handle, but Hannah knew she wouldn't come in. Kate and Hannah had been roommates for long enough to know *exactly* what was going on behind the door. Hannah giggled as Will straightened his clothing, giving the door the evil eye.

"Come back later?" Hannah asked, stepping back into her shoes.

"If you don't come with me now, Randy will be the next person to knock on this door," Kate said. Hannah could hear her tapping her foot impatiently. "Your guests are waiting for cake."

"One second," Will said, his voice resigned.

"Do I look okay?" Hannah asked, smoothing out her dress. Will's clothing suffered most of the damage. Her dress was pretty unflappable, but she had a hard-enough time getting her hair to stay in an updo when she wasn't making out against doors.

Will tucked a strand of hair behind her ear, his fingers lingering on her cheek. "You look beautiful, Hannah."

Her insides stirred at the soft inflection on her name. She inclined her head into his hand for the briefest of moments before linking their hands. "Let's go cut our cake, husband."

Chapter 30

Hannah

"Can you straighten it a bit?" Madison asked.

They sat next to each other on one of the lounge ottomans in the former study. There was a lot of dancing after the cake cutting, but the energy keeping Hannah from noticing the ache in every part of her body, especially in her knee, had dissipated.

Hannah extended her leg and felt Madison's hands come up under her dress and settle on her knee. That was all Jonathan and his guests needed to see—Jon's fiancée feeling up Will's wife.

"It's not swollen," Madison said. "We'll work it out in the morning if it still hurts, okay?"

She nodded and leaned her head against Madison's shoulder. "Thanks."

The number of guests had dwindled exceedingly, but more than enough socialites were mixed among their family and friends. Eddie stood near the fireplace with a small crowd, most likely telling the story of Will and Hannah's wedding day by the way Kate kept interjecting. Stephanie and Charlotte were in the dining room, tangled in each other's arms, swaying to the ballad that played lightly over an unseen speaker system. No one else danced, but Charlanie didn't seem to care.

Madison nudged Hannah and pointed to a spot across the room. Hannah followed her finger and smiled. Jon, Will, and Daniel were laughing and toasting with another shot.

"Great, he'll be snoring tonight," Hannah said, despite knowing her cheeks were flush from her second glass of wine.

"The boys can share a room," Madison said. "We'll steal Kate and Charlanie and have a girls' night with pillow fights, wine, rom-coms, and whatever you want."

"That's called a bachelorette party."

"Not like we had the chance to give you one."

"Ouch. You're a mean drunk."

"Sorry," Madison said with a shrug.

Grayson and his wife, Maggie, walked by, their teenage son beside them. Hannah watched them until they rounded a corner and were out of sight.

Madison wrapped an arm around Hannah's back. "I'm sorry your parents didn't come."

"It is what it is," Hannah said, packing false confidence behind her words. She couldn't get weepy in the middle of her own party.

"That's big of you," Madison said. "I would've dragged my parents here kicking and screaming."

Hannah was sure she would've. Not that she would've needed to. Her parents had come to support their future son-in-law's brother when they'd had other plans. But that was never Hannah's relationship with her parents. The spontaneity they'd lauded in Stephanie, they condemned in Hannah. On some level, she understood that she'd taken something from them by not including them in the wedding, but it didn't warrant *this*.

And what if she and Will lasted? Will was the one person, even more so than Kate in some ways, that just *got* her. There was no pretense or hesitation with him. He was her person—the one who could come back after five years and fit naturally into her life. What if her person was also her true love? Her parents would never be able to take back their snub.

"I'm choosing to look at the people we do have here," Hannah said, scanning the room again for her friends. Jon and Will weaved through the crowd, leaving a frazzled but polite-looking Daniel chatting with a young woman and her father, Jonathan standing close by.

She waved Kate, Patrick, and Eddie over and shot a text to Stephanie, who was still completely lost in her wife. She didn't want to directly disturb them. It wasn't often they had a kid-free night.

"Dad's trying to sell Daniel to the highest bidder," Jon said, wrapping his arms around Madison's waist.

"It's a Thorne rite of passage," Will said, tugging Hannah close to him. Her body lit up at the touch, remembering their hidden moment earlier and the way Will had looked at her when he told her she was beautiful. She kissed him, noting the faint smell of whisky permeating his skin.

Kate and Patrick joined the group, hand in hand. It was still weird for Hannah to see Kate with a boyfriend. She hadn't been serious about anyone in so long, but even though it had only been two months, she was clearly into Patrick. There was a recent calmness to Kate that Hannah recognized in herself since Will. *Bitching about Boyfriends* was about to get super boring.

"So, where's the afterparty?" Kate asked.

Hannah laughed, but Will and Jon put their heads together and started whispering about rooms.

"I'll get the booze," Jon said, heading over to the bar.

"I'll get the rest of our guests." Madison scooted away to round up Charlanie, Eddie, and Daniel.

Will fell into an elegant bow. "And if you'll follow me..."

Hannah looked around the group again, her heart overflowing with love. If this was who she and Will had in their corner, it would be more than enough.

"COME ON," WILL WHISPERED, grabbing her hand.

Hannah glanced around at their group of friends sharing stories and playing some weird drinking game—they were all but oblivious to the two of them. "Will they notice?"

"Do you care?" he asked, his eyes gleaming.

She lifted the ice pack off her knee and followed him out of the room, through the silent house and the remnants of their party until they reached Will's bedroom. Tension swirled between them—the air sparked with it.

He tugged the door shut and turned the lock before leaning her back against the hard wood. "Where were we?"

She smirked and pulled him into her. "Right about here."

The moment their lips met, the playful nature of their banter shifted intensity. Their tongues danced to a new and powerful tune. Her hands undid the buttons of his shirt and pushed it off. She ran her fingers down his chest and unbuttoned his pants. He kicked out of his shoes and unzipped her dress, his fingers tracing her spine with each inch. His lips never left hers, except to nip at her ear, suck at the most sensitive part of her neck, or leave a trail of kisses down her collarbone. Hannah arced against him as his hand slipped under her bodice and cupped her breast.

"Will," she said with a moan, pushing his pants down.

He picked her up and out of her dress. She wrapped her legs around him, feeling his hardness against her softest places. Another moan escaped her as they fell back onto the bed. Will's eyes were wide as he lay beneath her. She leaned down and kissed him again, her hair falling free of its pins. His fingers tangled in her hair, and he unhooked her bra with his free hand, his mouth finding her nipple.

It was finally their moment. She could feel it in every touch and every kiss. There would be no stopping them tonight. Kate could knock, the earth could quake, and they'd stay here in this bed. And it felt so right. It wasn't clumsy or uncertain. It was every minute of every hour of every day since he'd knelt before her with that diamond ring. The pact hadn't been a mistake. It had been foreplay.

With soft hands, Will removed the rest of their clothing and flipped Hannah over so that she lay beneath him. His hand skimmed up her leg as she brought it around his hips. Their eyes met, and she pulled him down until every part touched. *Yes,* she said with her eyes and her hands and her tongue. *Yes.*

He didn't hesitate, and her world exploded as their bodies came together. How had she ever worried this would ruin everything? They were a perfect fit, as Will had said all those weeks before. She tugged him closer, breathing the same breath as their bodies moved as one.

Chapter 31
Hannah

"Hi, Mom and Dad. It's me, your daughter. Hannah, remember? You know, you're going to have to answer the phone one day."

Hannah slammed the phone back into its cradle. She'd been convinced if she called from her office phone that one of her parents would pick up. She knew they were home. It was Stephanie and Charlotte's wedding anniversary, and her parents were babysitting the boys. It had been nearly two weeks since the party—three since the awful scene at their house—and her parents remained silent.

"Everything okay over here?"

Hannah made her expression neutral before looking up at Dave. He was the last person she wanted to see right now. She'd spent the last few weeks trying to get him to hand over coverage of the Wilderness Weekend concert, but he hadn't budged. There wasn't even a Leonard Nulty interview accompanying the piece. It was concert coverage only. Anyone else would've handed the show to Hannah by now.

"Yeah, I'm fine," she said. "What's up?"

He held up a pair of tickets. "I have a peace offering of sorts."

Hannah reached for the tickets. Wilderness Weekend. *No way.*

"I'm not giving up coverage, but my sister-in-law, or soon-to-be, anyway, won these from a radio show," he said. "She didn't know I was covering the show, and she was so excited to give them to me that I couldn't tell her that I was already going. I've heard you cursing at StubHub for the last week about ticket prices, so I thought—"

"Seriously?" If it hadn't been Dave, she might have hugged him. As it was, she just turned her brightest smile on him.

"I mean, you owe me one, but yeah, they're yours if you want them."

She'd owe Dave seven if it meant these tickets were hers for free. "Yes, please.

Thank you!"

The moment Dave was gone, she picked up her phone. Will answered on the third ring. "I'm about to go into a meeting."

"You didn't get Wilderness tickets yet, did you?"

"No," he said, sounding deflated. "I can't find a pair within the negligible budget you set."

"Well, I got us tickets!"

Will laughed. "Of course you did. Listen, I have to go, but explain over dinner?"

"Sure, I'll pick up Thai on my way home from PT."

She tucked the tickets into her wallet. These were going right in the My plans are better than yours clip she'd made sure found its way onto Will's refrigerator when she moved in. Slipping on her coat, Hannah typed out a quick email to Riley requesting concert night off. It was a month away, but Hannah wasn't taking any chances.

STRETCH FOR THREE. Hold for three. Extend. Retract. Hannah had forgotten how tedious physical therapy could be. The itch to run returned with each session the further her knee got to full extension. But Madison had been very clear. No running—not yet. Hannah heeded this advice only because whatever Madison's plan was, it was working. Her knee felt better than it had in years.

"I brought you something," Hannah said, leaning back on her hands.

The studio was empty. The last client had checked out twenty minutes ago, and technically, it was after closing. But this was their time slot. Madison liked the privacy. She was more herself. The few times another therapist had scheduled a late client, Madison had been stiff and formal. This version of her—sprawled out on a mat, legs propped up on a foam roller, an incredibly tight TheraBand stretched between her hands—made the aches and pains bearable.

"Oh?" Madison rubbed her hands together. "I like presents."

"I know." Hannah handed over a pink cardboard box. The tiniest bit of frosting stuck to the clear plastic, but it had otherwise survived the walk.

Madison's eyes lit up at the cupcake. "You do realize I have to fit into a wedding dress in, like, five months."

"Don't act like you don't know the exact number of days."

Madison swallowed a giant bite of cupcake. "Fine. I have to fit into a corseted wedding dress in one hundred and thirty-three days. This is not going to help."

Hannah rolled her eyes. "It's *one* cupcake. We can go for a run, and it will be like you never ate it."

Madison shook her head. "Not until after your appointment. Which is when?"

"On January 17." Hannah could hardly believe it. It had been so much of the reason she'd even considered marrying Will, and soon, she was finally getting to see an orthopedist. And not any orthopedist but one of the city's best. Even as a resident, Daniel's name went a long way.

"Then on January 18, if you don't need surgery, we will try a run."

"No way!"

Madison grinned. "Yes way!"

"I'm bringing you cupcakes more often."

"Please don't," she said, stuffing the last bite of the cupcake into her mouth. "Actually, I kind of have something for you too. A proposal of sorts." When Hannah didn't say anything, she continued. "Jon and I were talking, and well, we'd love for you to be a bridesmaid in the wedding."

Whatever she'd expected, it hadn't been that. True, she was Will's wife, and she and Madison had quickly become friends, but Jon and Madison barely knew her. Not that it wasn't nice to be asked. They must have accepted her as part of the family. If they didn't, why risk having some random chick in all of their wedding pictures?

"But won't that throw everything off?" Not to mention the short timeline—Madison had said the bridesmaid dresses were custom ordered.

Madison shook her head. "Not really. Jon has been itching to add another groomsman, but I only have so many friends."

"You have more friends than anyone I've ever met."

"Not ones I would want in my wedding pictures for eternity." She rolled her eyes. "But we're going to be sisters, and I don't want you *not* to be in the pictures for eternity."

That was sweet and a bit comforting. Apparently, the act, which was no longer an act, was working. People believed in Will and Hannah. But still, the logistics of it worried her.

"Stop overthinking it," Madison said, hitting Hannah's foot lightly with her own. "I can already see your head spinning through all the to-dos to add two members to the wedding party this late in the planning. But Hannah, the rules don't apply to us. They'll make the dress. They will find the tie. They will accommodate us. We're Thornes—or soon to be."

Right. Thornes. For the foreseeable future, Hannah was going to be a bona fide Thorne.

"If you don't feel comfortable being in the wedding, that's totally cool too," Madison said, examining her fingernails.

Hannah shook her head. "I'd love to. Let me check with Will, but I would be honored."

Madison squealed, her hands clutched together in front of her chest, and just as suddenly, she turned a serious face back to Hannah. "Your first duty as my bridesmaid is to not bring me any more cupcakes—not even if I beg."

Hannah rolled her eyes. What had she gotten herself into?

Chapter 32

Will

Will flipped through the report, not taking in anything on the page. Not that it mattered—he'd already memorized the key parts that would cost the company too much money. Redeveloping brownfields was a lofty and sustainable objective—it also royally sucked for everyone involved except the Public Relations team. It would be fine. He could handle a little groundwater contamination. Endangered species and preserved wetlands were harder to defend.

A knock on his door brought Will to attention. In the seconds it took him to walk across his office, he hoped it was Hannah. A hot office make-out session was exactly what he needed to brighten his mood. But Hannah was busy finishing her section layout at work. Will didn't expect to see her home until the last caption was in place and every article had been read backward and aloud.

"Hey, Uncle Grayson," Will said, finding his uncle on the other side of the door. Will assumed he was visiting as his uncle and not as the CEO.

"I thought we could have lunch together." Grayson set a Susanna's bag down on the small table in Will's office, stacking some papers that were in the way—papers that Will's junior associate had organized into separate piles the day before. At least he'd had the sense to tag them with colored stickers. "I asked the staff there for your regular. Hope that's okay?"

"That's great, thank you."

"I can't believe you have me eating this bird food when Aunt Maggie's not around." His uncle poked at his salad. "How's Hannah?"

"Busy," Will said with an easy smile. "She's looking forward to dinner next week, though."

"Good. I know Aunt Maggie's looking forward to it too." They ate in silence for a few minutes. Will enjoyed the companionable silence, but at the same time, he knew this wasn't a social visit.

"Hannah's a good girl," Grayson said finally, "and the right people at that party noticed how she grounds you, how you are with her. I'm hearing only good things about you. I suspect that board seat will come along soon enough."

Will swallowed the bite he'd been chewing. The pact had worked on everyone except the person he needed to convince the most. His father would never see him as anything more than his emotional, whimsical screwup of a son. "Jonathan will never—"

"You leave your old man to me." His uncle put the cap on his barely eaten salad. "I can't eat this crap. You want anything from Tony's?"

Will shook his head, still a little shocked by the unexpected news. Things worked slowly at Wellington Thorne. "Soon enough" could mean in the next year, but it was better than never.

"Knock, knock."

No. Not today. He squeezed his eyes shut. Maybe this was a nightmare. Madison could *not* be standing in his doorway.

Grayson turned, his eyes widening at Madison's presence. *Fuck.* He stood and patted Will on the back. "Only good things, William. Don't make me regret backing you."

He walked past Madison with a cursory nod. At least Will knew someone would pick his side if it came down to it.

"What do you want?"

"Is that any way to greet your sister-in-law?" she said, shutting the door behind her.

Too many curse words ran through his head. "Door open. We don't have closed-door conversations anymore."

"So dramatic, William," she said but pulled the door open.

"Again, what do you want?" He leaned back in his chair and folded his arms behind his head. He had to admit, he'd expected her sooner. Pretty much since the second Hannah had asked if she should accept the invite to be in the wedding, he'd been holding his breath. *No. Hell no. Fuck no.* Except he couldn't exactly say any of that without also telling her about Madison. And again, he hadn't done it. How could he when things were finally where he wanted them to be with Hannah? He knew keeping the secret would only make it worse when he did tell her, but telling her now could blow up everything they were building. It wasn't a risk he was willing to take. So he'd nodded and smiled at her request, his stomach threatening to reject the pound of Chinese food he'd eaten for dinner.

"In about ten minutes, Jon's going to come in here and ask you to be the fourth for his poker night." Madison sat in the seat across from him, crossing her legs. Visions of other midday visits and more revealing outfits flashed through his mind. "You are going to say yes."

"Why would I do that?"

Madison smiled. "Did Hannah mention that we're having a girls' day after the holidays? We're going to get her measurements done for her dress and then brunch with the whole bridal party. It would be a shame if someone let slip that you and me... Women and mimosas are never good for secret keeping."

How was this his life? Everyone had screwed him over and lived happily ever after, and *he* was the one being blackmailed.

"Why do you care if I spend time with Jon?"

Her face lost its hard edge at the comment. She looked up at him with soft eyes, the same ones he used to get lost in. "Because he cares, William. Would it really be so hard to spend time with him?"

"Yes, it really would."

"You're married! To someone you've loved forever. Do you think I don't remember hearing about Hannah? Why does what happened even matter anymore? You won."

Will liked the sound of that. He liked the feel of it even more. He'd won. Had he really? Maybe, if he didn't mess up everything with Hannah. If that awfulness brought him here, would it have been worth the pain? He wanted to believe so. If it had been a normal betrayal—if it had been anyone other than his brother—things might've been different. But he wasn't sure he would ever truly forgive Jon. And trust? Trust was out of the question.

SUN. BRIGHT. NO. UGH. Never again. Will threw his arm over his eyes, blocking the strips of light slipping through the blinds. Why didn't his father invest in blackout curtains? He groaned and rolled over, burying his head under his pillow. Poker was officially blacklisted. He should've known better than to try and bluff his way through every hand against a bunch of financial experts. He flopped over again, sitting back against the headboard. There was a bottle of water on his bedside table. The bottle sat atop a napkin with Hannah's handwriting scribbled across the front. He took a sip and picked up the note. *Thought you might need this.* There was even a smiley face. Well, that was cute. Where was she? Her sneakers were still by the closet, as was her yoga mat.

He closed his eyes, willing his headache away. The gurgle of the coffee maker and the banging of pans sounded from the kitchen. That was new—they rarely cooked. Maybe they needed to try one of those preordered services. Cooking together could be messy and romantic. Hannah would be highly impressed by his superior chopping skills. He could be her sous-chef. His mind concocted an image of Hannah bossing him around their kitchen in a sexy chef outfit. He hadn't consciously known chefs could be sexy, but his subconscious knew. Oh, did it ever. He felt himself grow hard. Where was that year-round Halloween store? He would find it, and he would have that costume. He groaned and banged his head against the headboard.

"You okay over there?" Hannah leaned against the doorjamb, an apron tied around her waist. It only covered her bottom half, and spots of flour dotted her shirt.

"Why are you only wearing half of the apron?"

"Have you ever worn an apron?" she asked, tugging at the thin fabric.

"Yes," he said, remembering that weird period between college and Madison, otherwise known as law school.

"Well then you know they can be incredibly uncomfortable, particularly when they have all this lacey frill around the edges."

"True, and I was usually naked underneath."

A blush crept up her cheeks. She tried to throw words together, but nothing coherent came out. He loved that he had that effect on her.

"I don't even want to know," she said, shaking her head. "Breakfast is ready."

There was no way he could stand up right now. If the thought of him naked in an apron made her blush, the truth of the situation might make her swoon. "Awesome, let me just, uh, wash up."

She rolled her eyes. "Yeah, you do *that*."

That woman was going to be the death of him. He smiled at the ceiling. At least he had a date planned for today, and it was going to be epic. And she'd cooked him breakfast. He looked at the smiley face on the note again and sent up a silent prayer that he hadn't done anything too embarrassing last night. He'd been pretty wasted. The driver had handed him back his tip when he'd blithely slipped him a hundred dollars. Will would pay it forward in Rob's Christmas bonus.

"The bacon is getting cold!"

He pulled the sheets back with a laugh—*always so impatient*. She was lucky she was cute. After a quick stop in the bathroom, he slid into the chair across from Hannah. A coffee and a heaping stack of waffles awaited him.

"We have a waffle maker?"

"Someone sent it after the party—Martha? Margaret?" She motioned to the pile of gifts they had yet to open.

Apparently, a city hall wedding without a registry didn't stop people from buying them appliances. He'd expected more letters about donations in their name from his father's ilk, but that had not been the case.

"Supposedly you can make brownies and other delicious treats in this contraption and, oddly, crab cakes," she said, spearing a strawberry from the fruit salad. This apartment had never seen so much fresh fruit since Hannah arrived.

"Crab waffles?"

"So says the box."

He nodded approvingly. "Wow, this Martha or Margaret person went all out."

She took a sip of her coffee. "Yup. Now we have to write out thank-you cards. The first one is going to your dad—*thanks for the weeks of hand cramps, Dad*."

He forked two waffles onto his plate. "Leave it to my dad to find your weakness."

"Hey, hand cramps are no joke." She pointed at him with her fork, a piece of waffle dangling from the tines. "These babies are my livelihood."

"Well, the thank-you cards will have to wait another day because we have plans this morning."

She looked at him quizzically. Saturdays were usually their lazy mornings. On Sundays, they walked the farmers' market and did odds and ends for the week, but most Saturdays, Hannah binged the television shows of their youth in her pajamas, Will right by her side, cringing at the melodrama.

"Sweet," she said after a moment, a smile warming her features. "I'm officially off until after Christmas. This never happens—I might have to hug your father for insisting we come for the holidays."

"After you torture him for all the thank-you notes you have to write?"

She stuck out her tongue. "Yes, after that. So, what are we doing? Going to see the tree? Surprise tickets to the Christmas Spectacular? The market at Bryant Park?"

"Wow, someone has the Christmas spirit this morning."

Hannah shrugged, another blush rushing up to her cheeks. "I love Christmas."

"I am well aware," he said, glancing toward the oversized, overly decorated tree sitting in their living room. Fortunately, there had been a tree seller right down the street, but he'd still had to lug bags of lights and ornaments across far too many city blocks. So far, Binx had only jumped on the tree once.

An image of a sad little plastic tree tucked into the corner of Hannah and Kate's college apartment resurfaced. Hannah had wanted a real one, though they weren't going to be in town for Christmas or even New Year's. But Kate had put her foot down. In defiance, the little plastic tree had remained long after the holidays. He used to hang his socks on it for fun.

"Do you still have that little plastic tree from college?"

Hannah grinned. "It's at Kate's. The real one looks so much better, doesn't it?"

Will had to admit that it did. He hadn't put up a Christmas tree in years. But seeing the light in Hannah's eyes as she looked at that tree—he would put one up for the rest of his life if that light stayed. He would trek upstate to cut one down, kids trailing after him, fighting over who got to use the saw first. *Kids. Whoa.* His future materialized in front of him. He'd rarely thought about having kids with Madison, but with Hannah, the thought had come naturally.

"What are these mysterious plans?" she asked.

He grinned and held up one finger before making his way over to the hall closet. The clue—two overflowing bags of laundry—had been waiting for this moment for three days. Thankfully, Hannah was so used to laundry service that she hadn't even blinked at the empty hamper.

"We are going to the laundromat," he said, holding one of the bags up.

NO ONE IN THE HISTORY of laundromats had been as excited as Hannah was since he pulled out the heaping bags of laundry. Will was barely showered and dressed before she dragged him outside. The two bags were tucked into one of those carts old ladies used to tote around their groceries. Clara kept it in the hall closet, though he'd never actually seen her use it. But Hannah hummed the whole three blocks, a spring in her step as she pushed that cart. She added a bottle of Tide and a bag of snacks from Duane Reade to the top of the pile.

At the laundromat, she showed him the proper way to add the detergent. Teacher Hannah was adorable, particularly because she knew he knew how to do laundry. They'd done more than their fair share of loads together in college—until, of course, he'd found himself crashing on their floor and was able to sneak his clothes into Hannah's dirty clothes. The one time he'd tried that with Kate, it hadn't ended well.

Will glanced around the laundromat. There was a weathered waiting area with some battered toys and plastic chairs that had to be older than the two of them combined. What were they supposed to do? He hadn't really thought it through. This was *his* date, and he was failing miserably.

Without hesitation, Hannah plopped down in one of the ancient chairs. She crossed her legs and looked at him expectantly. He sat next to her, keeping his hands in his lap and away from any solid surface.

"You do realize this is, like, the cleanest laundromat I've ever seen, right?" She laughed. "I mean, it's older but clean."

Will's shoulders relaxed. "In my mind, this was a much better idea than it is turning out to be."

"What do you mean?" she asked, placing her hand on his knee. "I thought it was really sweet that you remembered that we were supposed to do laundry together and took the initiative to plan it. This is real couple stuff, you know?"

"I guess I imagined a brighter, cleaner place with a coffee shop or something." Even as he said it, the reality of how unrealistic that was set in. "Yeah, yeah. I watch too much television."

She handed him a water bottle from the cart and a package of fruit snacks shaped like Minions. "Come on, this is great! Have a fruit snack."

She pushed her chair against the adjacent wall and turned in her seat so her feet could rest on Will's legs. "Tell me about the Thorne Christmas traditions."

For all of his father's fuss about family gatherings, there weren't many things that Will considered traditions. Sure, his father had put up the trees, but really, it was just another extended stay—one marred by dysfunction. He thought back to the last few Christmases before the drama.

"I don't know if this qualifies, but we stay up until midnight on Christmas Eve to ring in the holiday," he said, leaning his head back against the wall. "One of the trees is in the back den, and we sit around the fireplace with the tree all lit up and drink and tell old stories—mostly about Mom."

He hadn't even thought of that as a tradition until right now, but he looked forward to it. It was one of the few times his dad was really just his dad.

"When we were kids—" *Wow*, he hadn't thought about that in years. "My mom loved French toast. We had it every Christmas morning—heaping plates of homemade French toast. We all piled into the kitchen and made such a mess. Granted, we had a live-in cleaning lady, so it's not quite the same. But still, half my Christmas presents were sticky with syrup every year."

"That sounds nice."

Grief swept through him, the tangible loss weighing on him. He cleared his throat. "What about you? What are Abbott Christmases like?"

Hannah's face froze. He realized his mistake too late. They'd done a fabulous job of avoiding the topic of Hannah's parents, but there was no avoiding it after that.

"You still haven't heard from them?" he asked to break the silence.

Hannah shook her head. "No, but I've stopped trying lately. I'm embracing my new identity as a Thorne."

"Hannah."

She looked at him, glassy-eyed.

Perfect. He'd taken her to a laundromat and made her cry. *Best. Date. Ever.* "Maybe you should try starting with your dad." He rubbed the back of her ankle, letting his hand rest just under the hem of her jeans. "He viewed my profile on LinkedIn the other day."

She rolled her eyes. "Leave it to Dad to not know about private mode."

"But he's obviously interested in me," Will said, turning on the optimism. "He could be your way in."

Hannah met his gaze, her eyes wide and full of hurt. "But what if he's not?"

"Well, I guess then you would know."

Chapter 33
Hannah

It was Christmas morning. At home, it had always smelled of the cookies they spent Christmas Eve baking. She'd never had a Christmas morning in her own apartment, and that was still the case. The Thornes' mansion didn't smell like cookies. From this side of the house, it didn't even smell like pine needles. And there were trees—*three* of them. Will had said they congregated at the one in the den, which made sense since the den seemed to be the life of the mansion. The tree was a beautiful Douglas fir, decorated in a silver-and-blue color scheme. It looked like it had fallen out of Pinterest. Still, it would've been nice to be at their own place, watching the Yule log, making out under the tree, and opening presents while forcing Binx to wear the Christmas sweater she'd bought him. Maybe next year.

True to his tradition, the boys had stayed up drinking and telling stories. She and Madison had taken the opportunity to exchange gifts since Jonathan had made it quite clear this was a men-only tradition. Will had stumbled in—weary with exhaustion, not intoxication—well after midnight. He'd smelled like old expensive whiskey, but his eyes were steady and his words clear as he crawled into bed beside her. She'd barely tucked her book away before he was asleep, his head on the pillow next to her, his arm slung across her chest. That was exactly how he'd remained all night.

It was early, and she suspected that the rest of the Thorne brethren would sleep in for at least a few more hours. But Hannah and Will had a mission to complete. She nudged him, but he only rolled over with a groan, taking the comforter with him.

She kissed him lightly. "Time to get up."

His eyes fluttered open and he smiled. "Merry Christmas, Mrs. Thorne."

"Ready?"

"Two more minutes?"

"Okay, but only two. I told Renata we'd be down by eight to get started."

Twenty minutes later, they stood in the kitchen. She was dressed in her morning worst with her hair clipped back in a loose half ponytail. Will had pulled a shirt on over his pajamas but otherwise looked like he'd rolled right out of bed. Renata dug items out of the fridge as Hannah eyed the coffeepot warily. She'd forgotten to smuggle in her own coffee grounds, and even if that little shop was open, Hannah had a strict no-shopping rule on Christmas, especially after so many years as a barista. If there was ever a day she could make her own coffee, it was Christmas.

"Stop glaring at the pot like that," Renata said from behind a stack of ingredients.

Hannah looked up from the text message she was composing. Will had suggested she start with her dad. A simple *Merry Christmas* seemed the easiest way in. She hit Send before pulling a mug down from the cabinet. "How do you drink it every day?"

Renata's laugh echoed off the vast stainless steel. "Pour a cup and see for yourself."

She didn't even have to pour the coffee. The mild and smooth smell of hazelnut hit her nostrils. "What did you do?"

"Rebels come in all shapes, my dear," she said with a grin.

"All this time, Renata?" Will asked, holding a hand to his heart in mock shock.

Hannah giggled and poured them each a cup. No matter what he said, she knew Will didn't actually like his father's coffee of choice. His cup always went back to the kitchen mostly full.

"Now, tell me what we are doing with all of this," Renata said, though the glint in her eye hinted that she knew.

Laid out in front of them were the makings of the best French toast assembly line ever. Though she might be biased.

"Will's most familiar with the recipe," Hannah said, taking an apron from Renata. Will was already tying one around his waist. "And I can't make French toast to save my life, so I figured Will can dip or dredge or whatever, you can cook, and I'll sprinkle powdered sugar on top."

"I see your evil plan," Will said, looping an arm around her waist. "Make me and Renata do all the work while you get to make everything look pretty."

She nodded and took her place at the end of the production line. "Sugar and then cinnamon, right?"

"Yes, Abbott," Will said, sticking the first piece of bread into the mixture with a grin.

A half dozen slices later, Will sent a bemused Arthur off to wake up the rest of the house. Arthur seemed so stiff when she had first met him, but his face lit up as he watched them make a mess of the kitchen. He'd even tried the first piece, given his nod of approval, and stolen a cup of Renata's coffee with a wink in Hannah's direction. Had Will known this side of the staff before that morning? Did anyone in the house?

They were nearly done when the kitchen door swung open. It was too soon to be Arthur returning from waking the rest of the household. She and Will turned at the same time, passing a dish towel between them to dry their hands.

Daniel stood in the doorway, still in scrubs. Bags ringed his eyes, and he had a sort of wired look about him. He must've had an overnight shift and come straight from work. "What's this?"

"How much coffee have you had?" Hannah asked, handing him a plate.

"Not that much, actually," he said, flipping a piece of French toast onto his plate. "Mom's Christmas French toast?"

Will nodded with an easy smile. "Yeah. It just felt like time to bring it back."

The kitchen door opened again, and Jon and Madison entered, chattering about being summoned to the kitchen. They froze once inside, taking in the trays of French toast, fruit salad, and the platter of bacon Renata was filling. A fresh batch of coffee—Jonathan's sludge—brewed noisily on the other counter.

Her father-in-law appeared at the other side of the kitchen. He must have come through the back entrance Renata had shown her. Hannah had never seen him in anything but his Sunday best, but there he stood in a dressing gown and slippers, looking like every TV dad she'd ever seen. His ever-keen eyes took in the spread before him. His face, which never softened, relaxed a fraction, and she swore she saw nostalgia in his eyes.

When Will had told her the story about making French toast with the biggest smile on his face, Hannah had the idea to bring back the missed tradition. His smile had been followed by an onslaught of emotions she'd never seen out of him before. She hadn't considered that the unexpected reminder might be too much for the Thorne men, that they had been repressing their emotions about their mother's death for a long time. But Will had been excited by the idea, texting Renata to pull out the old recipe book before she'd even finished her sentence.

Standing in the kitchen, Will was relaxed and happy. As Daniel slung an arm across his shoulders, Will's eyes stayed on his father, but not in the tense way they usually did. "Merry Christmas, Dad," he said, waving toward the spread.

It wasn't Jonathan who spoke next but Jon. "Man, I've missed that smell."

The spell broke with those words. The silence dissipated into conversation and the clinking of plates as everyone gathered around the counter.

Will pulled Hannah in and kissed her among the chaos. His eyes were light, his expression open and hopeful. "Thank you."

"It was nothing," she said, stealing a piece of bacon off his plate. "You did all the work."

He kissed her temple, leaning his forehead against hers. "It's everything."

Chapter 34
Will

"Ouch. Ouch, Will." Hannah stopped walking and rubbed a hand over her hip. "Can I please look now?"

He maneuvered her out of the path of the table and urged her forward, his hand still covering her eyes. "Two more steps. Nothing's in front of you, I promise."

Will dropped his hand as they entered their bedroom. It looked perfect in the dimmed lights and the glow of the little Christmas tree he'd acquired from Kate. Kate had added Christmas lights around the doors and windows. Under the tree sat presents and a bottle of wine with two flutes wrapped together with ribbon.

"How did you get the tree?" Hannah asked, her eyes taking in the space.

"A courier."

"Courier?"

"Yes." He straightened a bent branch, making the light come into full view. "I made a few calls to a certain mutual friend of ours, who brought the tree to our apartment while we were in the Hamptons."

"Kate brought the tree all the way uptown for you?" Hannah sat down and trailed her hand across the plastic branches. Will could almost imagine what she was remembering because he was remembering it too.

"I earned some goodwill by letting her watch football here a few Thursday nights while you were covering shows," he said. "And promised her she could stay and watch Sunday Night Football on the big screen."

"You know, if you weren't you, it would be really creepy that you hang out with my best friend without telling me."

"Kate's my friend too," he said, meaning it. He had missed both Hannah and Kate separately and together, each in their own way. "Technically, I think I was her friend before I was your friend."

Hannah turned a betrayed glance at him. "You did *not* just go there."

He laughed. "After this morning, getting the tree back hardly seems like an effort."

Her cheeks flushed at the compliment. "So, it was a good Christmas?"

"It was the best Christmas." He sat down next to her, letting their toes touch. "I think you may have made a believer of Jonathan."

"That's because it's undeniable." She climbed onto his lap. "I'm crazy about you, Will Thorne."

He loved when he said his name like that. "And I you, Hannah Abbott."

She cupped his face, and her expression softened, becoming shy. "Hannah Abbott-Thorne."

Wow. His heart skipped a beat. "Really?"

She looked up, and their eyes locked. He understood everything—everything they hadn't said, didn't need to say. Her lips came down to his, and in all his life, Will had never felt so loved. Hannah had seen behind the curtain. She understood the burden that came with the Thorne name, and she wanted to bear it with him.

"Really," she said, a gleam behind her eyes.

"Best. Christmas. Ever." He grinned and planted a giant, wet kiss on her forehead. "Can I give you a present now?"

He leaned over and picked up the small jewelry box wrapped in red Santa paper.

"Clara wrapped this for you, didn't she?" Hannah said, pulling at the fold gingerly as if she didn't want to mess up the wrapping paper. It was pristine, after all.

He shook his head at her accusation. "'Only neat corners will earn you a buck.'" He pitched his voice high and affected a Southern accent, wagging a finger at her. "Miss Lauraine's gift-wrapping crash course."

Her nose scrunched as the memory came back to her. She laughed and shook her head. "Is there anything you don't remember?"

"Not when it comes to you."

Another blush crept up her cheeks. She turned her focus to the box in her hands. The discerning look in her eyes made it clear his disguise had worked—she was expecting jewelry. She pulled the lid off, her eyes narrowing at the two laminated sound check passes. It had taken a lot of phone calls and owed favors, but he knew what it would mean to Hannah to meet Leonard Nulty. For all the times they'd seen Wilderness Weekend, for all the merch they'd bought, they had never met him.

She ran a finger over the passes, a smile lighting her face. "No freaking way."

"I figured we might as well make a day of it," he said, grinning. "Go to sound check and meet Leonard Nulty then head back that night for the best show of our lives. We also have a reservation at that restaurant you like near Astor Place."

This time, when he looked at her, he was certain there were tears in her eyes—happy tears, he hoped.

"Best. Christmas. Ever," she said, parroting his words. "Thank you."

He wrapped his arms around her waist, his fingers digging into the thin fabric of her dress. "Anything for you, Mrs. Abbott-Thorne."

Saying the words was so much more powerful than hearing Hannah say them. Desire rolled through him, his whole body alight. He pulled her into him. Their lips collided, hard and desperate. He inched her dress up over her hips, his hands sliding up against the sensitive skin of her thighs. Her fingers curled into the short hair at the back of his neck as she trailed kisses down his chest, her hands working the final buttons of his shirt. He pulled the dress over her head and she pushed him back until they lay on the floor. He quivered under her touch, goosebumps sprouting on his arms as she skimmed a hand down his chest, over his hips, and lower. Every touch was kindling, and Will wanted to burn.

Chapter 35

Hannah

Hannah tapped her finger to the beat of the song playing in the restaurant. They had picked a restaurant near Penn Station to make it easier on her father, but that meant it was more crowded and that her father's tardiness didn't go unnoticed. The waitress had been giving them dirty looks for the last ten minutes, even though she and Will had ordered drinks and an appetizer—not that she thought she could stomach food right then.

"How was your dress fitting?" Will asked, though she knew he didn't care. "Did you end up meeting the rest of the bridal party?"

Hannah shook her head. "No, Madison decided not to do that. I guess I'll just meet them at the bridal shower or something." She looked around the restaurant again but didn't see her dad. "The dress is... well, I'm glad I'm not paying for it."

"I'm sure you will look beautiful."

"Honey, hey!" Her father strode up to the table with an apologetic smile. He was alone. She hadn't expected anything else, but it still stung that her mother couldn't be bothered to make the trip. He slid into the open spot next to Hannah. "Sorry I'm late. I should've taken the car."

"You hate driving in New York," she said, feeling herself relax. There was no preamble with her dad, not even now.

"Not as much as I hate taking the train anywhere."

"That's sacrilege on this side of the river," Will said jokingly, taking a sweep of the restaurant.

Hannah laughed and turned to Will. "My mom once had this brilliant idea to take the train to Florida."

"It took thirty hours," her dad finished. "We could've walked there faster."

"How old were you?" Will had a smile plastered across his face that was unmistakably filled with amusement, but then, this was a part of her that he'd never experienced. She could see why the way she played off her dad would delight Will. It was the basis for so much of her sense of humor.

"Thirteen. Stephanie was nine," she said, remembering how Stephanie had run up and down the aisle for an hour straight. The other travelers in their car had been saints.

Hannah's eyes wandered toward the door. A gaggle of women with bridesmaid sashes had just come in, and behind them were a few loners in business clothes. She tried to see them better through the gaps in the bridal party. They were only young businessmen, not her mother.

"She's not coming." Her dad frowned. "I'm sorry, Hannah. She just... needs a little more time."

Hannah nodded and pulled a piece of bread onto her plate, afraid that if she made eye contact with her dad, she'd burst into a million little pieces.

"So, I didn't get the full story last time," her dad said with a hint of sarcasm that it was probably too soon for. "How did you two end up at the altar?"

She exchanged a look with Will and wondered briefly what would happen if they told the whole truth. "I'll let Will take this one," she said instead.

Will didn't miss a beat. He walked through the story they'd crafted together, but this time, it was sprinkled with truths from their marriage—how they crashed a wedding on their honeymoon, how he'd taken them to a laundromat on a date because of some silly quip she'd made. She watched them fall in love through his eyes. It was beautiful, it was theirs, and it was real.

"What made you say yes?" her dad asked, returning his full attention to Hannah.

"She liked my butt," Will said before Hannah could answer.

She shoved him, a blush heating her cheeks. "He was sweet, and we were in love."

"My daughter, the hopeless romantic? I never thought I'd see the day." He held a hand mockingly to his heart. "Charlanie rubbed off on you."

"You too?" Will exclaimed with a laugh.

"It's just so damn catchy."

Hannah didn't know how to feel about her dad's statement. There was no malice in it, but she had never been cold or jaded. In fact, she'd put in a great amount of effort to not let any of her past relationships taint her feelings on love. No matter how sideways things with Brian had gone, it wasn't for a lack of trying. Sometimes you picked wrong. And sometimes you got Will. Maybe one had to happen before the other.

She listened to Will and her dad talk about work, football, and some new phone that was supposed to come out next month. They were a good fit. Her dad would enjoy having someone to watch sports with—someone who cared, at least. Hannah placated him, but half of the time, she had no idea which team had the ball. The longer they talked, the more relaxed she felt. This was how she'd imagined it.

"How's your knee doing?" her father asked as they were finishing up their entrées.

"Surprisingly well! Madison—Will's brother's fiancée—is my physical therapist, and"—she pushed her leg out from under the table—"I can straighten it and everything."

"Wow," Will and her dad said at the same time.

"I have an appointment with an orthopedist next week, and then I'll know if I need surgery or not."

"Hopefully not," Will said, squeezing her hand. "Madison is good at what she does, and Hannah has been diligent about doing all her exercises at home."

"Madison kind of threatened my life, but yeah. I'm looking forward to getting back out there," she said. "Will's a runner, and he's been totally rubbing it in my face that he can go for runs every day."

Will's eyes widened, and his gaze swiveled to her father. "I swear I have done no such thing."

Her father's laugh filled the restaurant. "You two are fun. You know, the New Jersey half marathon is in April. Perhaps the Abbotts and Thornes can team up."

The memory of runner's high coursed through her. Was that even a possibility? Back on the pavement by April? They'd have to add Daniel to the team. She'd be so outpaced. But maybe. "Team Thabbott!"

Her father waved his hand in front of his face as if wafting away a bad smell. "Oh no, no, honey. That's just awful."

Chapter 36

Hannah

Hannah redialed Riley for the third time. Riley was going to be so annoyed when she picked up, but that was what she got for scheduling meetings unannounced while on maternity leave.

"Why do we have a two o'clock scheduled for today?" Hannah asked when Riley finally answered, her tone calmer than expected.

"Because we need to... hold on." Hannah could hear the high-pitched and aspirational sounds of a Disney movie playing in the background as Riley shuffled the phone around. "Sorry, Jo is being needy."

"Is there any other way for an eight-week-old to be?"

"Yes," Riley said amidst more shuffling. "Anyway, we need to talk, so you're coming to me at two."

"You're on maternity leave."

"Which is why you are coming to my house."

"That's all I get?" Hannah asked.

Much to her disbelief, Riley had stayed away during this maternity leave. With Cecilia, she'd been in the office constantly, baby strapped to her chest in one of those weird wrap things. She couldn't stand to be home or away from her first baby. But the bigger, more experienced staff seemed to help keep her at home this time.

"See you at two!"

Hannah ended the call, staring at her phone incredulously. What could this possibly be about? Godmother duties, a fatal flaw in the latest issue, or health insurance finally coming through? No—Riley could email about all that. Hannah would have to worry about it later—and she'd have plenty of time while she sat in an MRI machine. Today was the day. Riley had better hope for good news if she was about to drop a bomb.

Hannah stared up at the hospital towering over the East River. She hadn't been there since the days following her accident. The sight of the building filled her with trepidation. What if the news was bad and time made everything worse? She shook her head. This was why she married Will. She couldn't lose more time. *New Jersey half in April. Team Thabbott.* She kept those thoughts in her mind. Whatever the outcome, she needed a goal.

"Hannah!"

She turned at the sound of Daniel's voice. Will hadn't been sure about Daniel's schedule, but there he was, scrubs and all. At least they weren't blood splattered.

"Ready?" he asked, enveloping her in a hug.

It still amazed her how quickly Daniel had taken her into the fold. Jon was warm but still distant. Not that she expected anything else—even in a normal situation, it had only been a few months. But Daniel seemed genuinely excited by her existence.

"As I'll ever be," she said, wishing again that she hadn't told Will she'd be fine on her own.

"Listen," he said as they entered the hospital through the main entrance. So far, it was much more welcoming than the emergency room—less chaotic and not so frightening. "I know my brother is trapped in some god-awful meeting right now, so I was thinking..."

"I'll be fine."

He laughed. "I don't doubt that, but if you'll have me, I'd love to accompany you."

"Doing an ortho rotation?" She leaned against the rail in the elevator, watching the numbers go up. There would be no getting rid of him, but a good ribbing never hurt anyone.

"If it makes you feel better about it, then absolutely."

Part of her wanted to do this on her own. That was why she'd shooed away both Will and Kate's offers to go with her. Maybe she wanted the opportunity to take it in by herself—to be able to have whatever her reaction was going to be without an audience. Maybe she wanted the chance to lie about whatever the doctor said. Probably both.

But after an hour of scans, Hannah was glad Daniel had agreed to stay with her while she waited for the doctor. She would be mighty bored otherwise and probably panicking.

"Tell me what you saw on the scan." Hannah lay back on the exam table, the paper crinkling under her weight.

Daniel sighed from his perch on the stiff plastic guest chair in the corner. "I'm no expert, but your meniscus is still torn."

"Fuck." Not that she hadn't been expecting to hear that.

"It didn't look that bad to me, but let's see what Dr. Annabelle has to say."

"Thank you for staying with me." She meant it wholeheartedly. Daniel had less time off than the rest of the Thornes, and he was spending it with his brother's wife in the hospital where he already spent the majority of his days.

"That's what you do for family..."

Hannah couldn't see his face from where he was sitting, but the end of the sentence had started to trail off, and the silence that followed was heavy with racing thoughts.

She sighed. "Just say it."

"What?" he asked with a short, nervous laugh.

"I can hear you thinking all the way over here," she said, closing her eyes for the briefest of moments.

"Right," he said, clearing his throat. "I just wanted to thank you, really."

She sat up too quickly, and all the blood fled from her head. She kept her eyes closed until her equilibrium returned. When she opened them, Daniel stared back at her, an amused expression on his face.

"Thank me?" she said after another moment.

"Listen, I don't know why you and Will got married. Maybe it was because you needed this appointment." He held up his hand as she started to protest. "I was there after everything happened. There is no way he met you and fell in love the way you two said. When you supposedly ran into each other, Will was so drunk every day he could hardly function."

There was no proper response to that, so she remained silent, lacing and unlacing her fingers. She knew things had been bad, but hearing it outright from someone besides Will made her heart ache for him.

"I don't need to know why," Daniel said, looking up at her. "That's between you and Will. But whatever your reasons, you make him happy. And in a *real* way. You've brought him back to us."

"He makes me happy too," she said, her cheeks heating up to what had to be a flaming red.

"I can see that," he said warmly.

The door to the exam room opened, and Dr. Annabelle swept into the office. And he was younger than she expected for someone who Daniel called his mentor. He was most likely in his midforties, dark skinned, with close-cropped hair and a verifiable goatee. A gold wedding band gleamed on his left ring finger every time he flipped a page in her chart.

"I was able to get ahold of your old scans," he said, finally looking up at her. His smile was friendly and comforting. She took that as a good sign. Her old doctors had been all serious faces and grimaces.

He held up the scan she had memorized after the accident. "What do you see, Dr. Thorne?"

"Grade two, maybe three." Daniel stood and pointed at a spot on the scan. "I would've recommended a closer look with the possibility of surgery."

She looked between the two of them, waiting for the bad news to drop. Surgery would get her back on her feet in the long-term. It would also prohibit her from attending concerts for the foreseeable future. She had avoided acknowledging that for too long.

"This is your scan from today," he said, holding it up.

Her breath caught in her chest. Even to her untrained eye, it looked better—not healed, but the tear wasn't as defined. She'd felt the difference in her time with Madison but assumed it was simply because she was working it out consistently rather than breaking out her TheraBand when it rained.

"Wow."

"Wow, indeed, Ms. Abbott," Dr. Annabelle said with another smile. "Dr. Thorne tells me you've been working with a physical therapist?"

Hannah nodded. "For over two months now."

"Let's continue that," he said, typing something into the tablet hidden under her chart. "But pending any further injury, I think your knee will heal itself with proper rehabilitation."

"So I don't need surgery?"

"Tentatively, no. I'm comfortable, if you are, with you continuing to work with your PT, and we can revisit this in three months."

Hannah's heart raced. She didn't need surgery. At least not yet. "Can I run?"

He paused for a moment then nodded. "I wouldn't run a marathon or even a 10K, but yes, if you take it easy, I think you can work a run or two into your weekly routine. Dr. Thorne can go into further details with you."

Daniel put a hand on her shoulder once Dr. Annabelle left the room. "We'll have you out on our Saturday-morning run in no time."

She grinned. "Will said no girls allowed."

"True, girls have cooties," Daniel said, cringing at her.

She poked him. "Oops, now you do too."

RILEY, DANNY, AND THE girls lived in a Park Slope brownstone. It was just big enough for the four of them if Cecilia and Jo shared a room. Riley had talked about upgrading, but that would mean moving to the suburbs, and they were city dwellers through and through. At least that's how Hannah always imagined them. Though even household meetings in Westchester would be preferable to making the trek to Brooklyn.

She pulled a note off the door of the brownstone. *If you ring the doorbell and wake the baby, I will kill you.*

Hopefully, this was intended for Hannah and not some poor, unsuspecting deliveryman. The knob turned easily. She taped the note back to the door and peeked around the block. There was no sign of a delivery truck of any type. Hannah did not want to be in the house if someone rang that bell, especially if she was the one who took the note down. She'd experienced Riley during the newborn phase, and now she had a toddler as well. The click of the door was barely audible, but Riley stuck her head out of her office, which was right off the front hall and far away from Jo's room.

"Sorry for the death threat," Riley said. "We've got those damn cable salesmen wandering around. Yesterday, they rang the bell three times."

"That's persistent." Hannah fell back onto the couch and tucked her feet up under her.

"So, is surgery in your future?" Riley asked, glancing from Hannah's knee to her face.

"Definitely not in the next three months," Hannah said, still not quite believing it. She knew her expression must match all the grinning emojis in her texts from Will, Kate, and Madison. "After everything, my knee has started to heal."

"That's amazing. And how's married life?"

Hannah narrowed her eyes at her boss. "We're great, but please tell me you didn't make me come all the way to Brooklyn so we could talk guys."

"All that banter and no time for chitchat." Riley shook her head. "I have some news."

Hannah tried to mentally calculate if it was even possible for Riley to be pregnant again, but she knew little to nothing of Irish twins except that they existed.

"Stop trying to do math you don't understand," Riley said with a laugh. Hannah really needed a better poker face. It was seriously amazing no one important had figured out about the pact. "It's magazine news."

"Magazine news you couldn't tell me about over FaceTime?"

Riley swiveled her chair until she was facing Hannah. The chair gave her a bit of extra height, and Hannah sat straighter to try and match it. Whatever this news was, it was big. And for Riley to have to bring her here, it was a game changer.

"We've received funding for the Boston edition," Riley said without further preamble. "It'll start with just a few city-specific pieces as an inset and be fluffed with our bigger features from the other issues, much like how New York started."

"That's huge!" The higher-ups had been working on Boston for so long, and it was finally here. "Where did they find the money?"

"The magazine received an anonymous donation last month specifically designated to expansion," she said, flipping through some paperwork. "It's going to be threadbare—just an editor and one or two interns. The idea is to cover as much as possible so we have enough material for a few issues while we're staffing up."

"Are they sending Nate out?" Hannah asked, thinking of the managing editor of the Los Angeles edition, who oversaw all expansion efforts with Riley. Riley would never leave her girls for an extended period of time.

"No," she said plainly. "Nate and I discussed it, and we'd like for you to head up the effort."

"What?" She hadn't meant to say it—not like *that*. But there it was. This was the opportunity she'd been waiting for, wanting, and needing. The chance to make a real change, to shape her career and the direction of *Deafening Silence,* and to become her own version of, well, Riley.

"You heard me."

Several iterations of the word "yes" ricocheted her around her mind, but slowly, her brain recovered from the shock of the offer. How could she move to Boston? It wasn't her and Binx against the world anymore. There was Will, who she had committed to for at least a year, who needed her as she needed him and who loved her. Could she ask this of him?

"How long is the assignment?"

"A little under two months to start," Riley said, her eyes searching Hannah's. "Just long enough to get everything set up and running while we find a managing editor."

Two months in Boston. It was the chance of a lifetime. Will would do this for her.

"We'll pay to relocate you, Will, and Binx for that period." She scanned the notes in front of her. "Nate's working on finalizing a sublet."

"When would I have to leave?" Hannah asked, thinking of the long weekend in the Hamptons, the Wilderness concert next week, and the zillion wedding tasks Madison had added to her calendar.

"If Nate had his way, you'd leave tonight," she said. "But I know you're not going to miss the Wilderness show, and I'm sure there are things to figure out. So, first thing Wednesday morning?"

It was Thursday. How could she move her whole life in six days? A promotion hadn't even been on her radar, especially not one that included moving out of the state.

"Hannah?" Riley stared down at her with a pained expression. She knew the gravity of this news and the damage it could do—to both *Deafening* and Hannah's marriage—if not handled properly.

"I don't know, Riley." Hannah clasped her hands together. "I have to talk to Will, and I just don't know."

Riley placed her hand on top of Hannah's. "That's a perfectly acceptable answer."

Chapter 37
Will

Will glared at the stack of reports littering the coffee table. He promised to be home for dinner, but he couldn't drop everything either. He could've pawned all this off on the junior staff—that was literally why they existed. But after his misstep with his last big case, he needed to do his own work. That meant reading the reports and not just the note summaries.

He had a whole plan—champagne, chocolate-covered strawberries, and a brand new pair of sneakers—but there'd been no time to find the perfect running shoes. He'd take her to the store another day and let her pick them out. It would be an experience that way, something she might remember longer than the life of the shoes. At least that was what Eddie was always telling him—make *moments*.

Will turned at the sound of the front door opening. Hannah entered, balancing a pizza box on one arm and holding several bags in the other. He followed her into the kitchen, his stomach growling as the scent of garlic, tomato, bread, and cheese hit him.

"It was like the entirety of the Upper East Side was at Frankie's tonight," she said, putting the box down on the kitchen table.

He waited until she dropped the rest of her stuff before sweeping her into a hug. "When is our first run?"

She laughed against him. "Probably Sunday morning. We can get in a workout instead of a *workout*."

"I think we can work out and then *work out*." He raised one eyebrow suggestively, which made her laugh harder.

"That kind of sweaty is not sexy," she said, handing him a plate with a slice of pizza.

Will swallowed his retort. It would be better to prove her wrong and absolutely more fun.

They sat down to dinner, and for a few minutes, the only conversation centered around passing each other more pizza and refilling water glasses. Tonight, the silence felt heavy, and every time he tried to catch Hannah's eye, she turned away. Had he not heard from Daniel about her knee looking better, he would've suspected she was lying about the outcome.

"Everything okay over there?" He let the tips of his fingers mingle with hers across the table.

She straightened and let her fingers slip out of his. "Riley offered me a promotion today."

"What? Way to bury the lede—pun totally intended."

She shook her head. "It's interim editor in chief of *Deafening Silence Boston*."

The words didn't sink in at first. Not all of them. *Interim editor in chief.* Pride swelled in him. She'd made it. Her dreams were coming true. His wife was going to be editor in chief. Then the rest of her title hit. *Boston.* She couldn't manage the Boston edition from New York.

"Whoa."

"Yup."

"When do you leave?" he asked, even though the last thing he wanted was to hear the answer. Because if she was telling him now, then the answer was soon, sooner than a year. Too soon for all the plans he'd started making.

"Will," she said, reaching for his hand.

"Do you want out of the pact?" he asked, eyes trained on the table. He couldn't watch her say she was leaving him.

"Come with me." She scooted her chair closer to him, cupping his hands in hers. "It's only for a few months until they hire a full-time editor. And I love you, so come with me."

"You love me?"

She rested her forehead against his. "Yes, Will Thorne, I love you. I have always loved you."

He'd been waiting a decade to hear those words. He kissed her, long and deep, putting every ounce of his love into it. "Me too," he whispered against her lips.

"You too, what?" Hannah asked, her eyes locked on his, searching.

"I love you, Hannah Abbott-Thorne," he said, cupping her face.

"Then come with me to Boston."

Timing was such a bitch. Getting allowance to relocate, even temporarily, would've been difficult at any time. Wellington Thorne wasn't exactly known for being up with the times.

He kissed the hand that still covered his. "I wish that was possible, Abbott, I do. But there's no way my uncle's going to let me move to Boston in the middle of this case."

"Then I won't go." Hannah's voice was steady and determined. Her eyes, glassy with unshed tears, bored into him.

"I can't be the reason you turn this down," he said, his voice cracking.

She pressed their entwined hands against his heart. "And I can't do this without you."

Chapter 38
Will

Light snow dusted the ground, and the night sky twinkled. He hoped it wouldn't stick, at least not until Hannah arrived safely in the Hamptons. She and the rest of her team were covering an indoor music festival on the Island all day. Will had dropped her off, and Daniel had agreed to drive her the rest of the way after his shift. Once Hannah was safely in his arms and he could smell the sweet scent of her skin, then bring on the snow. It would at least give him a solid block of time to convince her to take the Boston job. As of that morning, she was planning to turn it down, but she had agreed to wait to give Riley a final answer.

He stared down at the journal he kept in the Hamptons, sometimes in his room, sometimes in his mother's room. For once, he didn't feel like visiting with her. He lay back on his bed and sketched Hannah's name into the margin. Hannah loved him. He'd hoped when he knocked on her door with that ridiculous ring that this would be the outcome. But the reality was better than his dreams. His wife was so much more than he could've imagined.

A knock at the door pulled him out of his reverie. Hannah wouldn't knock, and his father had long since retired. Whoever was on the other side of that door was someone he didn't want to see. Today had been better, but that didn't mean he was up for late-night heart-to-hearts with either Jon or Madison. The knock came again, softly—*Madison*. He banged his head against the headboard twice. *Why?*

Against his better judgment, he made his way over to the door. He could feel Madison's presence, thick and desperate. If they hadn't been in the Hamptons, the date might have swept past him without consideration. His mind was knee-deep in reports and Hannah—always Hannah—but it was hard to forget their old anniversary when the person who'd shattered his heart had been sitting across the room all day and was knocking on his door.

He leaned against the doorframe and hid his face in his arm. He didn't want to do this. She had chosen Jon over and over for months, and she chose him still. And Will's heart belonged to Hannah. It always had. He chose Hannah. He would always choose Hannah.

"Will, please," Madison said, so quietly it was like she knew he was standing on the other side of the door.

He took a breath. He could do this. Madison's hold on him was gone. It was just another night. The knock came again, and he knew she wouldn't leave until he opened the door. Hannah would find her crying outside his door, and then there would be questions. He pushed the image of Hannah to the forefront of his mind. Her eyes had been so full of love when she told him she was adding his last name to her own. They were perfect together, and nothing Madison said could ever change that. He pulled open the door.

Madison straightened, lifting her eyes to his. Tears stained her cheeks, and her eyes were filled with more unshed.

The harsh "make it quick" he'd planned on saying died on his lips at her tears. "Maddie," he said, the endearment slipping out unintentionally. "What's going on?"

"Jon and I had a fight," she said, wrapping her arms around herself.

He tucked his hands into his pockets. "About?"

"He thinks I'm still in love with you."

Well, that was something. He hadn't thought Jon even gave him a second thought when he'd decided to steal his girlfriend. "And you thought showing up at my door after your fight was going to assuage his fears?"

She sniffled, he thought to cover a laugh, but then a sob racked her body. "He's right, though."

Shit.

"It should've been you," she continued. "I thought... I thought we'd be together for always, like we promised, and I know—*fuck*, I know I messed it up."

"You didn't mess it up," he said, trying and failing to keep his voice steady. "You fucking blew our relationship to pieces."

The anger he'd long since digested roiled in his stomach. His hands clenched into fists. Was she serious? He felt the tautness of his control.

"And then you agreed to marry him! You didn't even talk to me about it."

"I knew you would never forgive me." She paused. "Would you have—could we have gone back?"

"We're not doing this. I'm married. You're engaged to my brother." He took a breath. "You made your choice. And I made mine. Whether you regret it or not is not my problem. Besides, I thought you and Hannah were friends."

"This isn't about Hannah," Madison said, tears continuing to stream down her face.

"This is entirely about Hannah."

"I love you, William."

A gasp echoed down the hall. Will didn't have to look to know it was Hannah. He'd known she was almost here. He'd opened the damned door. Will and Hannah's eyes met, with Madison, the embodiment of his cowardly secret, standing between them.

Chapter 39
Hannah

I love you, William.

God, was she ever going to get that image out of her head? Will had been leaning against the doorjamb in his pajamas, a pained expression on his face. Madison had been close—too close—tears streaking down her cheeks. *Madison* was Will's maligned ex. Of course she was.

Hannah stopped at the front door, dropping her bag onto the floor. Several sets of keys hung from hooks in the mudroom. She pulled Will's down and slid them into the pocket of her hoodie. She couldn't stay here.

Her stomach churned. She leaned against the door, willing herself to stay on her feet as a sob wracked her body. Why hadn't he told her? Worse yet, how hadn't she figured it out? Hannah had seen it, had felt the weird tension between the two of them for months. It explained Will's hesitation whenever she asked a question about Madison and his awkward encounter with Madison's parents at the party. He'd been filtering his answers *the whole time.*

Fuck. She was such an idiot.

"Hannah."

"Leave me alone, Will." He must have followed her. Why hadn't she thought to hide in one of the million rooms in this house?

"It's not—"

She whipped her head up. He had to be kidding. "It's not what it looks like? You mean Madison's *not* your ex, and she's *not* still in love with you?"

"Just listen to me, Abbott."

No. He didn't get to call her Abbott or Mrs. Thorne. He didn't get to explain. Not then. Maybe not ever. Hannah pulled open the front door and stepped out into the frigid night air. They'd had the coldest temperatures all season this week, and she was in a hoodie.

"Hannah, wait! What are you doing?" Will grabbed her arm, stopping her in her tracks. "Please don't go. I love you."

"Don't say that to me." She turned to face him, and for a split second, she worried about him being out in the snow in only his pajamas. He wasn't even wearing shoes. "You don't get to say that to me."

"Madison is just upset. She doesn't mean it."

"Are you serious right now?" she yelled, pushing him away from her. "Screw Madison! How could you lie to me this whole time? Did you think I would never find out? That I wouldn't care that you married me to hurt her?"

She watched him try to come up with an answer. Finally, he shook his head and looked at her with sad eyes. "I didn't marry you to hurt her." He reached for her and she flinched. He dug his hands into his pockets, his eyes imploring her to listen. But she couldn't. "Please come back inside."

She shook her head. "I trusted you with everything."

Without waiting for another response, she turned and ran to Will's car, barely able to see through the tears. She climbed in, started the engine, and threw the car into reverse in one beat. Hannah peeled out of the driveway, refusing to look back at Will. She drove for miles and miles, the road ahead of her blurry from her tears. She didn't even know how to get home from here, but she couldn't stop to find her phone. If she stopped, she'd lose the small ounce of sanity keeping her hands steady on the wheel. If she stayed on this road, it would lead her to a highway eventually.

Will and Madison. *Will and fucking Madison.* Had this been a joke to them? Some weird foreplay before they decided they were destined for each other. Every moment of the last three months blackened—had any of it been real? The thought alone brought an ache to her chest. It had to be real.

A horn honked, and a splash of light sparked in her periphery. Hannah jerked the wheel to the right, narrowly avoiding a car in the oncoming lane. Her car screeched onto the shoulder. She threw it into park. *Shit.* She breathed heavily, trying not to hyperventilate. How was this her life? She screamed in the silence of the car, hitting the steering wheel over and over. Tears stung her eyes. There was no escaping the truth—Will, the last boy she'd truly trusted, had lied to her.

She took a breath. Music, directions, Riley, in that order. Scrolling through her music app, she selected Dashboard Confessional. Lyrics filled the small space.

Next, the unnatural voice of her GPS navigation sounded: "Turn left in one thousand feet."

Hannah hesitated for only a moment before opening her text exchange with Riley. *I'll be in Boston tomorrow afternoon.*

Part 3

Chapter 40
Will

Will stared at the note, reading the simple sentence again and again. *I took the job in Boston.* Hannah hadn't even signed it. He'd rushed out after her, going back inside only to get dressed and grab Daniel's keys, but the effort had been fruitless. An accident on the Southern State Parkway had stranded him, and by the time he'd gotten back to the apartment, she'd gone. He knew she was at Kate's. She had nowhere else to go in the middle of the night. But that note stopped him. Her words echoed in his head—*You don't get to say that to me. I trusted you with everything.* The way she'd looked at him, as if she didn't know who he was anymore, haunted him. Hannah had been the one person who'd never looked at him like that.

It had been three days with no word from her. He hadn't been back to work because the energy required was too much. People, namely Jon, were starting to ask questions, but Will didn't care. It wasn't his place to tell Jon what Madison had said, what she had done. He no longer owed Jon anything. He knew he needed a story—one grounded in truth—for why he'd left the Hamptons so suddenly and why Hannah was mysteriously absent from New York. At least he could tell the truth on that one—she had taken an unexpected job opportunity in Boston, and they were figuring out the details. They had to figure out the details. That couldn't be it.

She loved him. She'd said it first and with such weight behind her words. She'd been willing to give up her promotion to be with him. And he'd repaid her by lying and by opening that damned door. The romantic in him wanted to fly to Boston and demand she hear him out. He would confess his love for her, beg her to take him back—whatever it took, he would do it. But her look had killed the romantic. If Hannah had wanted to save their marriage, she would've left more than a note, and she wouldn't have taken Binx.

The apartment door creaked open. Will didn't even turn toward it, just kept staring at that note. It wasn't going to be Hannah.

"William," Daniel said, putting his hand on Will's shoulder. "What are you doing?"

He handed Daniel the note. "She left me."

"She'll come back," Daniel said, folding the note into neat squares. "Hannah loves you. You just have to give her some space. Make some changes. Get Madison the fuck out of your life."

Will dropped his head into his hands. "Jon and Madison are a package deal."

"Then maybe... you need to tell him. He's a big boy, William. And if he stays with her, then he can get out too. We don't need him."

Will pulled Daniel into a hug, his shoulders shaking under the weight of his tears. "Thank you."

"Pack your stuff," Daniel said, holding Will tighter. "You're not staying here alone."

WILL WISHED, NOT FOR the first time, that his office door had a lock. He'd gotten through the last week by keeping his door shut all day, every day. And it had worked for the most part. Only his junior associate, Sean, and various administrative assistants had stopped by. He wished that the seclusion had helped him finish reading the report Frank had finally sent over or line up the best expert witnesses he could find. But it was Monday again, and Will was still spending most of his time playing *Minesweeper* and staring at his cell phone.

Hannah hadn't answered a single one of his calls or texts. He only knew she was safely in Boston because Kate took pity on him.

After a week of silence, Will couldn't have his calls go unanswered any longer. It hurt too much. He typed out a simple text: *I love you, Hannah.* It was a final plea to save his faltering marriage before it had even really begun. He hit Send and slid the phone into his desk drawer. Either Hannah would answer him or, more likely, not.

The handle on his door jiggled, then Jonathan stood in front of him. He was dressed in a full suit and tie for the first of two days of the quarterly executive board meeting this afternoon.

"Good afternoon, Jonathan," Will said, standing in greeting.

His father waved the formality away and sat down in the chair across from Will. That was unexpected. In all Will's time at Wellington Thorne, his father had never sat down in Will's office. "Hello, son."

Will blinked. Jonathan never called him that when dressed for work. It couldn't be. His uncle couldn't have worked that fast.

"How are you?" Jonathan continued. "I hear Hannah is in Boston? That must be... difficult for you two."

Will swallowed before answering, tempering his tone. His father was baiting him, trying to trick him into giving out information that would prove his marriage was a sham. "It's been rough. She's busy, but I'm needed here, as you and Grayson pointed out when I asked you to allow me to go with her."

"Yes." Jonathan nodded. "I was glad to see you stayed true to your work ethic and didn't let your heart ruin your career."

Will furrowed his brow. Had what appeared to be his dedication to Wellington Thorne gotten him a seat at the table?

"It's only two months," Will said slowly. "Then she'll be back, and it'll be like we were never apart." The words hurt him to say, but he got them out steadily, cockily, and confidently. Jonathan wouldn't ruffle his feathers today, and no one was dictating the end of his relationship except Hannah herself.

"We'll see." Jonathan's eyes narrowed, glinting. An unsettling feeling grew in Will's stomach. He knew that determined look. It was never good and always underhanded. "Either way, come along. We don't want to be late."

"Late?" Will asked calmly. His father's meaning was clear: there was only one place they'd been going. But Will wanted his father to have to say it—to invite him into the fold.

"William," his father started while getting to his feet. He rebuttoned his jacket. "I'm pleased to escort you to your first executive board meeting. It's time you took your place alongside the other Thorne men."

Chapter 41
Hannah

Hannah closed the door behind yet another intern candidate. This one had been the worst of the bunch. He didn't even listen to alternative rock. Technically, it wasn't a prerequisite, but Hannah needed someone who knew their way around the pop underground. A working knowledge of Coldplay's discography wasn't going to cut it. There'd been one promising graduate student. Hannah would call her tomorrow. She didn't have any energy left to put on the act that she was okay or to pretend she wasn't crying herself to sleep every night—if she slept at all.

Hannah curled on up on the couch, pulling Binx onto her lap. He hadn't loved the long car ride, but over a week in, he was adjusting well. He lounged in front of the balcony window by day and slept by her feet at night. Binx purred, the soft vibrations of his small body offering the tiniest of comforts in their strange new habitat.

Nate had secured a two-bedroom sublet in Cambridge, with the second bedroom meant to be the headquarters of *Deafening Silence Boston*. It was nice, homey, and owned by someone who liked all types of media. The sound system was fancy and new, DVD cases lined the shelves in the living room, and video game consoles from Nintendo to PlayStation were hooked up to the television. She'd even tried her hand at *Mario Kart*. It had always helped Brian on his worst days. And these were desperate times. To her surprise, it *had* helped a little.

Hannah turned on the sound system, and Wilderness filled the space. She should've attended their anniversary show with the love of her life last week. Instead, she had spent the day unpacking, perusing intern applications, and cuddling with Binx while crying. The rest of the week had been much the same, except she'd had interns to interview and concerts to attend. With only two months in Boston, she had to hit the ground running.

The opening song reached its chorus, and Hannah leaned back against the couch, letting the music wash over her. The music she had loved for a decade both soothed and hurt her. But she wanted to feel that pain. If there was pain, then it had been real. She lay down on the couch, Binx sitting on her chest. He leaned his head into her hand, and she scratched behind his ears the way Will always had.

Will. Pain burst through her. The ache that hadn't left her chest since she'd seen the pair of them standing together throbbed now. *I love you, William.*

Why did she have to hear that? *Fucking Madison.* Madison, who wouldn't stop calling no matter how many times Hannah sent her to voicemail. Will had stopped calling two days ago. He'd left two voicemails she couldn't bring herself to listen to, and then yesterday afternoon, he'd texted her a message that broke her heart in its simplicity: *I love you, Hannah.* She still hadn't responded. She didn't know how.

A knock sounded on the door. Hannah stared at the stack of resumes on the coffee table. Had she forgotten about an interview? No, definitely not—she hadn't been *that* distracted. Her heart sped up. *Will?* It would be like him to just show up. He would see it as a grand gesture. But if he was coming to Boston to get her back, he would've been there by now.

Or maybe it was one of those pesky cable salesmen. She got up and looked through the peephole. A woman with graying brown hair and a striking resemblance to Hannah stood on the other side of the door. It couldn't be.

Hannah opened the door and found herself face-to-face with her mother. She blinked a few times, but no, she wasn't hallucinating from sleep deprivation. Her mother stood in her doorway in Boston on a Tuesday, the busiest day of her mother's week. If Hannah had ever gotten sick on a Tuesday, she'd been her dad's problem.

"Your sister is pregnant," her mother said by way of greeting.

Hannah gripped the doorknob. "I know."

"Your sister is pregnant, and you're married." Her mother looked up at her with a wry smile. "How did I get so old?"

"A twenty-two-year-old called me ma'am today," Hannah said, stepping back to let her mother in.

"Authority will do that."

They weren't a touchy-feely family, but Hannah couldn't ignore the fact that they hadn't hugged. Part of her wanted to jump into her mother's arms and cry her eyes out. Something about her mother's stance and her first words—about Stephanie—stopped her. It was exactly how she would've started a normal conversation, except that she hadn't returned a single phone call in all this time. There was nothing normal about her showing up in Boston.

"What are you doing here, Mom?"

"I could ask you the same thing," she said, picking up a picture of Hannah and Kate from the entertainment center.

Hannah counted to three in her head before answering. "I'm working."

"Where's your husband?"

"Mom."

Her mother held up her hands. "What happened, Hannah? Your father told me you two were madly in love—perfect for each other. It hasn't even been a month since you had lunch, and now you're in Boston looking like a tractor ran over you, without a single picture of the man in sight." Her mom stepped toward her and put a hand on her arm.

The simple touch had lasted no more than a few seconds, but each second had felt like an eternity. Tears welled in Hannah's eyes. She didn't want to tell her mom about Will like that. She'd wanted a happy family event, with laughter and storytelling and everyone important around her. Their love had deserved that. But after everything that had happened, Hannah didn't have that luxury.

"You can talk to me, honey." Her mother took a seat on the couch and motioned for Hannah to follow suit.

"I don't know if I can, Mom."

"Don't be ridiculous. What did you think I was going to do when you showed up at our house with a husband?"

"I don't know," Hannah said. "Not accuse me of being little more than a paid escort."

Her mother opened and closed her mouth. Hannah could hear the correction that she didn't say—*the "paid" is implied in escort, honey.*

"You've never done an impetuous thing in your life. It's just not in your nature. You're a planner. So no, I don't believe you fell in love and decided to get married in six weeks without telling anyone but Kate. And don't even try to tell me that Kate didn't know. Let's just say, for today, I accept your version of events."

It was the best she was going to get. Hannah sat down, curling her legs underneath her. Physical therapy had paid off—not that it mattered now. Telling her mom about the Will and Madison situation might help. She had years of life experience to bring to the table. But how to start? Hannah played around with several openings. Finally, noticing her mother's growing impatience, she just threw it out there. "Will and I—we got married so fast. We'd been friends for so long... but I just found out he lied about part of his past."

"Meaning?"

Hannah clasped her hands. "His ex-girlfriend cheated on him—I knew that. But he didn't tell me that the ex-girlfriend is Madison, his brother's fiancée—my soon-to-be sister-in-law."

Her mother nodded. "So, he omitted the details."

"Yes. And to make matters worse, Madison and I were friends. Or I thought we were. But I caught her telling Will she was still in love with him."

Her mother put a hand on top of hers. "What did Will have to say to that?"

"He didn't really get a chance to respond." Hannah laughed bitterly. "Their conversation ended kind of abruptly."

"What did he say when you talked to him about it?" her mother asked.

Hannah sighed. "I haven't spoken to him about it."

"At all?"

"No. I came home, got Binx, and came up here." Hannah stared down at her hands, for once not speckled with ink. Band-Aids covered three of her fingers—stupid cardboard boxes. "I couldn't talk to him then, and now, I don't know what to say to him. I feel like such an idiot."

"Sounds familiar," her mother said with a small laugh.

Hannah met her mother's gaze. "Like mother like daughter."

Her mother fidgeted on the couch beside her before straightening and wrapping Hannah's hand in her own. "In this case, I don't think that's a good thing."

Hannah wiped away the tears brimming in her eyes. This was how it should've been—not weeks of silence. "I don't know what to do."

"I think..." Her mother paused, and a battle played across her face as she decided what to say. "Did you know that Dad smoked when we first met?"

"You're kidding," Hannah said. She wasn't sure where this was going, but her mother wouldn't have handed out that information lightly.

"I knew he smoked. We ran in the same circles," she said with a shrug. "But he'd told me he quit—was quitting. And I believed him. To his credit, he never smoked around me. About a month after we got engaged, we were talking about the wedding. I joked that he was allowed the customary cigar with his brothers. He declined and said something like it hadn't even been a year since he'd last touched a cigarette."

Hannah did the math in her head. Her parents had dated for two years before they got engaged. "He lied about smoking for a year?"

"Yes, he did." Her mother put a gentle hand to Hannah's face. "Relationships are built on moments—a million moments big and small and in between. And I decided—over lots of tears and wine—that I wasn't willing to throw all those moments away over this new information. I don't think I would've left him had I found out he was still smoking, and he'd lived in a fraternity house where everyone around him smoked. I should've known. I *did* know but turned a blind eye. That's not to say I wasn't hurt. It was something we had to work past, but that's what marriage is."

"So, you think I should forgive him?"

"I think you should at the very least talk to him." Her mother sighed. "You went in knowing he had a broken heart. That much he didn't lie about. Would you have made a different choice if you'd known the identity of his ex?"

Hannah tried to reconfigure her acceptance of the pact with the knowledge that Madison was his ex. She would've had different questions, more questions. She hadn't even asked about his ex. For all she'd known, Will's ex was still in his life—perhaps a coworker at Wellington Thorne, a family friend that he had no choice but to still see. She hadn't asked.

"You'll figure it out," her mother said, patting her shoulder. Hannah sniffled. Her mother clasped her hand between her own. "You will. Just don't let your anger at Madison cloud your anger for Will. They are two different hurts. Make sure you remember that."

Hannah tucked herself into her mother's arms, her head resting on her shoulder, somehow still the perfect fit. "I'm glad you're here, Mom."

Chapter 42

Will

For Will's whole life, he'd been groomed to sit on the executive board and help run Wellington Thorne. Jon would always be the heir, destined to take over after Grayson stepped down, but Will would become his brother's trusted advisor as general counsel. When that future started to seem less likely, he'd been set adrift. Hannah had righted his world and set him back on track. She hadn't even had to try.

But after two straight days of board meetings, Will almost wished he had been barred for life. The meetings were tedious, and it had become clear in the first five minutes that Will was not going to get a word in edgewise. Jon had barely spoken, and he'd been on the board for four years. Jon and Will might be the future of Wellington Thorne, but the table of old men running the show wasn't about to let the younger generation set the pace. Not yet—and certainly not while the tension between Jon and Will was palpable.

It was usually Will glaring at Jon, but for the past two days, Jon had sat across from Will, a permanent scowl on his countenance. Will had wanted to ask him what the issue was. It should have been a welcome surprise to find Will here in his rightful place when Jon had spent so much time trying—and failing—to spend time with his younger brother. Will could guess at his brother's discomfort, but Madison couldn't have been that reckless. In telling Jon even half of the truth, she would both implicate herself and threaten the tenuous hold she had on the Thorne name.

Will walked out of the board room at the next break, stretching after hours of sitting. He felt Jon's eyes glued to his back. Even Jonathan had noticed, giving his eldest son no less than two reproachful glares in the last hour. But Will couldn't care less about Jon's turmoil and why it was directed at him. Jon certainly hadn't cared about Will's when he'd asked him to give a speech at the wedding. If Jon expected Will's marriage to magically absolve him of all his crimes, then his brother would need to get over whatever slight Will had unintentionally spun into motion.

"William. My office. Now." Jon's voice was fierce and left no room for rebuttal. Will hesitated only a moment before turning on his heels and following his brother.

Unlike Will's enclosed space with solid walls and privacy, Jon's office had glass spanning the front and did little to keep sound from slipping through into the larger office. This was a mistake. Will felt it deep in his bones. He sat down across from his brother, who paced behind his desk.

"What in the world is going on with you?" Will asked when his brother showed no sign of standing still.

Jon stopped midpace. His eyes bored into Will, fury rising behind them. He clenched his fists, and his voice when he spoke was ragged with anger. "You kissed my fiancée."

Will sprung to his feet, the fight in his fight-or-flight response winning out despite Jon's threatening stance. He clenched his hand in an imitation of his brother, his own face turning stony. Madison had finally started her war.

"Madison told me how she came to you after our fight. After she told you she was letting you go for good, you kissed her."

"And you *believed* her?" Will's voice rose at the incredulity of Jon's statement and his staunch belief that Madison, the same woman who had cheated wholeheartedly on Will, would be telling the truth.

"It's more than obvious that you still love her."

Will laughed, a cruel undertone curdling the sound. "I stopped loving her the moment I saw her wrapped around your dick. I saw her for what she was then—a liar and a whore."

He'd known his words would have an effect. He hoped it would feel like a punch to the gut and wake Jon up from his blind love of a woman who didn't know how to love him or possibly anyone. But when Jon's fist connected with his face, Will was caught by surprise. He put a hand to his cheek. Nothing was broken, but it was still tender. He stepped back from his brother's rage.

"You're such an ungrateful pissant," Jon said, also taking a step back. "I backed you with Grayson so you could get your seat on the board. We kept your stupid secret from Hannah. Madison even became her friend, fixed her knee, put her in our fucking wedding. Madison did everything you asked even though it hurt her. She felt we owed you after everything."

"You do owe me, you asshole." The words spilled from Will. "You stole my life."

"Boys!" Jonathan's sharp voice caught both of their attention.

Will came back to reality—they were doing this at Wellington Thorne, in a glass box. They knew better. But he didn't care anymore. "You took everything from me," he said, his voice rising. He grabbed Jon by the lapels and pushed him back against his desk.

"William," Jonathan hissed.

Will ignored his father. He wasn't hiding for the sake of the company or appearances—today or ever again.

"Madison and I were together for years. *Years*. You knew how I felt about her. You helped me pick out her engagement ring. And all the while, you were fucking her behind my back. And you're not even sorry about it. Not once have you expressed one regret about throwing our entire relationship away. Did you ever stop to think what your affair would do to me? To us? To this family?"

Will glanced at his father, finding him stone-faced and immovable. He didn't seem to care that his sons were in pain. He'd never cared for a second. Will turned back to his brother, whose anger had faded to a pain he was all too familiar with.

"I didn't kiss your fiancée," he said wanly. "She came to my room uninvited on our old anniversary and told me she still loved me. *She* ruined *my* marriage."

Will's voice rose on the last sentence, and as he reached for his brother to shake some sense into him, Jonathan stepped between them. "Now is not the time for this, William."

Will shook his head. There would never be a time for it. Not in the Thorne family. They weathered the storm—they didn't chase it. But this storm would never pass.

With a final withering look at his family, Will walked out of the office, stopping on the threshold for the briefest of moments. "Consider this my resignation."

Chapter 43

Hannah

Hannah watched her intern, Camila, skip down the street to her car from the window of her apartment. She'd never met anyone as happy as Camila, especially not someone who also loved emo and punk rock. But Camilla was like that every time Hannah had seen her in the few days since being officially hired. That morning, she had shown up with Starbucks in hand, having already memorized Hannah's order. They had worked through lunch, trying to cover the top three finishers from the Battle of the Bands they'd attended the night before. Camila had taken the runner-up, her favorite of the three and a band she'd seen more than once around the city. Hannah had decided to let her off early to get her weekend started after all her hard work.

Once Camila reached her car, Hannah returned to her desk and opened a blank document. She checked the clock. It was nearing two in the afternoon. Hannah didn't know the nap schedule at Riley's house, but this seemed like the usual time. Still, she shot Riley a text just in case. God help anyone who called and woke the girls. Riley hadn't left a message when she'd called during Camila's interview. Camila was good—raw but talented. She'd be a great asset to *Deafening Silence Boston* if she wanted to stay on.

Hannah rolled out her yoga mat and fell into Forward Fold, shaking the tension from her arms. Two Sun Salutations later, Hannah's phone rang. Riley's voice came through, abnormally high pitched. "Are you sitting down?"

Hannah stepped back into standing from her Downward-Facing Dog and then sat cross-legged. "I am now."

"We have a cover article for you." The pause between Riley's sentences was weighted, and Hannah sat there for what felt like forever before Riley continued. "Leonard Nulty has granted us an exclusive for the Boston launch."

Hannah gripped her phone. "What?"

"Surprise!"

Holy. Shit.

"Are you there?" Riley asked, laughing.

"When?" Hannah croaked. She could barely breathe. This was *everything*. Already, the panic was setting in. Leonard was notoriously awful to interview. He gave dry answers without room for follow-up questions. His music was personal enough, so in interviews, he kept to the basics. But an *exclusive*? He'd never—to her knowledge—granted anyone an exclusive.

"Later next week. I'll email you the details."

"Okay," she said, barely able to get the word out. She had an exclusive with Leonard Nulty. *Holy shit.*

"Hannah?"

"Yes?"

"Breathe." Riley hung up.

Hannah pulled her laptop down onto the floor with her and stared at the empty Word document. She was supposed to be writing an article about... Hannah's mind went blank. Who cared about whichever no-name band she'd just interviewed? She had an exclusive with Leonard Nulty. She had to call Will. The thought came to her unbridled before she could stop it. She'd heard her mother's advice loud and clear, but she still hadn't found the strength to call him. She would. Soon. But when she did, it had to be about him, and right now, it wouldn't be.

Hannah FaceTimed Kate from her laptop instead. She stretched a leg out in front of her and folded over herself. Both her legs straightened under the pressure.

Kate picked up on the third ring. She sat at her desk and held a steaming cup. She was bundled in a cowl-neck sweater that Hannah knew was paired with those brown riding boots they'd found on super clearance right after Christmas.

"Hey, Bostonite."

"I'm a New Yorker, remember?"

Kate laughed. "One who lives in Boston."

Hannah smiled. She missed their Kate-and-Hannah banter. She missed Kate and Hannah. Between wedding planning and the Thornes, Hannah had spent most of her free time with Madison, and when she'd seen Kate, it had almost always been as part of the trio they'd been becoming. Anger boiled under the surface, and she shook the thought of Madison from her head.

Kate's eyes shifted from Hannah's face to her legs, and she nodded approvingly. "It's nice to see you with both legs on the ground."

"I'm interviewing Leonard Nulty next week." The words flew from her mouth in an excited yelp.

"Holy shit."

Hannah laughed. "That's what I said."

"I'm so proud of you." She paused, and Hannah could already anticipate her next question. "Are you going to tell Will?"

Hannah nodded. "Yes, I just... I don't know what to do about him yet."

"Answering his calls would be a start."

Hannah met her best friend's eyes through the screen. "Do you think he still has feelings for Madison?"

Kate sighed. "If you're asking me if I think something is going on between Will and Madison, then no, I don't. He loves you and only you. That said, of course he still has feelings about her. Wouldn't you?"

The words weighed on her heart with their truth. Madison, Will, Jon, and even Hannah would always be bound to each other once Madison became a Thorne. Hannah had separated her anger with Madison from her issues with Will as her mother had suggested, but even so, they were tangled together irrevocably.

Kate met her eyes through the camera, her expression gentle and sympathetic. "You trusted him enough to marry him. You need to trust him now."

Levelheaded and sound advice—exactly what she'd expected and needed from Kate. Hannah opened her mouth to respond but found Kate staring down at her phone, her expression twisted with concern.

"What's wrong?" Hannah asked, her heart rate ticking up a beat.

"I just got a text from Madison."

The words slammed into Hannah, denting the armor she'd built. "You're still talking to Madison?"

Kate gave her an incredulous look as if to say that wasn't the point before her expression softened. Hannah could almost feel the hand that would've been on her shoulder if they were face-to-face. "Hannah," Kate said, "according to Madison, Will's in the hospital."

Hannah was on her feet in an instant, looking for her phone. If Will was in the hospital, someone would've told her—someone other than Madison.

"She's lying to get my attention," Hannah said, grabbing her phone from her desk. Kate responded, but Hannah couldn't hear anything over the buzzing of her phone. Her vision narrowed, fixing on the contact flashing across her screen—*Daniel*.

Chapter 44

Hannah

Traffic was mercifully sparse on the drive back to New York, only picking up when she neared the city. She'd made it from Boston to New York in incredibly good time for a Friday, and Daniel had promised to keep Will held up with tests and observations until she arrived. Will would be annoyed at being detained at the hospital for hours over a fainting spell, assuming Daniel's account of Will's incident was accurate. At least they hadn't called an ambulance.

Hannah stared up at the emergency room entrance, her phone clenched in her hand. She'd never been so thankful for an intern as she was for Camila, who'd agreed to cover all shows for the weekend and take care of Binx—all free of charge. Whoever took over in Boston had better hire Camila full-time. Hannah would have to talk to Riley about it.

Hannah spotted Daniel waiting for her outside the secure entryway.

"He's fine," Daniel said, giving her a hug. "I think he had a panic attack and then fainted. Grayson overreacted."

"What was he doing?"

Daniel's eyes shifted to his hands. "He was in a private meeting with our uncle. Things have been a bit tense this week."

She wanted to ask more questions, but it was clear that Daniel was planning on protecting Will's privacy on the matter. She followed him through the door to the ER and attempted to prepare herself. It was no use. Seeing Will would shake loose everything she'd been keeping in, and seeing him again for the first time in a hospital bed wasn't going to help.

Daniel pulled back the curtain on E10, a space tucked into the back corner of the room. Will looked up with contempt in his eyes and a complaint on his lips, but when his gaze panned to Hannah, he clamped his jaw shut.

A pain—both sharp and dull—settled in her stomach. He looked ashen and crushed. A fading bruise crested his cheekbone. Gone was the brightness that was innately Will's.

"I told him not to call you," Will said as Daniel removed his IV. Will's voice was rusty with disuse, and the gentleness he always used in his words with her was replaced by an unfamiliar sharpness. He didn't look at her. He kept his face downcast, watching Daniel's hand work at the tape marks on his arm.

Daniel's brow furrowed, and he ran a finger over the puncture site. "I told you not to play with your IV. This is going to bruise."

"Can I go now?"

Daniel nodded. "Let me print out your paperwork."

Will chafed at his brother's words.

"Ten minutes max, William."

Will lay back on his small hospital bed, a hand over his face. Hannah stood awkwardly, equally afraid to say something and stay silent. Had she done this to him?

"Are you okay?"

"You shouldn't have come." Even muffled by his arm, his statement was more than clear.

"I'm your wife. Of course I came." She kept her voice steady, but she felt shaky all the same. After two weeks of silence, she hadn't known what to expect, but it wasn't this.

He looked at her now, his face drawn and cynical. "We both know *wife* doesn't mean what it should."

Ouch. Someone was on the warpath.

"It still means something to me."

He shrugged. "You being my wife didn't seem to matter two weeks ago when you walked away."

Hannah crossed her arms. The middle of Daniel's ER was not the place for this conversation. "I'm invoking Rule 5."

Whatever response Will was trying to elicit from her, he hadn't planned for that. Hannah could literally see the effect on him as his face scrunched in consternation. He knew what Rule 5 was. *Our friendship is the most important thing. No matter what, we stay friends.*

WILL SORTED THROUGH his keys, his fingers finally settling on the one he wanted. He unlocked the apartment door and pushed it open without ceremony. Stale air greeted them. He had given little explanation as to why they couldn't go back to the penthouse on the drive downtown. Hannah wanted to push the topic, an uncomfortable seed of worry rooting in her, but his mood had only slightly improved since the hospital. Instead, she had sat with her hands in her lap as they drove into Tribeca. There was so much to be said, but fighting with him then seemed like an awful idea, and she didn't want to send him back to the hospital with a second panic attack.

"Welcome to my apartment," Will said, stepping aside so she could enter the space.

She knew it was going to be fancy after seeing the lobby, but the sheer beauty amazed her. She couldn't even fathom what he must pay for a space like this. A pang of jealousy ran through her. She would've loved living here instead of the penthouse. Binx would have never moved away from the floor-to-ceiling windows gracing the living room. The furnishings were patently Will, more so than anything she'd seen at the penthouse. Had any of it been his?

Will shuffled around in the kitchen. "Do you want something to drink? I asked Clara to restock the place last week, so I'm sure there's wine."

"You moved back in?" she asked, picking up a figurine. A similar one had adorned Madison's dresser in her apartment with Jon.

"No, I'm staying with Daniel right now, but I can't do that forever. And despite what you may think, I can't afford two rent payments." Will offered her a glass of red wine and placed a water for himself down on the table. Annoyance came off him in waves. He didn't want to be here. She couldn't blame him for feeling that way, but this was his fault.

She picked up a family photo, spotting Madison in the mix. Madison sat on his lap near the beach. Her arms curved around his neck. Jon and Daniel stood behind them, arms slung casually over each other's shoulders. Will looked different—younger, happier. There was a light expression on his face that she hadn't seen on him since college. The truth of his relationship slammed into her more than it had after Madison's profession of love.

"How could you not tell me?" she asked, anger backing her words despite her earlier resolve to avoid an argument.

Will took a sip of his water and looked up at her calmly through his eyelashes. "So much for Rule 5."

"Rule 5 doesn't mean we can't argue," Hannah said sharply. "It means we can't be cruel about it, which was exactly what you were being at the hospital."

"Says the wife who—"

Hannah pinned him with a death glare.

Will held up his hands in supplication. "I wanted to tell you, but then Madison was your friend—"

"Madison was not my friend!" The only thing she was certain of in all of this was that Madison was not, and never had been, her friend. "Friends don't tell friends' husbands they are in love with them."

"Hannah."

"I deserved to know that she was your ex-girlfriend."

"And I deserved a chance to explain before you simply moved out, but here we are," he said, his tone turning icy. "What good would've come from you knowing about Madison? You never would've let her help you through PT. Every family event would've been completely awkward. We still would've been forced to be around them."

"Exactly!" she exclaimed, her hands flying frantically above her. "I wouldn't be friends with someone who is in love with my husband. With someone who has the gall to declare that love despite the ridiculous triangle—square—or whatever we're all in now."

A hint of a smile played on Will's face despite the circumstances. "I promise you there's no square." She watched him battle with his own memories and frustrations before he looked her directly in the eyes. "I love *you*."

His words were slowly snaking their way into her, but she wasn't ready to acquiesce. She couldn't. "Then you should've told me."

"I know that."

She stepped closer to him, still maintaining a safe distance from any chance contact. "Tell me now."

He stared at her for too long and then took a breath. "I dated Madison for three years before everything happened. And when I found out about Jon, things got complicated..." Will paused, and it felt like a hole had been punched through her.

"Complicated how?"

He palmed his face before looking up at her resignedly. "She used to call me for sex. It only happened once. Right after everything happened with her and Jon. Months before I proposed to you."

Hannah sat down on the couch, afraid her feet wouldn't support her as a fresh onslaught of tears spilled down her cheeks. "Did you use me to get her out of your system? To get revenge on them? Was that what this whole pact was about?"

"No. It was never about revenge or cleansing. You know... I've made it more than clear how I feel about you, how I've always felt about you."

"Then why?" She couldn't keep the whine out of her voice. If he'd just told her, they wouldn't be here. They'd be happy and in New York. They'd be together.

"The last nine months of my life have been hell. You are the only bright spot in all of it. My girlfriend cheated on me with my brother for a year. I've had to support them through all these wedding events, put a smile on my face, and laugh at stupid jokes his friends make. Jon asked me to give a speech—a *fucking* wedding speech—to smooth things over." He closed his eyes, a pained expression coming over him. "You were the one person in my life who didn't look at me with complete pity. I couldn't lose that."

Her pain at Will's betrayal was mirrored in his eyes but a thousand times worse. She reached across the table and wrapped a hand around his. Warmth seeped through. It would be so easy to let this pass, but they needed to work through it, not around it. She had to know the truth. "Do you still love her?"

"No." He walked around the table and came to sit next to her. Her senses awakened at his closeness, and she breathed in his scent as he wiped a tear off her cheek. "If you believe anything I said, believe that nothing is going on with Madison, and I don't want there to be. You are my future. I love you, Hannah."

The memory of who Will Thorne had been to her—the last boy she'd truly trusted—was tarnished. Trust was why she'd agreed to marry him—her perfect boy. But the man standing in front of her wasn't perfect. He was flawed and broken, and she had fallen in love with him, wholly. She couldn't walk away from him any more than she could go back to being just friends. "I love you too."

Chapter 45
Will

Tell me about Madison. It had been a simple request, but Will hadn't expected it. He wasn't sure how detailing his history with Madison was going to help either party, but if she wanted to know, he'd tell her everything. Had they been deeply in love? Yes. Had he planned to marry her? Yes. Did he know she was still harboring feelings for him? *Hell* no.

Hannah had peppered him with questions throughout the morning. Over a perfectly enjoyable cuddle session, she'd asked how they'd met—at a townie party in the Hamptons over MLK Jr. weekend. During an episode of *Scrubs*, she'd inquired about the state of their relationship when things started with Jon—totally and perfectly normal. They'd just gotten back from a ten-day trip to Wellington Thorne's newest island resort. Ten minutes ago, she'd wanted to know if Madison had ever explained why Jon happened in the first place. He could only guess at this, but something always told him it had to do with Madison's thirtieth birthday and the lack of an engagement ring on her finger. Though how exactly an affair was supposed to help with that problem, he couldn't say.

He stretched his arm across the back of the couch. The unease he'd first felt over returning to the apartment dissipated the longer he was there with Hannah. Madison no longer hid in every corner. A story didn't unfold from simple objects. Still, it would never be solely his, and he would be happy to give it up at the end of his lease. Despite her admiration of the apartment, he could tell Hannah didn't love being here either, particularly after the way she'd eyed the bed last night as if she wished to set it on fire.

Hannah rested her head against his shoulder—perhaps that meant no more questions. He relaxed for the moment. They were almost through *Garden State,* a movie Will hadn't watched in nearly a decade and that Hannah swore by. Somehow that didn't surprise him. On-screen, Zach Braff, Natalie Portman, and Peter Sarsgaard stared down a landfill and lamented the poor guy who had to argue for the right to destroy a natural phenomenon.

That had literally been his job for years. Fighting for the right to build hotels wherever they wanted. Reading the reports, advising on the costs, ignoring the hole the job was ripping through his soul every time he read about relocating the flora and fauna. But not anymore.

"I quit Wellington Thorne yesterday."

She bolted upright, her eyes panicked. "You can't."

"It's done." The words terrified him. But for the first time in his life, he felt the chain that bound him to the Thorne name and all that came with it loosening, breaking. He could be free with a few more strategic tugs on that poor, deteriorating connection. The thought sent a spike of panic through him, as it had yesterday in Grayson's office when his uncle had looked at him squarely and asked if he knew what he was doing.

"What will do you now?" Hannah asked, surprise and concern mixing in her voice.

He took her hand in his and met her gaze. "Kiss you."

"Will," she said, staving off his advances and scooting to the far end of the couch.

He laughed. "I'm still William Thorne, one of the best corporate environmental lawyers in New York, Wellington Thorne or no Wellington Thorne. I'll make some calls. With any luck, I'll soon be on the partner track at a small firm, still practicing corporate environmental law."

Hannah nodded as if that sounded exactly right. He loved that she knew it did.

"I have some news, too, actually," she said, a tentative smile on her face. "We got an exclusive for the inaugural issue."

Will didn't even have to go through the list of Boston-based artists. There was only one who would have Hannah unnerved, but he would play along because this was her moment. "Really? Who?"

"I'm interviewing Leonard Nulty next week," she said, a giant smile brightening her features. "When I think about it, I can't even breathe."

His wife had arrived. Editor in chief of *Deafening Silence Boston* and an exclusive with the illusive Leonard Nulty himself. "Congratulations."

She shrugged. "I didn't really do anything."

"But you will." He squeezed one of the feet resting in his lap, the only part of her he could easily reach. "Maybe I should make some calls to firms in Boston?"

It was a Hail Mary. They were barely over their argument and in no place to talk about big moves. Without the legally binding marriage between them, Hannah might not have come back, Rule 5 be damned. It tethered them to this relationship as much as their feelings did. But if she'd have him, he wanted her to know he was all in.

"Boston is a beautiful city, but I don't think I could live there indefinitely. I love living in New York. I loved Queens—a city outside the city, you know? But I've always pictured myself in a brownstone in Murray Hill. Or maybe in Long Island City with a view of the river?"

"So you are, in fact, a New Yorker?"

"I guess so," she said with a small, contented smile. "Not that I could ever afford to live in either of those areas."

"If we hock your engagement ring, we could piece together a down payment." Murray Hill and Long Island City were less expensive than the places he'd lived before, but Hannah wasn't exactly making bank at *Deafening*. Maybe he could make it happen—he would have to do something since he would officially be homeless in the next few months.

"Was... was it supposed to be Madison's?" Her voice stuck on the name.

Will stopped the mental calculations in his head and caught up to her line of thinking. "No. I sold Madison's ring and bought this much bigger one when I decided I was going to initiate the pact. I figured the bigger the better. It might sway your decision."

"It didn't. Actually..." She paused. "The ring itself didn't entice me to marry you, but the fact that you had a ring—and quite a large one—made me think you were serious about the whole thing."

He glanced down at her left hand. Her wedding band adorned her ring finger with its simple, classic perfection. "Is that why you hardly ever wear it? Because you thought it was meant for someone else?"

She bit her bottom lip. "Partly... yes. After I had the wedding band, which I knew you bought for me specifically—and it's so perfect—pairing it with the engagement ring made it feel more fake. And then as we became us, it was this reminder that you were supposed to marry someone else."

"Maybe I wasn't," he said, leaning in until their foreheads touched. He tangled his fingers in her hair. "Maybe that's the whole point to all of this. Maybe I was meant to be with you."

"You're such a hopeless romantic."

"You love it," he said, sitting back against the couch.

Hannah smiled, but her mind seemed elsewhere. She worried at her bottom lip. "I've been thinking."

"A dangerous pastime."

She rolled her eyes but played along. "I know."

She paused and then took a breath as if deciding she was going through with whatever she had to say. He steeled himself for her next words.

"I think you should tell Jon what happened," she said, meeting his gaze. "You keep things from people to try and protect them, but they still get hurt. I got hurt."

Will opened his mouth to tell her about the argument with Jon, but she put a finger to his lips to keep him quiet.

"And the thing is, I don't know why you didn't tell me. I would've married you anyway. I could've helped you deal with the fallout instead of—"

"Jon knows," he said, cutting her off. He motioned to the bruise on his face. Hannah's eyes widened, but she didn't say anything. He kissed her cheek, the first time his lips came in contact with her since before Madison's confession. "I'm sorry I hurt you. It was the last thing I wanted."

"I know," she said, her eyes open and questioning.

He kissed her then on the lips, hesitantly, afraid she might reject him. But she deepened the kiss, parting his lips with her own. He pulled her onto his lap, his hands sliding up the back of her top. She leaned into him before pulling his shirt off. With each caress, he felt himself heal. Hannah's tears flavored their kisses, and he knew she was healing too. And in the final moments, with his name on Hannah's lips, his heart sewed itself back together.

Chapter 46
Hannah

Hannah sat down on the couch with a steaming cup of coffee and her laptop. Will had gone out to pick up breakfast. She'd asked to stay behind to do some work. The thought of being alone in this apartment that showed the reality of Madison and Will's past wasn't one she relished, but she needed a Will-free moment. Hannah wasn't naïve enough to think that one argument and make-up sex was going to fix their relationship. That would take time, which was a luxury they didn't currently have. She was due back in Boston the next morning to cover a show the following night. Regardless, Hannah couldn't deny the tug on her heart—she wanted to be with Will. They needed to adjust to their new normal, to rediscover exactly who they were—in general and to each other—starting by getting through the next few weeks apart. It pained her to think about leaving Will again, but she wouldn't ask him to come. He needed to stay in New York to put his life back together.

She couldn't regret her rash decision to relocate—she was interviewing Leonard Nulty after all. *But shit*—it messed everything up. The assignment would most likely be shorter than expected with the Nulty exclusive since they wouldn't need as much padding. Even so, she wasn't enjoying the experience as much as she expected to. She had taken for granted sharing the ups and downs of her life with Kate every day, of Will waiting up no matter what time she rolled in. Hannah had her dream job, but at what cost?

Boston wasn't pressing pause on a relationship. Madison's revelation had threatened more than a break-up. *Divorce.* She repeated it in her head. *Divorce.* That's what they were facing if this didn't work out. And not because of a fight or a misunderstanding or because the year on their pact was up. It would be because they didn't put in the effort to make things right. There would be no coming back from that.

For the first time, Hannah appreciated what it was Riley did every day for the last five years—how she balanced everything, never letting any of the responsibilities she juggled fall. Hannah could do this. She would channel Riley and learn how to do it all—fix her marriage and kick ass at managing this launch. She would live the dream and keep her life in New York. Somehow.

A ding from her computer brought her attention back to her task. Journalists didn't get weekends, and her inbox was brimming with messages.

The message was from Riley. *Subject: Boston Things.*

Well, then.

Hannah scrolled through the large email chain Riley had forwarded—because it wasn't awkward reading through other people's emails. Hannah scrolled through the information about her schedule with Leonard. He had his photo shoot in the morning, and they would do their interview after lunch. She made a mental note to bring wine. At least it was a short rider. She continued scanning the email. *Boring, boring, amusing, boring, bor—*

Hannah reread the next line: *Everything should be charged to the Boston account. Use code 5479-JT.*

She stared at the words on the screen. No charge code she'd ever used had had "JT" attached to it. NYC, BK, QN, SI, LI, and BX sure, but those were obviously the boroughs. *JT.* Her heart hammered as her mind wrapped itself around those initials. *Jonathan Thorne?* It made perfect sense. There'd been a large anonymous donation right after she and Will had wowed all of Jonathan's party guests. They had convinced everyone they were in love, and Jonathan had needed to make a move. She closed her eyes, willing away the knowledge that Jonathan Thorne had funded the Boston edition.

Riley, her mentor and friend, hadn't told her. Had that been why she'd gotten the call? Hannah *was* the most senior person at *Deafening* under Riley, not in title or responsibility but in time on staff. She'd been there since day twenty-three. But Riley had never mentioned growth like this before. Hannah had never considered that she was being groomed to run another edition of the magazine. She was always going to be a step under Riley. When she'd been offered the position, it had made staying at *Deafening* worth it. It had been the big payoff. What if it hadn't been about her at all? Hannah couldn't believe that. Riley wouldn't do that—not to her. But what if she had?

Hannah picked up her phone. She had no idea if she planned to call Will, Riley, or Jonathan himself, but she needed to do something with this information. Maybe she shouldn't start with Will. Things were so tenuous between them, and the fact that his father was still meddling in his life would break him. At the same time, she couldn't keep it from him. The lies were getting them nowhere.

A key sounded in the door. Hannah looked over her shoulder to see if Will needed help with the bags. He always over-bought when on his own. The blood froze in her veins at the sight of Madison in the entryway, a set of keys dangling from her left hand. She still had keys.

"What are you doing here?" Hannah asked, even though the answer was written all over Madison's ridiculously calm face.

"I came to see how William was doing," she said plainly.

"He's fine, no thanks to you." Hannah stood up and faced Madison head-on. She had gotten the full story about Will and Jon's fight the night before. The depths that Madison stooped to were beyond Hannah's understanding.

Madison didn't react, except to shrug out of her coat. "I'm surprised you came back."

"He's my husband," Hannah said incredulously. "I was never permanently gone."

Madison pulled a face. "I think maybe you were."

"Get out," Hannah said, anger coursing through her.

"You can't kick me out of *my* apartment." Madison stepped further inside and dropped her coat on a nearby chair. The door was still open behind her, but it was clear she wasn't planning on honoring Hannah's demand.

"It's Will's apartment." Hannah walked around the couch, effectively blocking Madison from gaining more ground.

Madison held up her hands placatingly. "It doesn't have to be like this."

"You attempted to destroy my marriage. So yes, it has to be like this."

"I'm done apologizing," Madison said. "I called you dozens of times. I begged and cried and tried to explain."

God, Hannah didn't want to fight. Yet oh, how she wanted to. She'd avoided Madison, but here she was—front and center—asking for it. Except all the words had fled from Hannah's mind. All the pretend conversations and mean things she'd planned to say faded away. "Have you tried apologizing to your fiancé? Or to Will? Don't you think you've messed their lives up enough? To go back and do more damage—"

"Why does it matter?" Madison's voice rose, and the words came out almost as a screech. "He picked you. He *married* you."

"This isn't just about Will! You betrayed *me*! We were friends. I let you into my life, and you tried to steal my husband."

"I loved him first," she said, her voice quiet.

It was that simple to Madison. Hannah was expendable—Will, apparently, was not. Hannah shook her head. "That doesn't mean you have permission to mess up his life."

"*Me?*" Madison's face turned cruel. "What about *you?*"

"What *about* me?"

"Do you think I didn't know about you? Hannah from college—the one who got away." Madison made a disgusted face. "The pinnacle that every other woman was held to. You messed up Will's life long before I came around. And then you marry him when he's at his lowest. Maybe if you'd taken more than two seconds before hopping into his bed, you might have known who I was from the beginning, and maybe you would've thought twice about making a complicated situation worse."

"It shouldn't have been complicated!" Hannah said. "You made your choice the moment you kissed Jon. Leave Will alone. Go be a Thorne or don't, but stop trying to act like any of this is hard for you. You destroyed a family, Madison."

"Jon kissed *me*," she said plainly.

"And you kissed him back. You lied to both of them—cheated on both of them. You pretended to be my friend." Hannah shook with frustration. How did Madison not feel the magnitude of what she'd done—to the Thornes and to Hannah? "Do you even remember how to tell the truth?"

Madison's mouth flattened into a thin line. "How's this for truth? You're in love with a boy who doesn't exist anymore. And when you realize the man you married isn't your precious college crush, you'll leave him."

Hannah shook her head. "I'm not going anywhere. I love Will, and he loves me, here and now. And even if that weren't true, he will never love you again."

"I want to see him," Madison said, her voice a low growl.

"Madison?" Will stood in the doorway, a reusable shopping bag in each hand. He looked from Madison to Hannah and back again, his face paling. "What are you doing here?"

She had the audacity to look hurt as she picked up her coat. "I wanted to make sure Jon didn't mangle your face." She reached out as if to touch Will's bruise.

Will backed away from her. "You shouldn't be here."

Madison frowned as her gaze, blazing with anger, passed between the two of them. She started to respond, but Will cut her off.

"I'll need that key back," he said, holding out his hand.

Hannah waited for the backlash, but Madison simply unhooked the key from the ring and shoved it into Will's hand. She brushed past him and turned to look at them when she reached the threshold. The look she fixed on Hannah was one of such hatred that Hannah wondered how Madison had ever appeared to be her friend.

"Madison," Hannah said, her anger reaching the tipping point. "I'll get the RSVP in the mail for your records, but we won't be able to make the wedding."

Will shut the door before Madison could reply. From inside the apartment, they could hear her stomping down the stairs.

Rage ran through Hannah's veins down to her toes and up to her fingers. She wanted to throw something. She wanted to chase after Madison and shake some sense into her. The affable woman she'd known this whole time was gone. Hannah counted to ten in her head before loosening her grip on her cell phone—the outline of it was scored into her palm.

"I'm sorry," Will said, pulling Hannah into an embrace. "I didn't realize she still had a key."

"I'm fine, Will. Really."

"You're crying."

Hannah stepped away from his embrace, swiping at her tears. "I'm going to take a walk."

Chapter 47

Hannah

Thirty minutes and one impromptu jog through downtown later, Hannah found herself in front of Will's building again. Her head was clearer, and she'd shaken off the specter of Will and Madison's past. She had to tell Will about his father's investment. He'd already freed himself from Wellington Thorne and its shackles to his family. Maybe the news wouldn't hit as hard as it might've two weeks ago.

"Hey," Will said as soon as she walked in the door. He stood up in greeting. "Are you feeling better?"

She slid into his arms, coat and all. "I am."

"Good." He led her into the kitchen, taking her coat and hat as she shucked off her layers.

She could feel the tingle in her cheeks as the warmth of the apartment came into contact with her cold skin. She shivered.

"Here." Will thrust a mug of coffee toward her. She noted the logo of Madison's alma mater on it before taking a sip. "Oh, Clara brought your mail when she was here last week."

Hannah nodded and shuffled through the small stack. Clara had taken time to sort out Jonathan's mail and the daily mailers that flooded their mailbox each week. The menial task and the coffee would help calm Hannah further, and then she would tell him about the donation.

She stopped on a letter addressed to her. Her stomach turned over as she read the return address. Mail from her landlord was never good and usually resulted in her rent being increased by some exorbitant percentage.

Hannah scanned the letter—*ten-day notice, lease violation, unauthorized subtenant, termination of tenancy*. This was not happening. She flipped the envelope over to find the postmark dated two weeks ago. Had she been evicted? If so, where was her stuff? She crumpled the letter in her hand.

"Will," she called, even though he was sitting across from her at the table. Panic rose in her voice. "Does this mean what I think it means?"

Will took the wrinkled letter from her and scanned it. His expression darkened as he read. "Dammit."

"What happened?"

He held out a halting hand. "Your landlord found out about the sublet somehow. Maybe something broke, or there was a complaint. Did your landlord call you at all?"

Hannah thought of her neighbors. She couldn't imagine them complaining unless the person had been awfully loud. The older couple next door did not like loud neighbors. "No, but my landlord is always in the building, and the super lives there. And we have a doorman."

"Right—someone probably told your landlord that you haven't been around for a few months." He stopped. "Subletting isn't allowed in all leases, but as long as there are no major issues and the rent gets paid, people tend to look the other way."

She followed his train of thought with a sinking feeling. "We violated the lease?"

He picked up the envelope and cursed under his breath. "Technically, yes, but it should've been no different than if you'd let a friend crash for a few months. Everything was still in your name. You still paid all the bills."

Panic bubbled in her chest. "Can we fight it? Or pay a fine or something?"

Will pulled a face. "Possibly. It depends on how badly your landlord wants you out of the building. Is it really worth it?"

Something in Hannah cracked. All that anger and resentment and fear she had yet to sort through from the past few weeks mixed with Madison and Jonathan and Will's god-awful apartment. She had trusted him when he said it would be fine. Kate had backed him up. They both told her nothing would go wrong. But something *had* gone wrong.

As if sensing her panic, Will reached out and stroked her arm. "Hannah, it's fine. I'll call the landlord. We'll get it figured out."

Hannah jerked away. "I needed that apartment. I can barely afford the prices in Queens, and now no one good will want to rent to me. We can't all quit our jobs and not have to worry about keeping a roof over our heads. Our home is gone, this apartment is tainted, and now *my* apartment, which I worked so hard for, is being ripped away from me." She slammed her hands down on the coffee table. "Do you have *any* idea how hard it is to find a decent pet-friendly apartment in this city? One that a journalist can afford? If this"—she motioned between the two of them—"doesn't work out, I'll have nowhere to go."

"You mean *when*."

Hannah froze. All the energy drained out of her. Those words and thoughts and fears hadn't been for Will's ears. They weren't for anyone but Hannah to pine over in the middle of the night alone in Boston.

She met his gaze. "What?"

"You meant *when* this doesn't work out, right?" He took a step back. "You need your apartment. Why? Because you can't get past the Madison thing? Or because you never thought we'd make it a year?"

"That's not what I said."

"It is *exactly* what you said."

"It's not what I meant. That's not how I feel."

He held his hands up, stopping her advances. "I think that *is* how you feel."

"Will, don't." She wanted to put as much energy into her denial as she'd put into the vitriol she'd spouted at him, but she felt helpless. The last weeks had taken everything from her. And now they were taking Will. She couldn't stop it. She'd said those things, and a part of her—no matter how small—had meant them.

He picked up his phone and keys from the table. "I've got to go."

She grabbed his arm. "Please. I didn't mean it. It's just—"

"No," Will said, his expression completely closed off. "Whatever you're about to say, whatever excuse you're trying to make, I don't want to hear it. Not right now."

She released his arm and wrapped herself in a hug. "Where are you going?"

"I'll be at Daniel's."

"Please don't do this."

He reached for her but then seemingly thought better of it. "Be safe in Boston."

The door closed behind him. Hannah stood there for a long while, watching that closed door. It should've opened again. That was how these things worked. The guy always turned around and came back or was waiting on the other side of the door. But this was real life, and Will was gone.

Chapter 48
Hannah

Will was gone. Hannah had climbed into his bed two hours ago and hadn't moved since. She swallowed a sob as a fresh waterfall of tears wet her pillow. Their fight ran through her mind on repeat. It wasn't just that she'd voiced doubts—of course, she'd had doubts—but she'd been cruel. They'd bound their lives without thoughts of the consequences or how they fit together. But they'd risen above it, and for a few blissful weeks, it was perfect. The last two weeks in Boston had illuminated how reckless they'd been. Coming back to New York had reinforced that idea, but it also showed Hannah that she was in this relationship for better or worse. If she walked away, she would do so with regrets. She never wanted to regret Will Thorne.

Hannah pulled her phone back out. She knew better than to call Will, though she itched to do so. It had taken him being admitted to the ER for her to answer his calls—she could give him one night. They'd still be married in the morning. There was, however, one thing she did have to do—call Riley. Maybe she'd gotten the assignment as a stipulation of Jonathan's money. Maybe not. Either way, the Nulty interview had to be perfect—to prove them right or to prove them wrong.

Riley answered on the second ring. "Good timing. Danny's got Cee in the bath, and Jo is in a milk coma."

"Which means I have like three minutes before someone is screaming?"

"Ninety seconds, if we're lucky."

Hannah paused, bolstering her confidence. "Were you going to tell me that my father-in-law was the backer for *Boston*?"

"What? How... *oh my god*, I'm such an ass. It was in the chain, wasn't it?" Riley's voice took on a weepy edge.

Crap. Hannah hadn't prepared for the baby blues. "Is that why you picked me?"

"No. Oh, Hannah, no." Riley's voice cracked. There was no doubt about the tears coming. Her boss might even be full-on crying. "How can you even...? No. You were my first thought when I heard about it, and that never wavered. I told Nate it was yours if you wanted it. He didn't even tell me who the backer was at first—probably for that exact reason."

Hannah breathed easy for the first time in hours. It *had* been about her. But there was still the matter of how it looked. "People are going to talk."

"Fuck 'em," Riley said, her voice suddenly firm.

"Riles."

"I'm serious. You didn't ask your father-in-law to support our magazine. And anyone who questions your right to run the Boston edition can have a little chat with me. The New York office wouldn't be where it is today without you. You are the only one who knows how to start a magazine, because you did it with me five years ago. Even though your beat is Long Island, you have the most covers of anyone on staff. That isn't happenstance, and it isn't favoritism."

Okay, she was going to cry too. *Dammit.*

Riley sniffled. "You are the *only* one I trusted with this assignment."

Hannah wiped at the tears brimming her eyes. Riley had always been her champion, but she'd never had to champion for her before. "Thank you for believing in me."

"Always." There was a weighted pause between them. Not uncomfortable, but Hannah could feel a question burning in Riley. "Do you know why he invested?"

Hannah wasn't one for airing dirty laundry, but this was Riley. Did it matter that the investment had been an underhanded attempt to destroy Hannah's marriage? Jonathan had taken a calculated risk. He'd had no guarantee that Hannah would be the one sent to run the Boston edition, and he wouldn't have guessed that Hannah almost turned it down, because he still thought she and Will were acting. He was wrong, but his risk had paid off anyway. The truth wouldn't hurt Jonathan; it would only hurt Will.

"No," she said finally. "I have no idea why he decided to invest."

Chapter 49
Will

Will stared at the two messages in his inbox from Hannah. They had arrived the morning after their fight. Two days later, he still hadn't opened them. The emails could be about anything. Maybe it was her explanation and apology. Maybe it was her admitting that she wanted out. Either way, he wasn't ready. Everything about that afternoon still hurt. He'd gone to his apartment only to check that Hannah was officially back in Boston, and then he'd returned to Daniel's love seat to await the call from his real estate agent.

Will closed his laptop and picked up the business card sitting on the table. Someone at Wellington Thorne, probably Grayson, had boxed up everything in his office and sent it to Daniel's place. After years at the company, he had a single box of belongings to show for it. The contrast spoke volumes. Will pulled out his wedding photo. He needed to read Hannah's emails, and then he needed to talk to his wife. Her silence after the Madison debacle had been thunderous. It had broken him in ways he was still processing. He didn't want to do the same to her.

He pulled a card out of his Rolodex, surprised that it had made its way from his office and hadn't be confiscated as company property. It was another sign that Grayson had sent the stuff over. Jonathan would have included a seething message about how his son was a complete and utter letdown, and Jon would've burned everything in effigy.

Will tapped the card against his leg, working up the courage to pick up his phone. Brady Douglas had been trying to get Will to leave Wellington Thorne for years. His firm recruited the best, and Will was nothing if not the best.

He dialed the number, his hands shaking. Maybe it had all been friendly banter from a competitor, something to ease the silence between opposing counsels. Will hit the call button and prayed for the best.

Twenty minutes later, after scheduling a lunch date with Brady Douglas and another with his top competitor, Will reopened his laptop. Hannah's emails greeted him, bombs waiting to be detonated. It had been Will's words, *his* insistence, that led them here. He could've heard her out. But her words that afternoon had spread through him like venom, poisoning the faith he'd had in their reconciliation. He clicked, starting the countdown to destruction. His vision blurred—it couldn't be a goodbye.

I wrote this email, deleted it, wrote it again, and deleted it again. There's so much I could say, so many explanations—excuses—I could give. But I won't. You were right to walk away. You—we—deserved better than that cruel tirade. I'm more sorry than I know how to express. I do want to make this work.

If you believe nothing else, believe that I love you.

Will leaned back against the couch, a small smile loosening the tightness in his jaw. *If you believe anything I said, believe that nothing is going on with Madison.* She'd called back to his own sentiments from when he'd been at fault—when she'd had to take him at his word. Hannah was asking him to do the same. Except he didn't doubt that she loved him. He doubted whether she loved him outside the confines of the pact. Those were fears he'd created himself the moment he initiated the pact instead of simply asking her out on a date. They were fears he hadn't anticipated—there was so much he hadn't anticipated. Her loving him at all had been wholly unexpected. There was only one fix, but putting it into motion risked the fragile equilibrium of their relationship. It was the only way to save their friendship.

He clicked on the second email, curiosity getting the better of him. What could Hannah possibly have had to add to that first email?

Jonathan funded the Boston project. I know things are a mess, and we have so much else to talk about, but I had to tell you. I didn't think... I was afraid you wouldn't answer, or you would, and we'd get sidetracked on other things. Important things, but not this. I don't know what to do with this information or if it even matters anymore. You left Wellington Thorne, and Riley assures me my assignment had nothing to do with the name of the backer. Do with this information whatever you must, or do nothing. I just thought you needed to know.

Will closed the email. *Fucking Jonathan*. The man never stopped. Will had thought, for the briefest of time, that the party and Christmas had assuaged his father. But no. Their unfailing love merely caused him to find a new way to get her out of the picture. It had been his father's last attempt after she'd refused to walk away. Whatever he invested in *Deafening Silence* was certainly less than Hannah would get in a divorce without a prenuptial agreement, and if she had been the one to leave Will, there'd be no money going her way. It was quite the move on his father's part. How perfect it would've been if Hannah had turned down the position as she'd intended. If that weekend in the Hamptons hadn't ruined everything, Jonathan would've funded someone else's future. God, he wished he could've seen that play out.

He hit the Call button, resolve building in him.

"Will?"

"Hey." The sound of her voice was a balm to the scorch marks she'd left on him. He could just say he loved her and everything between them was okay. It would be so easy. But no, he had to do this.

"I'm so glad you called," she said, her words tentative but her tone hopeful. "I'm sorry about your fa—"

"I want to dissolve the pact."

Chapter 50

Hannah

"I want to dissolve the pact."

"What? No. That's not what I want," she said, alarmed. He couldn't mean he wanted to end things—*to get divorced?*

Hannah turned to face the ongoing photo shoot. Panic was setting in at Will's words, but a portion of her mind still needed to pay attention to her crew. Everything seemed to be in order. No expense had been spared—*thanks, Dad*. She picked at the fruit she'd skimmed from the catering cart. Leonard didn't have much of a rider, so they'd had to improvise. Fortunately, Hannah had read enough Wilderness Weekend interviews and attended enough shows to have gleaned some idea of Leonard's foods of choice—at least she hoped. The shoot was wrapping up, and Leonard chatted with the photographer.

Hannah turned away from the scene, wishing there was somewhere more private to have this conversation. "Why are you doing this?"

"Because I meant every word of our vows. And I'm afraid that the pact is all that's keeping you in our relationship. You're stuck with me for a year, and it helps pass the time if you're in love with me. Added bonus that the sex is great."

"*You* wrote that clause in the rules, not me," she said, agitated. How could he throw that in her face?

"Exactly," he said. "I wrote in that we could date. You wrote in that our friendship was the most important thing. I may have needed to get married to get my family to take me seriously, to save my career, but I chose you because for me, there was no one else. I chose *you*, Hannah. I need you to choose me now."

Behind her, the sounds of equipment being put away grew louder. She stepped further away, noting that Leonard was still talking to the photographer. *Choose Will?* She'd chosen him when she'd suggested they share a bed. Then she'd almost turned down Boston for him. She'd even said she loved him first. "That's not fair."

"Maybe it's not," Will said softly. At least breaking her heart didn't seem easy for him. "But this is your out. Choose me or don't. The pact has been this safety net keeping us together, and if we're going to have any chance of abiding by Rule 5, it needs to end."

She hadn't thought of the pact as a failsafe, not once. Falling in love negated the one-year clause—at least, it had for her. "Rule 5 was a pipe dream, Will! We were always either going to get divorced or fall in love." *Or both.*

"I know that! Don't you think I know that?" Agitation finally showed in his voice. He clearly hadn't thought this through before calling her.

"You're not making any sense."

Will sighed heavily on the other end of the line, and Hannah knew his hair had to be mussed—she hoped he didn't have any interviews today.

"'If this doesn't work out, I'll have nowhere to go.' That's what you said. I know I came to you with the pact, but maybe I shouldn't have. Maybe I should've just asked you on a date like a normal person. Most people don't need to keep a second apartment in case things go wrong. They risk everything on the chance that it will work out. I need you to do that now, and the only way I'll ever believe you want to be with me is if we end the pact."

Hannah blinked back tears. Maybe he *had* thought it through. Maybe he was right. If they got rid of the safety net the pact afforded—that they wouldn't be jerks, would stay friends, and would be married for one year—they would either catch each other, or they would fall. Would their fledgling relationship survive without the pact tying them together? Were their hearts enough?

"Okay," she said quietly. "Let's end the pact."

Chapter 51

Hannah

Hannah stared at the blank screen on her phone. Had that just happened? Will couldn't have realized what day and time it was. He wouldn't have knowingly called her during the biggest interview of her career. And yet she had picked up. Why the hell had she picked up? She forced the conversation out of her mind, straightened her shoulders, and tried to refocus her thoughts. Leonard Nulty was waiting for her. Literally.

"Everything okay?" He was also standing behind her.

Shit. Hannah whirled around, plastering a smile on her face. "Yes, of course. Sorry, that was my husband reminding me to get him an autograph."

"Ah. Big fan?"

"We both are," Hannah said. Maybe he hadn't heard anything. She directed him toward a pair of couches where bottled water and wine waited on ice. "He introduced me to Wilderness, actually."

Leonard squinted in concentration. It was a face she'd seen plenty of times on tour, but up close, it was completely different. "Let me guess. Your wedding song is... 'Love Acts.'"

Hannah laughed. That would have most definitely been their song. "I wish." She palmed her face. "It's actually that new Ed Sheeran ballad, but I imagine under different circumstances, it would've been 'Love Acts.'"

He raised his eyebrows. "Do tell."

She shook her head—she shouldn't be telling Leonard Nulty about her love life. "That's a long story."

"I love long stories."

"I'm sure you do, but this interview is about you, not me," she said, pointing her pen at him.

"Right, right. Ask away." He sat back on the couch. His body language seemed open and relaxed.

"You haven't given an exclusive or any long-form interviews in over two years." Her hands shook as she spoke—Leonard wasn't any other celebrity. He was *her* celebrity. She clasped her fingers, resting them on top of her notebook. "Why now?"

"I'm retiring."

Holy shit. Another album, another tour, going solo—all of these she'd been prepared for. But retiring? The fangirl in her was screaming. Outwardly, she met his gaze with as professional an expression as she could manage. "Wow," she said, letting out a breath. "That was hard to hear."

He laughed softly. "I'm sure it was."

"Why give this to *Deafening*?" The question was out of her mouth before she had a chance to think about it. It was a fair question, though hardly appropriate in this setting. News like this, even with his midlist career, was worthy of much bigger venues.

He leaned forward with his elbows on his knees. "When we first started, we went out to LA to hit it big. We played in God knows how many small venues and Battles of the Bands. We made no traction." Hannah knew most of this, but she wasn't about to stop him. "And then one night, Riley Anderson—hell, she was younger than me—interviewed us for *Deafening Silence*. I'd only ever seen that magazine on the windowsill of the old records store on Sunset, but Riley was the first person to interview us, and she kept at it. She found us again and again. She's one of two journalists I trust."

"Who's the other?"

"My college roommate, Jackson Mendez."

No freaking way. "The editor in chief of *Talented*."

"The one and only. And I know your next question. Why not give this story to him, right?"

Hannah nodded.

"Well, as a fan, would you rather hear a filtered-down version of the story from an interviewer who drew the short straw over at *Talented* or, as Jackson put it, from 'one of the most talented writers on the alternative music scene'?"

Jackson Mendez knew who she was. She felt faint. That would be an interesting turn of events. She scanned her list of questions, more to give herself a moment to process the knowledge she'd just received than because she needed to. She'd memorized her list backward. None of them seemed relevant now.

"Why are you retiring?" Simple but effective.

He shook his head. "Before I answer that, Riley said you'd do right by me. That's why I agreed to the exclusive even though it wasn't with her. But if I'm going to bare my soul, I want something in return."

Had this been another artist, Hannah might have been concerned. As it was, Leonard was happily married. Nearly all his songs were about his wife. "What do you want to know?"

"For starters, you can tell me that story about your wedding song, and then we can talk about what really happened on the phone."

It was a good thing acting wasn't in Hannah's future. There was no harm in telling him about Will, and if it got him to answer her questions, there were worse things than talking to her musical idol about her love life.

She sat back in her chair, her notebook still resting on her lap. "On graduation night—"

"College or high school?" He sank into the cushions, leaned his head back, and closed his eyes.

"College. Will and I made a pact to get married if we were both still single when we turned thirty. About four months ago, he showed up at my door with an engagement ring. Five days later, we had a ceremony." The memory came back to her, the fear mixed with excitement. It felt like another lifetime, not four months ago. "We went on a honeymoon and crashed a wedding. Then we danced to that Ed Sheeran song."

He gave her an appraising look. "That's pretty badass."

She'd never thought of it like that. The pact had been a weighty secret that they'd kept. A truth—her truth—that she hadn't told. In a way, the secret had led to a sort of shame. Even if it worked out, they'd been stupid and reckless, and they'd hurt their families. But telling the story, out loud to an outside party, she felt exhilarated by that risk she'd taken.

"Why are you retiring?" she asked again.

"We started this band when we were nineteen—college freshmen at a school about as far away from the punk scene as you could get. You hope, but you never really expect to make anything out of a college rock band. But we went out to LA, and then we were signed. We had a hit here and there that broke mainstream. We toured all the time, and my wife, Veronica, had been there from the beginning. She traveled with us when she could. We made it work for a long time, but then we had Alicia."

He pulled up a photo on his phone of his daughter—all dark-brown hair and hazel eyes, wispy like so many kids that age. She sat with a guitar in her lap, her fingers splayed over an E chord. "She's four now, and every time I drag out the suitcases, she runs into her room and cries. She flops down on that little bed of hers and kicks her feet in such anger. This last time, she clung to my leg the entire time I packed. She tried to throw away my plane tickets. After that, it was an easy choice."

Hannah's heart swelled. This was why she loved Leonard Nulty and Wilderness Weekend. His love for his wife, his daughter, and his music came through in every line of every song. They were his inspiration, in the music and in ending it.

"You could stop touring," she said, the journalist in her knowing this was a good follow-up question and the fan in her dying at the thought of the end of Wilderness Weekend.

"Making the music without the tour would be a half-life," he said after a moment of hesitation. "That wouldn't be fair to anyone. Fans would miss it, I would miss it, and my family would feel that tug-of-war in me. That's not to say I'm done writing music. I'll write and produce. I'm sure a tune or two will find its way into the universe. But I'm tired of missing recitals and sleeping alone on tour buses. It took me a long time to decide this, but now that I have... there's no longer a place for Wilderness Weekend."

His words rendered her speechless with their weight and truth and the responsibility that was placed on her. She imagined reading those words in an article or on his blog—*there's no longer a place for Wilderness Weekend.* Tears would stream down her face while the angsty first Wilderness album played, followed by every album—with B-sides—in order. She would purge herself of the grief of never hearing those melancholic melodies again by hearing only them for a few hours. And Hannah had to be the messenger—her writing the channel to break hearts across the country.

"Will you do last shows in select cities?" It was a self-serving question, but she needed to say something, and all journalistic merit had left for the moment.

Leonard was sitting back and drinking his wine, but he was also taking her measure. He nodded. "They'll be in April—one in LA, one in New York, and the final show will be right here in Boston. I'll get you and—Will, was it?—on the list."

"We'd love that. We missed you in New York last month." *Had it only been last month?* Everything had gone entirely wrong so quickly. The pact was gone, leaving their relationship fraying at the seams, even if their marriage was still legally binding. She swiped at her eyes, relieved to find them dry. Crying in front of Leonard Nulty was unacceptable.

"Your turn," he said, repositioning himself on the couch. "I'm dying to hear how this pact played out."

She wasn't sure how much she would tell him. It would be easy to hit the highlights reel and move on. But as she started telling their story, it all spilled out. She walked him through Jonathan's disapproval and their laundromat date, through to Madison and Boston, ending at the phone conversation he had partially overheard.

"I'm worried that maybe I broke him," she said. "I promised myself when we got married that I'd be so careful with his heart, and I wasn't careful at all." She looked up at Leonard, who had been listening intently to the whole story. "What if I broke us?"

"Maybe you did. Maybe you both did. Love and careful rarely go together." He glanced around the room, but it was only them. The photography crew had long since left, and Leonard hadn't arrived with an entourage. "Six years ago, things with Veronica and I were the worst they'd ever been. We'd moved to a new part of town after *Lollipop Dreams* broke through to the mainstream. She'd made some really great friends, had a life and a career—traveling with the band on a smelly tour bus wasn't appealing anymore. I came home less often, and she flew out to fewer shows. One night after too many drinks and too many unanswered calls, there was this groupie—I hate to use that term—there was a woman, and I cheated on my wife."

Wow. Hannah sucked in a breath. She hadn't been expecting any of this. Leonard Nulty stuck to the music in a very dry and rigid way despite that his entire discography was autobiographical.

"I told Veronica right away, and I thought that was the end of things," he said without pausing, barely noticing Hannah's strife. "Could I have forgiven her for the same thing? I'm still not sure to this day. But my wife is a warrior and a goddess. It took a while—a lot of screaming and truth-telling and hard conversations. Our half-truths and omissions had led to resentment we didn't even know was building. But we worked it out. We had Alicia."

Hannah knew the time he spoke of—fans called it "the Blackout." Leonard had gone silent—no tours, no music, nothing for nearly a year. Then Alicia appeared on his social media accounts—a small, squished-up version of her father—and they'd thought it all made sense. They'd been wrong. Hearing the story from Leonard colored all the music that came after. The album that followed the Blackout had been one of his best. It had left behind the mainstream sound of *Lollipop Dreams* and returned to his punk and emo roots. It had felt like a love letter to the fans. It was a memoir.

"Who we are now together is so much stronger than who we were all those years before," he said. "Sometimes the way you fit back together after you've been broken is better than the way it used to be. Maybe that's how it will be for you and Will too."

"I hope so." Hannah laid her pen down on top of her notebook. "Do you want that off the record?"

A small smile played across his face. "Riley was right about you."

Chapter 52
Hannah

The Final Love Act: A Deafening Silence *Exclusive with Wilderness Weekend's Leonard Nulty by Hannah Abbott-Thorne.*

Hannah reread the headline. Her eyes stopped on what she hoped would still be her name after this was all over. *Hannah Abbott-Thorne.* It was a suitable byline for Leonard Nulty's goodbye and one of the few ways she had of letting Will know she wasn't going anywhere.

She scanned the article, already edited and partially laid out. Leonard had agreed to a second round of photos with his family. Once those were in, the layout would be adjusted, and in a few more weeks, this baby would go live, setting off a whirlwind of response in Boston and hopefully throughout his fanbase. Hannah could use a bit of fame by association. It had been a while since she'd had a story this big.

Riley sniffled from across the room. Hannah nudged her with her foot.

"Hannah, this is amazing. It's the perfect big headline piece we need to kick off *Boston*. When Leo told me he wanted to give us an exclusive, I never expected this. He gave me no warning. How did you keep it together? How did you get so much out of him?"

How *indeed*. Hannah hadn't told Riley that he'd agreed to swap one of his truths for hers. It wasn't that she had revealed anything scandalous, but it had been ingrained in Hannah since high school that reporters shouldn't insert themselves into the narrative. They were the storytellers, not the story. Riley would understand. Hannah had been around for the Robbie Cooper and Riley Anderson show. It had ended with Robbie in rehab and Riley engaged to Danny. Okay, maybe the rehab had been a few years later, but Riley had had a personal hand in launching Robbie's career with her in-depth interviews—in-depth because she'd had insights from the bedroom.

"We just talked," Hannah said. "He knew I was a fan, so that was an in. Plus, since this is his farewell, he wanted to get it all out there."

Riley sniffled again. The printout she was reading crinkled in her grip.

"Riles, why are you crying?" Hannah placed her hand lightly on Riley's knee.

"It's just—you don't understand! This story, your work here. It's like watching my baby grow up. I mean, you were my first intern in New York, and now you led the upstart of the Boston edition. And with an exclusive like this! Nate's already agreed to run it on the cover in both New York and LA."

"Are you serious?" Hannah had had plenty of covers before, but none of them ran nationally. A coast-to-coast cover was a rare gem in a pile of costume jewelry.

"So serious that Nate wants you to run the Boston edition."

Hannah sucked in a breath. *Run the Boston edition—be Riley.* Riley had given everything to the magazine. Hell, she was spending three days in Boston away from her three-month-old daughter. Hannah hadn't understood why she was coming up, but she didn't mind the company. She'd spent the whole last week working on her article, going to concerts, and worrying over Will—nothing more, nothing less. But then Riley's decision to make the trip to Boston sans baby made sense. It was a once-in-a-lifetime opportunity that she got to offer to the intern she'd brought up through the ranks. Six months ago, Hannah wouldn't even have hesitated. She would've left Brian, hugged Kate, and headed to Boston full-time. But life had taken an unexpected turn. *Hannah Abbott-Thorne.*

The last few weeks in Boston were everything she had ever dreamed of professionally. The assignment had taken everything she'd had. It had tested her abilities and proved to her that she deserved all the faith Riley had in her. But it had strained her relationships and pulled her away from the people who mattered. Hannah couldn't give everything forever. She couldn't be Riley. More importantly, she didn't want to be.

Hannah wanted to go home. She wanted to kiss Will and work on her marriage. Talking to Leonard had given her perspective. As she told her and Will's love story for the first time, she had realized exactly how she felt. She loved him forever. Maybe they had broken things—both of them in their own ways—but they could fix it if they were together.

"Did you hear me?" Riley asked, putting her hand on Hannah's shoulder.

Hannah blinked, refocusing her gaze on her mentor. "Sorry. Yes, I heard you. And I'm honored. It means more than I can articulate at the moment that you and Nate trust me to do this, but—" Hannah paused, a part of her still unable to believe what she was about to say and what it would mean. "I'm going to have to pass."

Riley smiled, tears gleaming in her eyes. She shook her head and pulled Hannah into a hug. "That's what I told Nate you'd say."

Chapter 53
Will

Will placed their wedding picture down on the corner of his new desk. This was the third place he'd set it, but it didn't seem right. He moved it to the other corner. That was better. His eyes would fall on it whenever he looked up. He'd officially joined Flannigan O'Hare Mahon as their new junior partner yesterday. The day had been full of meetings, paperwork, lunches, and drinks. If only all junior partners got this reception. He knew that his move to the firm felt like a coup, even though Will would never work a case against Wellington Thorne.

Brady had given him his first case that morning, and he couldn't wait to dig in. For once, he wasn't fighting to build a hotel that would displace the local flora and fauna. There'd be a learning curve, but he would master it. He was living the dream—he wouldn't forget that. Next, he just needed Hannah to come home—come home and choose him. He still couldn't believe he had dissolved the pact and given her an ultimatum. They hadn't spoken much since then, both agreeing that it was best to ride out her time in Boston. It would give them each the chance to consider what they wanted and how ending the pact had changed things. Yes, they were still legally married, but that was probably the easiest thing to fix about their situation.

"Sir?"

Will looked up at his associate. They always looked so young. He didn't remember looking that green out of law school. "What is it, Matt?"

"You have a visitor." Will looked past his associate but couldn't gather who was standing in the threshold beyond the fact that it was not Hannah.

"You don't need to deliver guests to my office."

The young man nodded. "I was coming to give you this, actually." He handed Will an overstuffed file. "Everything on the Lancosta case."

As Matt walked out, Jon walked in. Will stared up at his older brother incredulously. Had he really stepped foot in Flannigan O'Hare Mahon on Will's second day?

Jon sat down in the chair across from him. After giving his brother a once-over, Will swallowed the anger roiling in his stomach. Dark circles underlined the dullness of Jon's eyes, his skin was pallid, and the boisterous demeanor that defined his brother was absent.

"What are you doing here?" Will asked, leaning back in his chair.

Jon slid a file folder across the desk. "Dad tried to get rid of Hannah. He had me quietly get annulment papers together the moment your marriage license hit the public record. And then he asked me to set aside funds—he used them to invest in her magazine."

So their father had known about their marriage all along. Will wasn't surprised. Jonathan paid a great deal of money for information, monitoring the public record for anything that might tarnish the Thorne name. Will glanced at the paper, shaking his head at the number Jonathan had been willing to pay to break his son's heart.

"Why are you telling me this?" For whatever reason, Jon was extending an olive branch, but Will wasn't sure he wanted to take it.

"You deserved to know, and so does Hannah." Jon looked up, his expression heavy with regret. "I didn't know you really loved her."

"More than anything," Will said, dropping the folder back on his desk. There was more to this gesture than either of them would say aloud. Jonathan was stubborn. He wouldn't want to let Will just go.

But what Jon had handed Will was sizeable leverage should he need it.

Jon stood to go. He ran a hand through his hair, making it stand up and reminding Will of a much younger version of his brother. "That night with Madison... when Hannah... It wasn't the first time, was it?"

Will hadn't been expecting that. He shook his head, not trusting his words.

"Did you two ever...?"

"Yes."

Jon cursed, but there was no anger behind it, only dawning recognition.

"It was so early on, Jon—before she was ever your fiancée."

Jon looked at his brother, his expression crestfallen. "She's not my fiancée anymore."

Will ran a hand through his hair before clasping both his hands in front of him. "Does she know that?"

Jon shrugged. "She will in another hour or so."

Could the whole saga really be over? Will closed his eyes. "I'm sorry about you and Madison."

The words rang true, and relief washed through him. Whatever he decided about where the Thorne family and all that came with its name fit into his new life, Madison would not be a part of it.

Jon hesitated, his hand on the door and his body already making to leave. The heavy set of his shoulders told Will he couldn't stay much longer without breaking down, and Jon wouldn't do that in public. He'd hadn't when their mother died, and he wouldn't do it then over a woman, no matter how much his love for her might have cost him. "For what it's worth, little brother, I'm sorry as well."

Chapter 54
Hannah

Hannah added a third box to the stack in front of her. If she never moved again, it would be too soon. Hannah and Binx were heading out in a few days. The inaugural issue of *Deafening Silence Boston* was off to design for finishing touches. The next issue would feature some of the interviews she and Camila had done this last month and a few Camila would do herself in the coming days. After that, the Boston edition would be led by another editor—they were sending someone out from the LA team to run it full-time. Any loose ends Hannah could tie up perfectly well from New York. She hadn't officially given her notice, but turning down the promotion had laid down cards that only led to the end of her time at *Deafening*. Hannah knew it. Riley knew it. Not that Hannah couldn't stay. She could—Riley had been clear. But *Deafening* had been a haven, and it was time to see what she could do outside of its walls.

She plopped down on the couch, unsettling Binx, who glared at her before slinking off to his food bowl. The sight of his crate put him in a mood, but she knew he'd forgive her by dinnertime. Binx was a fickle lover.

An unknown number flashed on her phone screen. She answered in case it was someone calling about an interview. She and Camila had put out a lot of feelers in the last month.

"This is Hannah," she said.

"Hi, Hannah. This is Jackson Mendez, editor in chief of *Talented*."

Hannah clutched the phone tightly to her ear. Why was Jackson Mendez calling her? She tried to keep her breathing steady. *Talented* was the real deal. If you wanted to work in entertainment journalism, there was no better option—not that they trended toward the artists she was used to interviewing.

"Hello, Mr. Mendez," she said, doing her best to sound normal.

"Jackson, please." He cleared his throat. "A little birdie told me that you're looking to make a move."

Riley had said she'd put out feelers, but Hannah hadn't thought that included Jackson Mendez. "I am."

"Then I'd like to meet you," he said. "We've been talking about expanding our audience, and that means interviewing more than pop artists. Atlas Genius, Dreamers, the Wombats—we want them all on our covers. We need someone who understands those bands, who relates to their fans, and who can build our audience. After talking to Leonard Nulty last week and following your career for some time, I think that person is you."

Hannah covered the mouthpiece on her phone and silently screamed, her arms and legs kicking out wildly. This was real life. This was *her* life.

"That sounds amazing," she said, her voice edgy and jilted. "Those artists deserve to be on your cover."

"That's what I like to hear. I'm very excited to see what you did with Leonard's interview. You made quite the impression on him."

"If only he hadn't been saying goodbye," Hannah said with a laugh.

"When he makes his comeback—oh come on, you know he will—I think you'll have first dibs."

The fangirl in her held onto the idea that Jackson Mendez, who knew things, thought there'd be a Nulty resurgence. If Jackson Mendez said it, it was likely to happen. He might write about the

A-list, but he most definitely knew the whole spectrum—maybe Leonard most of all.

"You're still in Boston, right? How about lunch tomorrow?" he asked. "I could use a trip to Boston. It's been far too long since I've seen Alicia. I am her godfather, you know."

That was another thing Hannah hadn't known about Leonard Nulty. His music told so much, but not everything—not nearly everything. Perhaps that was the point.

"Lunch would be great," she said, her hands shaking.

"Perfect. My assistant will be in touch with you."

After a few more pleasantries, they hung up. Hannah threw her phone on the couch and looked around the tiny apartment. It was possibly the biggest moment of her life, and she was in Boston, alone. She didn't even know who to call. Will? Her mom? Kate? In that order? She spun around, her arms out, before sinking back down onto the couch with a squeal.

Deciding to leave *Deafening Silence* had felt like the end of a love affair that had nowhere to go but forever. She hadn't even fully processed it or considered where she would go from there. But the universe had plans for her. It knew her dreams better than she did. *Talented* had been the dream. It had been one of the many internship rejections that had led her to Europe, away from Will, and to New York with Kate. It had led her to Riley. And Riley had led her back.

Chapter 55
Hannah

The brownstone smelled of paper. It always had, but Hannah had gone nose blind to it long ago. The scent hit her then, throwing her back in time to her early days huddled with Riley, typing and deleting and typing the same article again until it was Riley-worthy, a standard that became more stringent the more Hannah honed her craft. The bustle of every day at the magazine went on around her. Interns scrambling, editors arguing over article placements, Riley in the middle of it all—the conductor of the *Deafening Silence* orchestra. All that was left to do was sign some invoices, code some expenses, and dwindle the remaining hours she had left as a member of the *Deafening Silence New York* staff. She would always be family. She sat down at her desk where, almost five months ago, white carnations had appeared on her birthday. Nothing had been the same after that. Will had been the butterfly that set off the tsunami.

She dropped their framed wedding photo into the box on her desk. It was already spilling over. One of the interns had started packing her things for her. Desks were a hot commodity at their office. Emily wanted Hannah's desk, and Henry—who had officially become a staff writer—wanted Emily's desk, which was Hannah's first desk. Essentially, they were kicking her out.

She'd accumulated a lot of crap in five years. There was an entire box of every issue she'd ever been featured in, which, for New York, was all of them. It was quite the collection, and she hadn't even needed it for a writing sample. She added the photo of Binx as a kitten—sprawled out on the couch with his tummy exposed, his paws in the air—to the box. He'd been none too happy to be dropped off at Kate's, which was as unfamiliar to him as Boston, but at least he was out of his carrier. A box of cat toys would be in his future as penance.

Hannah wiggled her mouse until her computer came to life. Her inbox was eerily empty except for one new email that had come through since she'd checked at Kate's. She squinted at the sender's name—why was Leonard Nulty emailing her?

A little something from the home studio. You and Will deserve a Wilderness song as your wedding song. Have your second first dance to this. (If I find this on Spotify, I know your boss(es)!)

Hannah pulled her headphones on and clicked on the link. The familiar opening of her wedding song started, on piano, not guitar. And then Leonard Nulty's voice, scratchy and imperfect, broke through. He'd covered their song. She blinked back tears. He'd gifted them the one thing they didn't think they would ever have.

"What are you doing here?" Riley's voice cut through the music pouring out of Hannah's headphones but just barely.

Hannah pulled them down around her neck. "Remembering."

"Me too." Riley sat on the edge of the desk. "Are you staying long?"

Hannah shook her head. She hadn't even planned on coming here today. But after stashing Binx at Kate's, she found herself walking toward the subway. Everything about the trip there was nostalgic, from the ebb of the subway to the college students loitering in the park. She would miss that life. *Talented* was in midtown with a view of Radio City Music Hall. At least the MoMa and the tree at Christmas would be close by. Lunch breaks would never be boring. Not that they had been in the Village.

"Will's actually meeting me"—she glanced down at her phone—"now. I'll come back tomorrow to finish packing."

"I'll take care of it," Riley said, adding a cat-shaped sticky-note holder to the box.

"I can come back and do it."

Riley shook her head. "Let me do this for you."

"You've already done so much for me," Hannah said, wiping at her eyes. She was being silly. She'd see Riley in a few weeks at Jo's christening. She was godmother, after all. This wasn't goodbye, and yet, it was.

"Likewise, Hannah Abbott-Thorne. Likewise."

Chapter 56

Hannah

Hannah stepped out of the subway to a sky streaked with red, orange, and pink. It was a gift at the end of the blustery day. She glanced down at her phone. Will had responded with a thumbs-up to her running-late text, not exactly a ringing endorsement for their reconciliation. She reminded herself not to overthink it. A thumbs-up was just a thumbs-up.

She clicked on Kate's latest message. *So, I was thinking for episode 50, we need to go big. What do you think of Bitching about Boyfriends #50 – The Marriage Pact?*

Hannah stopped under the awning of Blue Jean's to take in Kate's message. Kate was half-kidding, Hannah was certain, but with a boyfriend as perfect as Patrick, she was running low on material.

Maybe, she typed. *If everything goes well. And AFTER I tell my parents.*

Kate's response was quick. *Everything will go fine, better than fine. Good luck! Love you! Send pictures!*

Hannah pocketed her phone and continued down the street. A few blocks later, Will came into view. He stood outside Kate's building, his hands in his pockets. Even from a distance, she could tell he was nervous. She picked up her pace.

"Hi," she said, stepping in front of him.

Up close, the nervousness extended from his antsy feet up to his eyes. She'd told him about the job offer. He was the second person she'd called after Kate—Kate first because Kate would know who Jackson Mendez was without context, and she had a list of selfie requests for a situation just like that. She'd lived Hannah's dreams with her. Will had been excited, but she knew he wondered what it meant for them given her new benefits package. But that had been the past. Will had asked her to choose her future. It was time she did.

"Hi, Mrs. Thorne," he said lightly.

Hannah's heart fluttered at the nickname. She had always loved it despite its teasing nature.

"Walk with me?" he asked, holding out his hand.

Hannah wrapped her scarf tighter around her neck. She didn't want to walk—she wanted to talk to him and hold him and make him believe—but she took him by the hand anyway.

They walked a block in silence. She couldn't help but notice the changes in him in the few weeks they'd been apart. He looked healthier, lighter. She imagined a weight had been lifted since he quit Wellington Thorne and started over. It hadn't been easy on him. She knew he was nervous from their limited conversations since they dissolved the pact. But Will would be happier out of his father's shadow. The boy she'd known in college had been free—anxious about the future but uninhibited. The man he'd become had been fighting to prove himself. But after stepping away from Wellington Thorne, he didn't have to prove anything to anyone—to be anyone but himself.

They stopped at a busy intersection. Unease grew in Hannah as the silence between them extended. She'd made her decision, but maybe he'd made one too. Maybe they didn't align.

"Are you still staying at Daniel's?" Hannah asked.

Will shook his head as they crossed the street. The path was familiar. She and Kate had walked between their apartments countless times in the last few years.

"Right now, I'm in a hotel. But I was thinking, maybe we could stay here?" They stopped in front of her building. Ronny waved in greeting and held open the door. He mouthed a welcome before turning his attention to the next tenant. "I talked to your landlord, and we're good to stay here until your lease ends if you want."

We. He hadn't given up hope. Hannah's gaze shifted from Will to the apartment as he unlocked the door. Nothing seemed out of place, except perhaps Hannah herself. She wondered if it had always been this small and where Will would fit among her things.

"Thank you. You didn't need to do this."

"I did, though," he said, walking through the small space. It was odd to think he'd been here so few times. That one of the biggest parts of her life had almost never been in her home. "Consider it my husbandly duty."

She shook her head and leaned back against the couch. "Do I get to go now?"

Will narrowed his eyes at her. "What do you mean?"

"I have something to tell you, but you won't stop talking."

He waved his hand in front of himself, clearing the path. "By all means, Mrs. Thorne."

She grinned and plugged her phone into her speaker system. She scrolled until she found Leonard's musical wedding gift. The opening chords started. Hannah led Will around the back of the couch to the same spot where he'd proposed. She dimmed the lights. Leonard's voice filled the small apartment.

"Is that...?" Will trailed off when Hannah got down on one knee, taking his hands in her own. "What are you doing?"

She smiled up at him. "Proposing, dummy." Clearing her throat, she continued. "When you came back into my life almost five months ago, I didn't expect this. I thought it would be like that semester of college where you crashed on our floor." She shifted on her knee. "God, this *is* really uncomfortable."

Will laughed. His eyes glistened with tears. "Five months ago, you wouldn't even have been able to kneel like that."

"I know," she said. Her hands trembled where they held his. "The more time I spent with you, the closer to you I wanted to be. I grew to love you, slowly and then completely. There is no other choice for me. It has to be you. Not because of the pact or our history but because of the man you are and the man you are working to become.

"I love *you*, William Anderson Thorne. I promise to choose you every day for the rest of my life." She stood up, looping her arms around his neck. "Marry me. Marry me again."

He nodded, and his lips crashed with hers for the first time in weeks. Their tears mixed, leaving a salty taste to the kiss.

"It would be an honor to stay your husband, Hannah Grace Abbott-Thorne." He held out his pinky.

Hannah kissed him again before linking her pinky with his.

Acknowledgements

Writing may be a solitary task, but the journey to publication is not traveled alone. Without the support and comradery of so many, this novel may never have found its home.

First, a very big thank you to Lynn McNamee at Red Adept for taking a chance on Will and Hannah and their crazy marriage pact story. And to all the staff at Red Adept—*When We're Thirty* would not be where it is without you. A special thanks to my amazing RAP editors Angie and Marirose for loving Will and Hannah as much as I do.

To my RAP mentor and friend, Erica Lucke Dean—you have made my path to publication so amazing. Thank you for full-day conversations on grammar, for brainstorming whenever I needed you, for my amazing cover and graphics, and for so much laughter. I don't think I'd have survived this journey without you.

A big thank-you to my early readers, who saw this book in its infancy and helped shape it: Alison, Tracey, Katherine, Natalia, Bradeigh, Robin, Lainey, and Kimberley.

For the last several years, I've had the absolute honor of being in a small, tight-knit online writing group. To all the ladies in the Ink Tank, my Fictionistas—I could not do any of this without you. Finding all of you has been a highlight of the last several years of my life. When this pandemic is over, I can't wait to give each of you a giant hug.

To all my fellow writers who have been with me on this journey through one organization or another—thank you for the love and support. Knowing you all (virtually or otherwise) has made this journey worthwhile.

To the 2021 debuts—we did it!

To all the authors, readers, and bookstagrammers—you have made my publication journey so much fun. Thank you for all the support and for making sure more than my family knows about my book.

To Danielle Burby—thank you for encouraging me to write this book and for helping me get here.

To the ladies of the On the Same Page Book Club—thank you for making me feel like a celebrity long before I ever signed my publishing contract.

To all my friends and family who have watched me write and write and write some more—thank you for letting me get lost in my own little world for all these years.

To my best friend, Katie—there's a reason Hannah has such an amazing best friend and that she's named Kate. I never imagined when we started writing our book in ninth grade that I'd be here one day.

To my mom—thank you for believing in me and my dreams and for giving me the chance to try everything so I could find my one thing.

To my husband, who has given up countless hours with me while I've written and edited and worked to make this dream a reality—your support has kept me going through the hardest of times. Thank you for embracing my dreams. I love you more.

And finally, to my daughter—you're the very best thing in my life. Your smile and laughter and love bring me so much joy and inspire me every day. Dream big, princess.

About the Author

Casey Dembowski loves to write stories that focus on the intricacies of relationships–whether they be romantic, familial, or friendship. Her novels focus on the inner workings of women and how everything in their lives leads them to exactly where they are, whether they like it or not.

The first story Casey remembers writing was in the second grade, though it wasn't until she turned twelve that she started carrying a battered composition notebook everywhere she went. Since then, there hasn't been a time when she isn't writing.

Casey lives in New Jersey with her husband, daughter, and their two cats. She has an MFA in Fiction from Adelphi University, and currently works in corporate marketing communications. In her (limited) spare time, she enjoys reading, baking, and watching her favorite television shows on repeat.

Read more at https://caseydembowski.com/.

About the Publisher

Dear Reader,

We hope you enjoyed this book. Please consider leaving a review on your favorite book site.

Visit https://RedAdeptPublishing.com to see our entire catalogue.

Don't forget to subscribe to our monthly newsletter to be notified of future releases and special sales.

Made in the USA
Middletown, DE
24 July 2021